Tiny Grievances

stories and a novella

Robert Thomson

Tiny Grievances by Robert Thomson

Cover and author photographs by Jodi Thibodeau

Published by HowNow Media
www.robertwthomson.com/hownow

ISBN: 978-0-9939932-0-6
Second edition, June, 2016

Library and Archives Canada Cataloguing in Publication
Thomson, Robert, 1964-, author
Tiny grievances : stories and a novella / Robert Thomson.
-- 2nd edition.
ISBN 978-0-9939932-0-6 (paperback)
I. Title.

PS8639.H6484T55 2016 C813'.6 C2016-902158-2

"The Ballad of Aunt Stabby" was excerpted in *Now... Where Was I?* (HowNow Media), although in a slightly altered form.

To those who start late and still finish.

Contents

THE BALLAD OF AUNT STABBY

Aunt Stabby was never really married to Uncle Trip, but that's not the story most people wanted to hear. She would never talk about it and some of us knew why. Her real name was Agnes, and Uncle Trip was really Tuck. What people wanted to know I was only too happy to tell them. Perhaps because Aunt Stabby was so tight-lipped about the events leading up to *the incident*, it was left to a select group of her friends and relatives to pass the story down to future generations and the morbidly curious.

She was always at a distance it seemed. Aunt Agnes would come for dinner every second Sunday, along with an assortment of other guests pooled from family, friends and, occasionally, co-workers. My roommate Douglas and I would have spent the better part of the day preparing for the dinner—traditionally roast beef, my recipe. Agnes, always on time and a real chatterbox no matter who the other guests were, would only be silent during the few minutes the roast was being carved at the table. Her cherubic face would light up, pink colour rising to the surface of her cheeks, and a moist smile widening in anticipation of a delicious meal that cost her no time, effort or money.

"It's one thing to have a delicious meal made by caring hands," she said one night over a glass of sherry, "but to be able to thoroughly relax afterwards is like having a slice of cake without calories. You boys treat me so well."

This particular Sunday Aunt Agnes arrived late. Both Douglas and I answered the door, leaving our other guests in the living room. Agnes looked up at us as the door swung open. Her face was bruised and swollen. Douglas drew in a sharp breath and flashed me a look. He grabbed my hand and then quickly dropped it as Agnes stepped through the doorway and into the foyer, taking unusually small, deliberate steps. She smiled meekly as she removed her coat and passed it to Douglas, who, in turn, passed it to me.

"Can you put Aunt Agnes' coat in your bedroom please, roommate?"

She stopped short, pain registering on her face.

"What is it?" I asked.

"Oh, it's nothing," Aunt Agnes said. "I've just twisted my ankle again."

"Are you sure you're all right?" Douglas asked.

"Yes, yes, Douglas. I'll be fine. I'd just like a minute to compose myself if you don't mind."

"Sure. Help yourself to my bedroom," he told her. "Dinner

won't be ready for another twenty minutes. Why don't you go have a little nap?"

"No," Agnes said, moving beneath the chandelier. I saw the light on her face and grabbed Douglas's arm, stifling my shock. "I'll just freshen up at bit in the washroom," she said above a whisper. And with that she closed the door behind her.

"Roommate," I whispered, nudging Douglas.

"What?" He pushed my arm away.

"Did you see her face? There's something wrong with her right eye. It's like—"

"Just put the coat away and be quiet. We've got other guests. Put her coat in the bedroom and I'll freshen drinks."

"Douglas!" I said, perhaps too loudly. He turned and looked at me, his impatience wafting like bad cologne. "She limps in here, half an hour late, and her eye is swollen up like a balloon."

"She said she was all right."

"Somebody beat up your aunt, Douglas! You can't just do nothing."

But Douglas had already slid into denial mode. "It's her makeup, Jack. You know she wears it thick. Now be quiet, for God's sake. She'll hear you."

"Roommate!"

Douglas sighed.

"Don't ignore this," I cautioned him.

"Watch me."

Douglas moved into the living room, pushing the drink cart in front of him. I crept past the bathroom—slowly—and heard Agnes sob.

"Are you all right in there?"

"Yes, John," she murmured. "I'll be out in a minute."

John?

I put her coat on my bed and went back to the living room where Douglas was serving drinks to our other guests.

We called Burt Ross my assistant at the magazine. On paper he was my assistant, but in reality he carried much of the weight on his shoulders except when it came to models and money. He didn't get much of either; I saw to that, and would deny all rumours to the contrary—if anyone were smart enough to figure it out and stupid enough to speak of it.

Gregory Finn was a food critic who worked for *The Burlington Banner*. That was the newspaper my parents bought in the mid-seventies, and when I left high school I worked there on weekends. It was where we met. Even though he was just a few years older than I was, Gregory was already working as an editorial assistant in the Entertainment section. He was one of the first Canadian journalists to syndicate a food column from a local newspaper. His first nationally syndicated article was called "Mac & Cheese Redux: Rethinking A Comforting Classic." I still use the recipe when I'm depressed or broke or both. Of course, I don't use the expensive cheeses when things are tight.

Rounding out our guest list was my friend Nora Grey and her new girlfriend Alexandra Pots. Nora was a relaxed and affectionate woman, so it made sense that her girlfriend was neurotic and uncommunicative. This was the first time they had been at one of our dinners together and, judging from the first few minutes, it would probably be the last.

"So how many boyfriends do you have this week, Douglas?" It was Burt asking. He had recently started taking anti-depressants and was becoming a new person, or at least a slightly less annoying one. It was surprising to hear him interacting with people when normally he would be happy to sit in the kitchen stirring the vegetables or trying to organize our kitchen cupboards.

"Oh, Burt," Douglas chuckled. "It's not how many I have, but how good they are."

Everyone in the room laughed. Except Alexandra.

"Do you want some more wine?"

"Yes, please. Who was at the door?"

Douglas looked at me as I sat down on the couch. "It's my Aunt Agnes," he answered. "She's just freshening up."

Alexandra looked quickly at Burt and then turned her head toward Nora. She whispered into her ear. Nora looked at Burt and nodded her head. Alexandra took her hand. The two of them sat in silence. Rude.

I moved to the stereo and asked, "How about some music everyone?"

"I cast my vote for the *Showboat* soundtrack," Burt said, knowing it was my current favourite.

"Excellent! Coming right up," I said, and turned around to find the disc. "We were listening to it just yesterday afternoon over cocktails. On the terrace."

Alexandra turned to Nora and whispered in her ear. Nora listened, then turned to me. "What's *Showboat*?"

"You're kidding." I said. Alexandra gave Nora an aggravated smile. "The smash hit musical?" I continued, addressing Alexandra directly. "Second only to *Phantom* in terms of box office, but believed by many to be superior. *Showboat*. Come on! 'Old Man River,' 'Bill,' 'Can't Help Loving That Man.'"

"Dat Man," Douglas corrected me.

"Yes, and where I come from people speak properly." I slid the CD into the tray and pushed play.

Just as the opening chords flooded from the speakers, Aunt Agnes hobbled into the living room. All I could see was her eye. It was as if she'd tied a deflated football to the front of her face and, despite her attempts to cover it up with layers of makeup, the purplish-black semi-circle was impossible to ignore. Everyone watched her make her way in to the room as *Showboat*'s "Main Title" played. I quickly turned the volume down, and moved to help Agnes into a chair.

A round of stunned faces focussed on her as she creaked down into a recliner. Nervous glances followed, this time directed at Douglas. He shook his head at them and smiled a fool's smile.

"Agnes, I'd like you to meet some of our friends," I said to her.

"Oh that would be lovely, John."

"Jack," Douglas corrected her, frustrated.

"Yes, Jack." Agnes echoed.

"You know Nora of course, and this is her friend Alexandra from Edmonton."

"It's nice to see you again, Agnes."

"Always a pleasure, Nora," Agnes said with the trace of a smile forming.

Agnes looked from Alexandra to Burt.

"And this is Burt."

"Hello Aunt Agnes," Burt said.

"Oh heavens, Burt, never mind the aunt business. Please, just call me Agnes. It's nice to meet you."

"The pleasure's all mine," he smiled.

"Burt is Jack's assistant from work," Douglas added.

Agnes shifted in her chair, suddenly energized. "Oh Jack, how nice of you to invite your employee to dinner," she said with an air of tolerant condescension and a discernable emphasis on the word *employee*. "You know in my day such things just weren't done."

Douglas threw me a quick glance and rolled his eyes.

"I'm mostly here to clean up afterwards." Burt said, winking at me. Agnes seemed pleased by this announcement. "Everything in its right place," he concluded.

Douglas pushed the drink cart over to Aunt Agnes and rolled up his sleeves. "No Radiohead in this apartment, Burt. Aunt Agnes?"

"Yes?"

"Drink, dear?"

"Oh, yes please."

"Sherry?"

"Yes, thank you, Douglas. That would be lovely."

Agnes took the glass from Douglas and gestured an elegant cheers before raising it to her lips. She emptied half the glass in one gulp and braced herself as she swallowed. Douglas pushed the drink cart back into the hallway and returned to the living room. He sat down on the edge of the elevated fireplace. "The last first drink has been served, roommate," he said. "That means the evening is officially underway."

"I'll drink to that," said Agnes, and downed the remnants of her sherry.

Alexandra glanced at the cheese tray on the coffee table before her and then whispered something in Nora's ear.

"What kind of cheese is that?" Nora asked Douglas.

"Oh, on the left is brie, and on the right is a medium white cheddar," I answered. Then Nora turned and whispered to Alexandra who seemed confused for a moment, and stared at the cheese tray again. She pointed at it and whispered once more in Nora's ear.

"Your left or my left?" Nora reiterated.

Two questions in and already Douglas had lost his patience. "I have some processed cheese slices in the fridge if that would make it easier."

Alexandra and Nora looked at each other. Veiled confusion and obvious discomfort.

"That's all right," Nora said, and then reached forward to pull a grape from the bunch. Alexandra did likewise, but slowly. Everyone watched her as she raised the single grape to her mouth.

"Of course, the times are changing," Aunt Agnes said and lifted her glass into the air. Douglas got up and moved to the hallway. "Isn't it marvellous that people of different classes can group together socially? It's very modern, I think." Suddenly she craned her neck and looked at her nephew. A frown when she realized he was getting her another drink. "Douglas, why don't you let Burt get the drinks? Sit down and relax, dear."

In a split second Agnes had turned this moment of our dinner party into one of those slow-motion scenes from a film from the early seventies where the soundtrack is marked by the ticking of a clock. Frozen in that moment, we watched as Agnes turned to Burt and gave him a nod. It was not a silent instruction, underscored by the previously mentioned clock ticking; it was an order. Agnes had ranked our guests hierarchically and decided that whoever was at the bottom would not only know it, but would work for the dishonour of it as well. The old bird had established her pecking order.

Douglas glanced at me quickly and smiled at his aunt.

"I'll check on dinner," I said, moving from my chair.

"I think I'd better help you, Jack," Burt said urgently, following me. As I rounded the corner I could see Douglas in front of the fireplace, drink in hand, not knowing what to do. He glanced from Aunt Agnes to Burt, to the cheese tray, and finally to the empty glass Agnes held close to her chest.

I slid into the kitchen and grabbed a bottle of Scotch from a cabinet.

"Give me some of that," Burt said as he rounded the corner. I filled his wine glass with Scotch. "Who is that woman and why hasn't someone told her it's 2002? We're in a new millennium and she thinks she's part of the ruling class!"

"Oh, Burt. She's an old woman. Let her be."

"That's your excuse? Honestly. People of different classes mixing together. In my day it simply wasn't done. Let Burt get the drinks! For fuck's sake, Jack. And with *Showboat* playing. I thought she was joking. At first I thought, oh great, we're having dinner with Phyllis Diller! This'll be fun—"

"Please don't be upset."

"I'm not upset. It's not my dinner party. But still... The first time you invite me over for a Sunday dinner and your roommate's aunt calls me trash."

"Well—"

Just then I realized I shouldn't draw attention to my dismay at our guests' behaviour and that maybe Aunt Agnes knew something I didn't about how to control party guests.

"Oh come on now. This doesn't seem like the new Burt I've noticed blossoming lately." I almost choked on my words, but raised my glass to my lips and took a hefty swig of Scotch to conceal whatever grimace I might be making. I didn't really care if it was convincing. He *was* my employee.

"There is no new Burt. It's just me, medicated so I have no sense to complain about how fucked everything is."

"Well, I've noticed a very different you in the office. And I won't say another word about it."

"I wish you wouldn't, Jack, really. I don't like people talking about what drugs I take. And I have a bad feeling about these anti-depressants. They make me feel like I've lost something."

"Just your annoying edge," I said, winking at him so he wouldn't take offence. But it's quite true. Sometimes I'd like to jam a rag in his mouth or lock him in a closet.

"Ha!"

"Did you see her eye?"

"Yeah," Burt said, opening the refrigerator door and peering inside. "Nice shiner. Hey, did Douglas put out name cards on the table?" He thrust a package of processed cheese slices toward me. I shook my head.

"Of course."

"Why don't we fix it so that I sit beside Auntie Mamed?"

I sputtered, laughing, sending Scotch dribbling down my chin.

"At this point in the evening, I think I'm going to need to have a little amusement. Especially considering you're almost out of Scotch."

"Oh, Burt, please don't upset Aunt Agnes. Something terrible has happened to her and Douglas only wants to maintain a sense of calm."

"Calm? Listen, I'll tell you what happened to Aunt Agnes. Someone punched her but good. And I don't think they should be held accountable for their actions." Burt tossed the cheese back in the fridge and turned around to face me.

"That's what I think, too. Quick, have some more Scotch before Douglas comes in. You know how protective he is of his Balvenie DoubleWood."

"Thanks," Burt said, extending his glass toward me. He reached with his other hand and opened the freezer and pulled out two ice cubes.

"You can't really blame him though," I said.

"Oh, come on. It's not expensive."

"I meant about ignoring whatever happened to his aunt."

"Oh, right," Burt replied. "Also, she's limping."

"I know."

Just then Douglas rounded the corner and barrelled into the kitchen.

"She's just asked for a third tumbler of sherry," he muttered.

"Didn't you just serve her one?"

"Two. She downed the second one while you two have been in here conspiring," Douglas said, inspecting our glasses.

"Conspiring to serve dinner," I said.

"I was just looking for my blender," Burt said.

"What upsets you more, Douglas?" I continued. "That she's asking for refills or that she's drinking sherry from the wrong type of glass?"

"Meow," Burt said, acknowledging the sudden flare-up of tension. Douglas frowned at both of us. "Too bad you don't have any Demerol to offer her," Burt continued. "Or do you?"

"Tumbler!" Douglas shouted at no one in particular before turning to me. "Who was it that broke our Riedels?"

"You did, roommate," I said. "Remember that night the models were here doing the underwear dinner party shoot?"

"Kill me now," Burt moaned.

"Shut up. It was the drum scanner."

Burt rolled his eyes back in his head. "When was the last time you had six of your friends over for a dinner party where the dress code was underwear only?"

"That night."

"They were doing tequila shots from the Riedel glasses. They cost more than what they were drinking," Douglas said, his voice rising.

"That was also the night you two—"

Douglas cut me off. "No," he said flatly.

"Almost consummated your—"

He interrupted me again. "I'll burn your potatoes." He nudged Burt and pointed to one of the cabinets. "Your blender is in there," he whispered.

"Roommate!" I scolded him. At this point, I wasn't sure whether the blender issue was a joke or not but it seemed a good bit to run with because it was, of course, at Burt's expense.

Douglas ignored me. "What's going on with Nora and her girlfriend?"

"The mute," Burt laughed and peered inside the cabinet.

"She won't talk to anyone," Douglas continued. "They just keep whispering back and forth, like the girlfriend, what's-her-name, can't speak English and Nora is interpreting! Gregory's going to fall asleep any minute and my aunt is expecting Burt to serve her her next round with the drink cart proper."

Burt moved toward Douglas and wrapped his arm around him. "Relax," he said. "You don't want to break a sweat in that linen shirt. Gregory's fine. He's very adaptable socially, unlike Miss processed cheese slices. He's only here because he thinks it will advance his career. If he really thought you were his friends he'd invite you over to his place for a private dinner of Lean Cuisine and backstabbing. That's how you know you've made it into his inner circle. He starts to do character assassinations of his other friends. You'll both standing in front of the microwave waiting on dinner and he just lets loose like it's backlogged diarrhea or something he can't control."

I couldn't help but let out a gasp. It's not as if I didn't suspect as much, but to hear Burt come right out and say it was a shock.

"He's so quiet though," Douglas said.

"So?" I said, a little perplexed by Douglas' naiveté. "He's a food critic and all he eats at home is Lean Cuisine. To me that's a little odd. And yes, it does seem as though he hates all his friends. The useful ones, that is."

Douglas made a tsk-tsk sound as he checked the roast. A wave of hot air spread out from the open oven door.

"Oh, please," Burt droned at Douglas. "Save the surprise for when you find out who decked the old lady."

"Does this mean you're not going to serve my aunt her drink?" Douglas closed the oven door and looked at Burt with a large fork in his hand.

Burt glared back at him, and then, finally, at me. "If you wanted me to serve tonight, you should have told me in advance and I would have worn my uniform. But since I'm a guest, I expect to be treated like one."

Douglas' face was ashen. "This is going to be our first disastrous Sunday night dinner party, roommate," he said, grabbing at my arm but glaring at Burt as though it were his doing.

Burt picked up the bottle of Scotch. "I'm so glad you both waited until tonight to invite me." He made a grand gesture with his arms spread open wide and glanced around the kitchen. "The atmosphere is—"

"It's like *Macbeth*," I cut in.

"Irwin Allen is more like it," Douglas said and shot me a look.

"And your aunt is Shelley Winters."

"A complete disaster, Jack. I hope you're prepared." Then he turned and grabbed the bottle of Scotch away from Burt. "I think you've had enough."

"Roommate!" I gasped.

"I don't know the meaning of that word," Burt replied to Douglas with a smirk. "I've taken the liberty of fastening my seatbelt because I expect it to get much, much worse."

"Oh relax, both of you," Douglas scolded, pouring what was left of the Scotch into his glass. Then he leaned forward and kissed Burt on the cheek.

Burt welcomed the kiss and smiled. "If I'd known your dinner parties were this surreal, I would have brought tequila and a Buñuel film."

"You're not allowed in our home with tequila," Douglas said, pulling away and pointing his finger directly in Burt's face. "You remember what happened last time."

"I fell asleep."

"At the baths. In the shower stall," Douglas said with a grin. "Just reporting the facts. Don't shoot the reporter."

"You stole my blender."

"I did no such thing," Douglas replied. "You said you brought it as a gift."

"Who brings a used blender with a crack in it as a gift?"

Douglas arched his eyebrows and frowned. It made him look like Joan Crawford.

"It was in a plastic bag."

"Well, I am aware that you're on a budget," I said half-seriously, hoping to prevent their jesting from becoming something more serious.

"So give me a raise."

"This is a social evening," I replied

"Social work is more like it," Burt said quietly.

"I don't see you complaining," Douglas responded.

"Would you like to? I've been remarkably restrained so far." Then Burt turned to me. "You really think I'd bring you a used, unwrapped, damaged gift?"

"Well, did you?" I stared back at him.

"All right you guys," Douglas said, stepping between us. "We've got company out there. Jack, turn down the potatoes. Burt, grab another glass for my aunt. The biggest one you can find. And both of you keep smiling. Let's not let this evening go down the toilet."

Burt scowled at me a moment longer and then began searching through the cupboards for a glass. He pulled out a beer stein. Douglas shook his head in resignation and moved to the hallway. Burt took the stein to the drink cart in the hallway and filled it three-quarters full of sherry. The three of us went back into the living room where Gregory was explaining the difference between using flour and corn starch when making gravy.

"Here you are, Agnes," Burt said, handing her the beer stein filled with sherry.

"Oh heavens," she said, smiling. "It's a biggie."

Gregory chuckled out loud and sipped his wine. We all took our seats and, for a moment, anyway, it seemed as though everything was settling down—until the conversation turned from gravy to the magazine. Aunt Agnes was at fault actually, having become increasingly preoccupied with Burt's responsibilities at work. He had no problem filling her in on the details, thanks to the Scotch he had consumed, but I knew he had ulterior motives.

"When I first started the job was very defined," he began. "But within no time I was taking on little bits of work here and there that I was too impatient to wait for someone else to do. And probably not as thoroughly as I wanted it done, so—"

"Impatience is often a thorny flower," Agnes interjected, batting her eyelashes. Everyone stared at her in silence, and then at

Burt. It was like a tennis match.

He smiled. "Well, if you have to be criticized for something, it might as well be for being thorough."

Shifting in her seat, Aunt Agnes turned and faced Burt directly. Her voice took on a rather serious, almost accusatory tone. "Tell me, how is it that you assist Jack?"

Burt flashed me a look. All I could do was manage a discreet shrug in response.

Agnes continued. "As an assistant, you should know your job description. I'd like to hear it."

Alexandra leaned over and whispered something in Nora's ear. Gregory uncrossed his legs and shifted in his seat. His fly was unzipped. I tried to catch Douglas's attention, but he was watching Burt, keenly. I could tell what was going on in his mind because his posture was lax, almost suggestive.

"Well," Burt said hesitantly, "I come up with most of the story ideas, I find writers who I think are a good fit with the material, get them to submit proposals, they execute the ideas and, once approved, I edit them, and give all the credit to Jack. Oh, and I don't get invited to any of the social functions. Except this one, as luck would have it."

"I had a job like that once," Alexandra said, surprising everyone.

"Really?" Burt smiled at her. "How long did you keep it?"

"Until I started pulling my hair out," she said. "And even that was too late."

"Well," Burt sighed. "It pays the bills. Some of them."

The room bristled with nervous energy. Aunt Agnes sipped her sherry and jumped in her seat when Alexandra's voice rang out again.

"Yeah, but it's eating away at you inside, I can tell. Have you taken any stress management seminars?"

"No. I have my own way of dealing with stress."

"And what might that be?" asked Agnes.

Burt gave a quiet smile as he answered. "I meditate."

Douglas laughed heartily. "Yes, I've seen him doing it at the YMCA in the change room. He's very good at it. Seems like there's always someone asking him to meditate with them."

Burt sipped his drink, extending his middle finger upward along the bowl of his wine glass for Douglas to see.

"Hobbies can be such fun," Agnes said. "And also a productive way of passing the time."

Alexandra giggled.

"And what might your hobbies be, young lady?"

The smile on her face fell. She flushed red, gazed at Agnes

and shifted her weight on the couch. Beside her, Nora gave her an encouraging pat on the shoulder.

"Photography," she mumbled.

"Oh, pictures!" Agnes exclaimed loudly. "Oh how marvellous! Douglas' cousin Max likes to take pictures."

"Of dead animals," Douglas added quietly.

Agnes glared at him. Douglas met her glance and then turned away. It wasn't until that moment I realized that Aunt Agnes was sloshed.

"I hardly think it matters, Douglas. Some of his work is quite stunning. I think he shows great promise as a creative artist. Uh... Photographer."

"He hunts animals and takes pictures of their carcasses."

"Well!" Agnes said in a huff.

"It's not normal," Douglas continued, making no attempt to hide his disgust.

"Oh heavens, nephew! Who are we to define normal?"

Douglas got out of his seat and crossed the room, heading for the kitchen. He stopped and turned to face his aunt. "Do you mean we, as a group, or me specifically?" His face turned red as he glared at her, but she remained silent. "Max can be charming when he wants to be, but it's an act. I bet even *he* knows there's something wrong with him." By the time he had finished speaking, he was in the kitchen and almost out of earshot.

"There's the pot calling the kettle black," Agnes said quietly.

I could imagine Douglas processing what had just passed between him and his aunt and how he should respond. "Family," I laughed, hoping to lighten the mood.

Agnes sipped her sherry.

"Can't live with 'em, can't kill 'em," Burt chuckled.

Agnes gave a bit of a cough and looked into the fireplace. "I think it's time for another log, don't you, Jack?"

"Indeed it is." I jumped up before Agnes had the chance to ask Burt to do it.

"I'm interested in photography as well," Gregory said to Alexandra, relieving me possibly as much as her. "I've had a few of my shots published in the magazine. More by accident than by design, I think."

"Or good luck," I interjected. Gregory smiled at me. I gave him a discreet shake of my head, hoping he'd drop the subject.

"It's just a hobby, really. But I like it. And it doesn't hurt when the boss here pays seven hundred dollars a pop. Or should I say click?"

Fuck!

Burt turned in his chair. "Really? Seven hundred dollars for a photograph. I'm in the wrong line of work."

"It's very generous, considering," Gregory smiled.

"I think I'll check on the—"

"They only pay me five hundred dollars a month to do the editorial," Burt said, deflated. "All of it."

"Goodness," Gregory chuckled. "They pay the girl who answers the phone more than that."

Burt looked like someone had just snuck up behind him and pushed him to the ground. Agnes smiled broadly and took a swig from the beer stein.

"To be fair, she also styles the photo shoots." I said.

"Oh yeah, picking out underwear is such hard work," Burt said, scowling.

"I love being able to capture that moment, you know?" Alexandra sat up straight, eyes focused on Gregory. "Especially when it's not a planned shot. Then you can look back on it later and so many things come back like the sounds and the smells, and emotional reactions. I've got quite a collection growing."

"We'll talk about this later, Jack," Burt said, his eyes fixed on me.

"She's taken some beautiful shots of the lakes and woodlands in Haliburton," Nora piped in. "Next time we get together we'll bring them along. Especially the ones from autumn, when the leaves are turning."

"Oh, that would be lovely," I said, knowing I'd just as soon pluck my own eyes out.

Nora put her arm around Alexandra.

"A rather expensive hobby though, isn't it dear?"

"Not as expensive as skiing," Nora answered Agnes with a tentative smile.

"What do you intend to do with your pictures then?"

"I dunno," Alexandra said. "Just keep them I guess."

"Agnes, do you still knit?" Nora asked, trying to shake off the snide tone in Agnes' questions.

"Crochet, Nora. Crochet. A world of difference, dear."

"Yes, sorry."

"Well, unfortunately I had to give it up. Rheumatism." She looked at the floor.

"Oh, what a shame," Nora said with a touch too much sentiment. "And you used to make such lovely doilies."

Burt let out a quiet laugh. I noticed Nora trying to conceal her smile. Everyone looked at Burt. Douglas entered the room and interrupted the awkward moment. "Jack, can you give me a hand in here? The roast is almost ready."

"Certainly, roommate." I climbed out of my chair and moved past Douglas into the kitchen, grateful to get away from the tension.

"You can take your seats at the table everyone," Douglas called out. "There are name cards in front of each setting. Burt, can you take care of the wine, please?"

"Yes, milord," Burt said, moving to help Agnes out of her seat.

In the kitchen, Douglas had pulled out all our good serving dishes and opened a new bottle of Scotch.

"I think we'd better slow down, don't you? And by we, I mean you."

He stopped and looked at me. "Maybe you're right. It's not going that badly now. I think everybody's warmed up a bit to one another."

"Except for your aunt's little digs. And Burt's salary. I don't know how I'm going to lie my way out of that one."

"I've told you this before," Douglas sighed. "If he accepted the salary when you offered him the job, he's got nothing to complain about."

"I know. But the receptionist—" I gulped down air, thinking... I don't know what I was thinking. "He does an awful lot of work, Douglas. I can't deny that."

Douglas stood up straight and puffed out his chest. "If he accepted the salary when you offered him the job, he's got nothing to complain about. Now. Feel better?"

"I will once this is all over," I said, spooning mashed potatoes into a serving dish.

"Maybe you should have invited each of them separately. You know, to a chicken wing night or something. It's far more pedestrian. At least for Burt anyway. And the girl doesn't know her cheese."

I gasped. "Wing nights are sacred, roommate. Nobody but you and I shall bear witness to wing night. It's a commandment."

"Well, the roast smells delicious, and your garlic mashed potatoes are perfect as always. But what can compare to my hand-cut French-style green beans?"

"My home-made gravy," I replied.

"My table setting?"

"Oh, I meant to ask you. Where did you get those dried flowers?"

"Stole them from the restaurant."

"I should have known."

Douglas and I had a laugh about the flowers. It was a lovely moment that I remember vividly. It's as if my brain has framed our exchange as the calm before the story, so to speak. As we put the finishing touches on the meal, we heard voices drifting in from the other room. It seemed as though the evening had found its own groove and didn't need any further prompting from its two nervous hosts. It was a good sign.

Douglas and I moved into the dining room, platters in hand and a song in our voices. "Here we are," we chimed out in unison. Everyone cooed over the beautifully arranged selection of meat and vegetables. Aunt Agnes' eyes lit up. She leaned over and kissed Douglas on the cheek after he had taken his seat beside her.

I sat down at the head of the table and presented the electric carving knife to Douglas, who was immediately to my left. He took it from my grasp as I watched Agnes unfold her napkin and place it on her lap.

Douglas stood up with the carving knife raised. He flipped the switch. An electronic whirring sound. Agnes looked at him and froze. I don't know if anyone else saw the look on her face, but I'll never forget it. Her lower lip quivered. Within a few seconds her chin and jowls were shaking. My eyes darted back and forth between her and Douglas, who was too preoccupied with the carving of the roast to notice what was going on around him.

My first instinct was to ask him to sit down because it seemed as if it had been something about his movements that caused Agnes to freeze, but I didn't want to draw attention to her if she was having some kind of lapse or, worse, a meltdown.

"Jack!" It was Nora. She looked at me as if I'd just stepped on her foot. I couldn't speak. "Earth calling Jack. Do you want beans?"

She thrust the gleaming silver platter piled with Douglas' beans into my hands. "Watch it," she added. "It's hot."

I served myself some beans using our antique silver tongs and placed a portion onto Douglas' plate as he carved the roast. I leaned over and passed the platter to Agnes. She had come out of her trance and took the platter with a quick nod.

"That ought to do us," Douglas said, turning off the knife and placing it in its stand in the centre of the table.

Burt was pleased that he'd managed to switch the name cards around and put himself directly across the table from Aunt Agnes. Douglas' original seating plan had Burt beside her. Obviously he had something up his sleeve. He watched her carefully as she passed the basket of fan tan rolls to Nora. I've never seen him more focused than he was when Agnes fingered the cloth napkin that she continued to place on the table then back on her lap, a repetitive motion that made me worry she was having a stroke. All the way through the meal Burt watched her, hanging on every word she said, waiting for a chance to pounce, but, for the most part, she ate her meal quietly. Perhaps his attention made her self-conscious. Or maybe she was just hungry. Perhaps she felt as though Burt was trying to befriend her because when she finally did join in the conversation, much of what she did say was directed at him.

"Nora, you're being unusually quiet tonight. Is something wrong?" Douglas asked as he mixed corn and gravy into his mound of mashed potatoes—something he wasn't allowed to do as a child that he now relishes at every opportunity, usually with company present. It makes me sick to see it, frankly.

"Just nervous I guess," Nora answered.

"No more nervous than me," Alexandra added, with a little chuckle.

"Relax and have another drink," Burt said merrily and offered her some more wine.

"It's a very good wine," Gregory said. "For a Pisse Dru. Usually I find them quite thin, but this has remarkable body."

I half expected him to add 'for its price range,' but this was Gregory in my house, not the other way around. He knew his place.

"The art of conversation is lost on the young people of today," Agnes said out of the blue. Before I had the chance to remind her that we were all over thirty-five, she continued. "I find that their social skills aren't nearly as important to them as the ability to lift large amounts of weights or where to get the best price for a pair of spandex trousers."

"Do you work out?" Alexandra asked. Agnes ignored her.

Nora lifted her napkin to her face and giggled silently.

"Oh, absolutely," Burt chimed in, smiling at Agnes. And then, raising his wine glass, he proposed a toast. "Here's to all the hot men wearing tailored tweed suits at the gym."

Gregory chuckled but quickly cut himself off. "The roast is delicious, gentlemen," he smiled.

Douglas turned his attention from his mashed potatoes to our dinner guests. His mouth formed a frown. He looked at his aunt and was about to speak when Burt started up again.

"Yes it is," he said with surprising authority. "And it is a tragedy that so many people are happy to consume alcohol and drugs instead of having an engaging conversation." He raised his wine glass in the air and directed his silent toast at Agnes. She blushed and took a quiet sip of hers, unsure of what he had just implied. "I wonder if the two things might be connected."

Douglas glanced at me nervously and then looked back down at his plate.

"I think next time we'll have roast potatoes, roommate," I said.

"Excellent idea, roommate," Douglas replied, again giving me his Joan Crawford look.

"I have a great recipe," Gregory offered. "Remind me to send it to you by e-mail."

"I will," I smiled.

"But surely," Burt began again, "You're not content to just point your finger at all young people as if they alone are responsible for their conversational ineptitude?"

Douglas squirmed and began moving uneaten food about on his plate.

"I'm sorry?" Agnes said.

"Unless it's due to an aberrant strain of DNA that's suddenly appeared in the last generation, the inability of young people to carry on stimulating conversation must be caused by something."

"Perhaps we should change the subject to something we could all participate in," Agnes said, a whip cracking in her voice. She shot Burt a look that everyone at the table saw and felt.

"Perhaps we shouldn't make sweeping, oversimplified statements without the statistics to back them up."

Silence. Burt looked at me and a smile broke on his face. He turned once again to Agnes. "I'm sorry, Agnes. You brought the subject up and I just tried to follow through. What I really want to understand is why some people are content to use their energy to complain about things and yet not put any effort into finding a way to resolve the things that they're complaining about. So, you say young people can't carry on conversations, and I'm following your lead by asking who, or what might be to blame for this situation, and how we might possibly turn *this* into a conversation itself?"

"I'm sure there are many reasons," Agnes mumbled, her face reddening.

"Such as?" Burt put his fork down.

Agnes looked at me, then at Douglas, who downed the remnants of his wine glass.

"Well, I'm sure there are many."

"Do you have a lot of conversations with young people?"

"Certainly none as belligerent as you," she blurted, her voice seething with equal parts anger and embarrassment, her cheeks crimson.

"Oh, so you'd like to be able to make a biased, condemning statement about all the people in this room and not have anyone challenge you? My dear, that's not conversation. That's dictatorship, and it doesn't swing at dinner parties."

"Burt, please," I whispered.

"What?" He was getting angry.

"There's no need for you to be so—"

Agnes stood up from the table and hobbled out of the dining room. Burt held his tongue until she was gone.

"Rude?" he offered, eyebrows arched.

"Yes," I said. I could feel the anger rising and knew I wouldn't be able to contain it much longer.

"Jack, here's what I'm doing, okay? I'm doing a number of things; engaging in conversation, being honest, and challenging what someone has said in an attempt to prove them wrong, which is only fair since their statement was wrong and unfair and, frankly, rather insulting. I haven't said any bad words. I haven't called her any names…"

"Oh shut up." It was Douglas.

"What did I say?"

"Exercise some fucking restraint," Douglas hissed at him, realizing he was out of wine. "She's an old woman for Christ's sake and this isn't the debate team. Now, open some more wine. Please."

"He's right," Alexandra nodded. "He was only confronting her. What she said wasn't very nice. And she's really snotty. Why should we all just sit here and let her have a picnic at our expense?" Burt smiled. "But she is an old woman, Burt."

Nora nodded her head. "You may not have said anything mean, but your tone of voice was insulting."

Burt's smile fell flat.

Alexandra chimed in again. "And what's going on with her face? Looks like she should be in a hospital."

Nobody answered her. Burt opened another bottle of wine and filled Douglas' glass to the rim, refilled his own and then offered it around the table. Everyone except me declined a refill. Douglas kicked me under the table and motioned for me to put my cutlery down. I tried to gesture that people were still eating, but he had his mind set.

"Goodness, I'm full," he chirped and bound out of his chair. He began clearing plates and cutlery. Above the clatter of china and silverware he addressed his guests. "I hope you all saved room for coffee and dessert." He finished clearing Gregory and Nora's plates and then nodded at me.

"I sure have, roommate," I said, rising from my seat and hoping that the evening would soon settle again. "I'll help you with the dishes."

I moved past Agnes' empty chair and lifted her plate gently. I never thought to see if she'd finished eating. I gathered my plate and cutlery, then Alexandra's, and signalled to Burt to join us in the kitchen. The only plate left on the table was his, so he stood up and carried it with him, leaving Gregory, Nora and Alexandra awkwardly grinning at each other.

When I rounded the corner and entered the kitchen, Douglas had already placed the dirty plates on the counter and was stooped over the sink. I heard a loud inhaling sound. I thought maybe he'd developed a sudden sinus infection, but then I smelt a familiar stench. I cleared my throat. Douglas wheeled about, pulling a small brown bottle away from his nose.

"Roommate!" I gasped. "Poppers? Really?"

"Yeah, and before dessert," he moaned.

Suddenly Burt was behind me with his plate, and even before he could see what was going on he gleefully called out, "Yay, poppers!"

Douglas looked mortified, but after a few seconds his eyes glazed over and a ridiculous grin spread across his face. "That was a delicious meal, roommate. Don't you think, Burt?"

"Yes," Burt said, squeezing past me. "I just wish I'd been offered seconds or had a chance to finish my firsts. You guys are too uptight about the old lady. I was just being honest, you know, trying to figure out if there was anything behind her theory or if she was just being a cu— I really hate that word but it applies. You know, whatever's wrong with her, she needs to sort it out for herself and not dump it on everyone around her." He put his plate in the sink. "Honestly, the art of conversation is lost on the young people of today. Imagine! If our elders weren't so fucking anal-retentive perhaps we'd know how to talk to them. The next thing she'll say is how much better things were when slavery was legal. Give me those poppers, Douglas. I think I need to be a little less conscious right now."

Douglas moved closer to Burt and passed him the brown bottle. "How come you and I never finished consummating our...?" he asked, putting his free hand up against Burt's crotch.

"Because Jack said he'd fire me if we did." Burt glanced at me as he twisted the cap off and pressed the bottle to his left nostril. Covering the other nostril with his index finger, he inhaled deeply. He switched hands and repeated the action. "Mmmmm. This is really pure. Holy shit."

"They're expensive as hell, but no headaches," Douglas said with a ridiculous, exaggerated grin, his body loose and weaving back and forth.

This is where I snapped. "Okay, enough with the poppers! There are other guests here and we really don't want them thinking we're serving glue with the cheesecake. Let's get the coffee and dessert ready."

Douglas reached forward and slid his tongue into Burt's ear.

Burt in turn grabbed at Douglas' right nipple through his shirt and squeezed. Douglas shrieked, recoiling. "They're very sensitive!"

"I'll make a note of it." Burt turned around and placed his hands on the coffee maker. "Where is my blender anyway?"

The phone rang. Douglas moved to pick up the portable phone on the counter. He looked at me as he pressed the talk button and said hello.

"Let's make some really great coffee," Burt said, dreamily. "Have you got Kicking Horse? I heard they're supposed to be going completely organic soon."

"Fuck!" Douglas pushed a button on the phone and slammed it down on the counter.

"Maybe later," Burt smiled.

"What is it, roommate?" I asked, afraid to know the answer, as if anything worse could happen to our dinner party.

"Cut off," Douglas said, gritting his teeth. "I hate it when that happens."

Burt pulled the glass pot out of the coffee maker's cradle and wanged it against the counter top.

"Now we know what happened to the blender," I said, taking the pot from his hands. "At least you didn't break this one." Before he had a chance to respond, I continued. "Look, why don't you two go back out there and crack open a window so our guests don't suffocate on amyl nitrate fumes? I'll take care of the coffee and dessert."

"You'll use the good dessert plates with the forkettes?" Douglas said, furrowing his brow for emphasis.

"Yes, I will, Martha. Burt, why don't you tell the story of how you got John Waters to do that interview after his press agent told you no?"

"That's my favourite magazine story," Burt smiled. "Except for the one about the receptionist who owns a mansion filled with men's underwear."

"I know, I know," I sighed.

"That was our best-selling issue even though everyone hated the photographs you chose to go with it. Even John Waters. He e-mailed me, you know? And he had a few choice words about your underwear dinner party layout as well. Fashion spread."

"Don't."

"He said they were so ugly he was jealous."

"How nice of him," I mumbled, hoping he would soon tire of the subject.

"Do you think Agnes would know who John Waters is?" Burt asked.

"If not there's always the *Pink Flamingos* DVD you gave me for Christmas last year."

"Probably still in its wrapper," Burt said. "You've never even seen *Female Trouble,* have you?"

"Can you speed it up a bit?" Douglas hated banter that excluded him.

"I ask you to always remember that you *are* in the presence of a star," Burt sighed dramatically, and pushed Douglas out of the kitchen.

I pulled the cheesecake out of its container after the coffee started brewing. Then I went back into the living room.

Gregory was talking about his life partner, Yan, the oncologist. Yan had discovered an effective mood elevator, and Gregory was now trying to convince Burt that he should switch. Aunt Agnes was nowhere in sight.

"What's going on with your aunt, Douglas?" Nora asked.

The phone rang again. Douglas jumped out of his chair. It rang only once. When he reached the telephone and picked it up, he quietly said, "Fuck," put it down again and returned to the table. He sat down, clearly agitated.

"I don't know, and I'd really rather not talk about it," he said. Then he stood up again. "I'll go get the cups." He left the table. On his way out he passed Agnes. She walked unsteadily into the living room and rejoined us at the table. I took a good look at her as she sat down. She looked haggard.

Before anyone had a chance to resume the conversation, a loud crash rang through the apartment. The woman in the apartment above us must have dropped something quite heavy on her floor. Agnes was tucking a curl of hair behind her ear and jumped at the sound. The sudden movement dislodged one of her earrings—clip-ons. It fell and landed in front of her. Douglas came into the dining room, both hands filled with coffee cups. The phone rang again. Douglas stopped dead and dropped two cups, both of which landed on the love seat, bounced and then landed on the floor. Neither of them broke, but Douglas looked devastated. He continued toward us, placing the remaining cups on the table.

"We don't have any more clean cups," he hissed quietly.

"Just rinse them out," I whispered back as the phone continued to ring. "But get the phone first."

Agnes reached forward and picked up the fallen earring. It left a red stain on the tablecloth. I saw it and immediately looked at Douglas, but he was racing for the phone. Alexandra was staring at the red spot where Agnes' earring had landed. The phone sounded again. I inched myself backwards in my chair, wondering who it might be and what could possibly happen next. Gregory fondled a piece of cutlery while he stared at Alexandra. Burt was captivated by something outside the window directly behind the dining table. Nora scanned the apartment looking for the phone. She turned to Alexandra and then followed her gaze at the stain on the tablecloth. She gasped. I sat frozen, watching Aunt Agnes clip the earring back on. Douglas reached the mantle and picked up the phone.

"Hello!" he bellowed.

I could feel the tension building again, rising along with my heart rate. Everyone's eyes were on Douglas. I'm sure he could feel them too. He turned his back to us.

"Oh, hi mom," he said, his voice lifting with relief. "Sorry, yes we're a little busy with dinner. Yes, she's here. We're having our Sunday night roast beef."

"Tell her I say hello," Agnes called out.

"What?" There was a long silence as he listened. He turned and glared at me, the colour of his cheeks replaced by a startling pallor. "Hold on a sec. I have to go to the kitchen." Douglas pulled the receiver away from his ear and gestured for me to go with him.

"Excuse us," I said, standing up.

Once in the kitchen, Douglas gave me a pleading look. He covered the mouthpiece with his hand and in a serious voice, said, "I'm going to need you to remain very calm."

"What? Why? What is it?"

"Sssssh!" he hissed, and then put the phone back to his ear. "Sorry, mom. I'm just trying to figure out what to do." He listened for a few moments. "Well that won't work because we have other guests. Four, besides Aunt Agnes, but they aren't very... Never mind. What should we do?" A tone of despair had crept into his voice. "We can't just ask them to leave. What will peop—"

"What is it?" I cut in. He shushed me with his free hand. "What's going on, roommate?"

Douglas just shook his head at me and kept talking to his mother. "How did you find this out, the police? Well thank heavens for that. Did she phone them? He phoned them?! How could he? This is unbelievable. Absolutely unbelievable. A night of horrors. No, she's in terrible shape! She looks like she was run over by a truck. No, I'm most seriously worried about her. There's no way around this, mother. I think you'd better just come over right now and get her. She's hammered, by the way. I'm sure that's not going to make this any easier. Right."

Douglas looked at me, shell-shocked, just as Burt walked into the kitchen. I could tell from his body movements that he, too, was drunk. Douglas lowered the receiver and blinked.

"What is it?" I practically shouted. "Roommate, I insist you tell me what's going on!"

"Temper, temper," Burt said, lurching toward the sink.

"That was my mother, calling from Aunt Agnes' house," Douglas began, bracing us for what was to follow. He continued in a lower tone of voice: "Uncle Tuck is dead." He punctuated the last word by gesturing with the telephone receiver in his hand. And then in a whisper, "Stabbed to death."

Silence.

Burt weaved back and forth, his eyes open wide. "Oh my God," he said. "How to ruin a dinner party. I can see the headlines now: Meat and murder! Quick! Send Gregory over to take a seven hundred dollar photograph of the murder scene and I'll go get a part-time job at McDonald's." I could just imagine it. I'd never be able to go into a McDonald's again if that were the case. Nobody has ever seen me merge a McChicken with a Big Mac, and perhaps it's best that way.

"Oh, and your coffee maker isn't working," Burt said almost gleefully.

"Must have been a gift," I sneered.

"Blood everywhere," Douglas whispered. "All over the kitchen and living room carpet my mother says."

Burt spun about and looked down at the floor around him. Seeing no blood, he grabbed the bottle of poppers and handed it to Douglas. "You go first," he said. Douglas pushed the bottle away.

"Oh my God," Douglas moaned. "Uncle Tuck is dead."

"Roommate, I'm so sorry," I told him and pointed at the telephone receiver in his hand. He seemed to have forgotten he was still on the call with his mother.

"So she stabbed him, did she?" Burt asked. "The matriarch is a murderess. Sounds like an Agatha Christie novella that never got published."

"Dead," Douglas repeated, loudly.

"Ssssh!" I put my hand over his mouth. "You don't want her to hear do you?"

"She's the one who just told me!" And then he clued in. "Right. Right." And he gestured with his head toward the dining room. Then he lifted the receiver to his face and spoke to his mother. "Gotta go, mom. Get here as soon as humanly possible, if not faster."

Douglas started to shake his head mournfully from side to side. "I knew I should have taken that public relations class at university."

"What are you talking about?"

"How do we deal with this? What will we tell everyone?"

"Is that what you're worried about?" Burt said, incredulous. "What about your poor Aunt?"

"Poor Aunt," I said. "You'd just as soon have eaten her for dinner the way you behaved."

"Eat or be eaten," Burt said, his face changing suddenly with the realization. A crooked smile. "No wonder she's been such a bitch."

Douglas shot him a dirty look. "Make yourself useful and clean the plates."

"Douglas!" I gasped. "You can't talk to our guest like that."

"Oh shut up, Jack. He always scrapes the plates when he's here for dinner."

"Yes, but he usually offers. You don't order a guest to help clean up."

"I think I'll have my dessert at the baths if you don't mind thank you very much," Burt said, weaving through the kitchen and out into the hallway. He poked his head into the living room and announced, "Everybody, the coffee maker has died. I'm afraid you'll have to settle for tea. And collective moan now..."

I grabbed him from behind and yanked him back into the hallway. Agnes let out a little sigh. "Oh, I'll miss my after dinner cup of coffee," I heard her say. "That's too bad."

"Do you have any herbal?" Nora called out. "I hope you have herbal. Alexandra's allergic to caffeine."

From the foyer, Burt let out an uproarious laugh. I leaned out and saw him shrug into his leather jacket. "Now I've heard everything!"

"Ssssh!"

"Yes, we have herbal," Douglas shouted.

"Bag on the side," Burt said at the doorway, and laughed again as Douglas paced back and forth in the kitchen. "Hey, you'll fit in perfectly tonight. No tipping." Douglas hushed him, but to no avail. "Okay, gents, I'm leaving now," Burt almost sang out as he zipped up his jacket, "To go have sex with someone I'll probably never see again. I hope you all will have as much fun. Thank you for the lovely evening, but I don't care to sink with this ship." And with that, he turned and left.

As Douglas poured milk and cream into small porcelain jugs, I discreetly took the bottle of poppers and dropped them into the garbage. With the milk and creamers set, Douglas tucked in his shirt and nodded at me. "Let's get on with it."

We approached the table together. Douglas placed cream, milk and sugar in the centre of the table. "The water is just boiling now. I'll be right back with the dessert."

"I think your employee Burt is a little unstable, Jack," Agnes said as Douglas left the room. "I hope his behaviour here tonight isn't a reflection of his abilities at work."

"Oh no, Agnes," I said, at this point grateful for any conversation. "He's a very good worker. He's just had too much to drink."

"Well, I certainly hope that if he's going out to do what he said he was going to do, he won't bareback."

Gregory's eyes grew wide. He looked to me for a reaction. I was too stunned to know what to say. Nora couldn't hide her laughter.

Agnes continued. "You'd think with all the pain and suffering the gays have gone through they'd have learned about the preservation of self and community. But no, the infection rate keeps rising. I told those people at ACT that they weren't doing their jobs, and it would be a cold day in hell before I'd donate my hard-earned money to them and their lackadaisical stance on human health. Risk management indeed." And then she let loose an indignant huff.

Gregory joined in. "Many people share your beliefs Agnes, but most of them don't speak of it openly."

"And why is that young man?" Agnes asked, sounding haughty like Maggie Smith on a really bad day. Gregory looked at me and then back at Agnes. "I'd like to know," she goaded him.

"Well. I think that's a matter of opinion."

"What's your opinion then, Gregory?"

Slowly, Gregory replied, choosing his words carefully. "I think people want to minimize the emotional and psychological implications of HIV and AIDS so not to offend or stig—"

"Yes, yes, yes," Agnes interrupted. "I know all this. What I don't understand is how anyone expects things to change for the better. Instead of changing the behaviour, they just want to take a pill. Well, a hand full of pills, really. Imagine calling *that* a cocktail."

"I'm surprised," Gregory said with a tentative smile on his face.

"Well, I have a personal interest," she answered back as Douglas entered with the cheesecake. "Douglas," Agnes said loudly.

"Yes, dear?"

"If I ever find out that you've been having unprotected sex, I'll kill you."

Douglas froze. All I could think was that Burt had missed Agnes's shining moment. How ironic.

"Really. I would hope that any relative of mine would have more common sense than that. And if you're positive and spreading this disease, then you're a lot more sick than anyone can remedy. I'd disown you lickety-split."

"Yes, ma'am."

The phone rang. Douglas spun around quickly and muttered,

"Saved by the bell," under his breath. "Jack, can you get that, please? I have to cut the cheesecake. And no cracks. Oh... Burt's gone. Never mind."

"Hello?" I answered on the fourth ring.

"Jack?"

"Yes. Who is this?"

"It's Burt. I'm downstairs in your lobby."

"What's the matter?"

"Nothing."

"Then why did you call?"

"The police are here."

"Then there's something the matter," I replied, trying to sound cheery and aloof even though a lump had risen in my throat. I don't know if I gasped loud enough for the others to hear me, but I certainly felt as though the wind had been knocked out of me. "Hold on a second. Roommate?" I carried the phone into the kitchen. Douglas was two steps behind me.

"What now?" he hissed at me inside the kitchen.

"Burt is downstairs in the lobby," I hissed back. "The police are here."

"But we haven't finished!" Douglas said, fishing the tea bags out of the pot. "Jesus H. Fuckpole! Tell him to fake a seizure and distract them."

"I heard that!" Burt shouted into the phone. "Thanks for keeping my secret, Jack. I have a familial—"

I covered the receiver with my hand.

"We'll take Aunt Agnes up to the roof garden and hide her," Douglas suggested.

"This isn't a Hitchcock movie, roommate. Besides, we wouldn't be able to get her up that tiny staircase," I said in a harsh whisper. "It's nineteen inches wide. I can barely get through it."

"We could grease the walls."

"What did you say?" Alexandra called from the dining room.

"Nothing. We'll be right out. I think we got the coffee maker to work."

"I take mine black," Agnes called out in a withered voice. "But I'm sure you boys know that by now."

"This is crazy," Douglas said, exasperated.

"Not our best party?"

"She used to tell us when we visited her home that it was extravagant to use more than three squares of toilet paper."

"Tissue, roommate," I scolded him. "Toilet *tissue*."

"Right," he acquiesced.

"There's never any good reason to make reference to the below areas, especially below and behind."

"No one ever asked her if the three squares rule applies when you have diarrhea."

"Or if you shit your pants," I added. Douglas looked at me and we both burst out laughing.

Burt's voice crackled over the line and interrupted our moment of fun. "Okay, if you guys are making jokes, I'm hanging up."

"You can't leave now, Burt," I pleaded into the receiver.

"The cop car is empty. They're probably somewhere else."

"Are you sure?"

"Yup. Car's empty."

"Probably crazy Catherine again."

"What?" Douglas said, wrinkling his brow.

"The police car is empty. I said I think they're probably at crazy Catherine's apartment again. She thinks her apartment is haunted."

"Yes, by her dead cat," Douglas monotoned.

"Thanks for dinner, Jack. And thank Doug for me. See you tomorrow morning."

The conversation ended with a click. I put the phone down on the counter.

Douglas picked up the teapot and signalled for me to follow. "Let them eat cake," he said with a devilish smile.

"What's going on?" Gregory asked as we entered the dining room.

"Nothing," I replied calmly. "That was just Burt calling from downstairs to say there's been some kind of disturbance in the building and the police are here. I bet it's Catherine again." I turned to glance at Douglas. "Remember last month when she tried to have that séance and the Redmonds called the police because of all the noise?"

"Yes I do, roommate," he said, placing the teapot down on the table. "Maybe she's trying again."

"Who knows."

"All that fuss over a dead cat."

Douglas moved to his chair and addressed the remaining guests. "Okay, the coffee maker is working again, but it'll be a few minutes. The tea is ready now."

"That Burt should be chastised first thing in the morning for causing such a disturbance with your dinner, Jack," Agnes said, indignant, as we settled back down at the table.

Douglas smiled and lifted a slice of cheesecake on to a plate and passed it to Agnes. Nora looked at the dessert, then turned and whispered something to Alexandra.

"I'll bet you know what that is young lady," Agnes said to

Alexandra, who immediately cast her eyes downward.

"Cheese-cake," Douglas said phonetically, loudly, glaring at Alexandra. I tried not to laugh.

Outside a police siren sounded, ominously close by. On the walls and surfaces of furniture in the dining room lurid reflections of flashing red lights danced. Aunt Agnes turned in her chair and looked grimly out the window, following the car with her eyes. I caught a quick glimpse of Douglas. He had broken out in a sweat. The lights and siren faded as the police car sped past our building. Agnes turned back with the most pronounced look of relief on her face.

"Yan and I have decided to move to Calgary," Gregory announced suddenly, and much to my delight. Until what he said had sunk in.

"What on earth for?"

"We're so very tired of Toronto. People are so unfriendly. The rest of the country hates us. I don't like the community here and frankly I've had enough of the pretension and icy contempt with which everyone treats one another. Also the restaurants suck unless you're a millionaire, or from Central America. Why there are so many places serving arepas I'll never understand. You might as well eat cardboard."

"Well I just don't know how to respond to that, Gregory," I said evenly. "But Calgary? Rednecks, cowboys, barren wastelands, those horrific winters? Are you sure about this?"

"I've already made the arrangements and secured a job with a paper there," Gregory answered.

"Nobody called me for a reference," I said, pouring tea into Alex's cup.

"I didn't need one. I sent them samples of my writing. That seemed to be satisfactory. I'll be working on my first novel as well. And Yan is looking forward to semi-retirement."

"In Aruba. But Calgary?" I asked, trying to stay focussed on the conversation.

"Well congratulations then," Douglas said. "I'll go get the coffee." And then the telephone rang. Douglas jumped and dropped the pie lifter. It clattered on the thick glass cake plate. "I'll get it," he said.

"Goodness. So much commotion," Aunt Agnes said.

Douglas and I left the dining area together. He stopped in the foyer and answered the phone as I crept into the kitchen.

"Hello" he said wearily. Then a pause. "Yes, come right up." Douglas moved the receiver from his ear and held it out before his torso. His right hand moved forward and touched a single key on the pad. I heard a faint electronic beep before he placed the receiver down in its cradle. In the kitchen I grabbed the coffee pot and we went back to the dining room.

"Who was that?" Agnes asked as we sat back down at the table.

"Mom and dad," Douglas said quietly to Agnes as I poured coffee into a cup.

"You'll need two more cups," Agnes said to Douglas.

"They won't be staying," he said far more gravely than was necessary.

I noticed Agnes' head was bowed a bit when I poured her coffee.

"Oh dear," she said in a ghost of a voice. She was looking at the red spot on the tablecloth before her. She lifted a hand to her left ear and fingered the earring there.

"Are you all right, Auntie?" Douglas asked. (Did I forget to mention that Douglas pronounces the word like a Brit? *Awntee*.)

Agnes moved her hand to her chin and looked at the dinner guests surrounding her. "Terr... Yes Douglas, I think so."

Voices and footsteps in the hallway.

"I…uh…" Aunt Agnes continued, her eyes thin slits behind folds of skin. "Douglas, I killed your Uncle Tuck, earlier this evening," she said gazing from Douglas to Alex, then Nora and then Gregory. "My husband," she clarified for non-family members. "He was... He was..." It was like she had had the wind knocked out of her. She sat there, deflated, perhaps a bit relieved. "I had to."

Gregory shifted uncomfortably and lowered his eyes. Alexandra sat frozen. Nora just looked at me. Aunt Agnes folded her hands together on her lap.

"Agnes," a voice called out. It was Douglas' mother. She hadn't even knocked.

"Oh, Carole, hello," Agnes said, her voice releasing all kinds of stress. "And not a moment too soon. I think perhaps you'd better take me to the police station. Just let me finish my coffee first, if you don't mind."

Agnes stood up slowly and finished the last of her coffee. She excused herself from the table, thanked us for a lovely dinner and apologized for the disturbance. And before leaving with her sister, she turned to me and said, "Don't forget what I said about Burt. He's a loose cannon."

When Douglas came back to the table and sat down he looked at Aunt Agnes' empty seat, his gaze fixed on the red smudge on the tablecloth. "That'll be a nasty stain," he said, then poured some more tea for Alexandra. I filled four cups with coffee. "I hope this won't affect my job," Douglas said as I reached for the cream. "I mean if word gets out. You know how people love to talk. And exaggerate. Especially where I work."

"Don't worry, roommate. Your parents will take care of things, I'm sure. And if not, you can always change your name."

Douglas' parents managed to keep the events of that evening relatively quiet. Aunt Agnes spent one night in detention and was released. No formal charges were laid against her. It turned out that almost since their first year together, Uncle Tuck had been abusive toward her, first verbally, and then, after they moved in together, physically. Apparently her doctor was suspicious about her bruises and abrasions, but she always managed to assuage his fears. We never found out exactly what it was that made her snap and finally defend herself. Some things, I guess, should remain private.

I don't remember who was the first to call Agnes Aunt Stabby, but I do recall Douglas' mother referring to Uncle Tuck as Uncle Trip on several occasions. How refreshing that she managed to show a sense of humour about such an unpleasant circumstance. Or was she being heartless? Six of one...

It was Douglas' mother who ensured that Uncle Tuck was buried in the cheapest casket possible. She only appeared at the funeral to accompany her sister. It was a very sombre but speedy service. No tears were shed. At the end of the service, Aunt Agnes thanked us for coming, then quickly got into a limousine that would take her and her sister to the airport for a two month vacation in the Virgin Islands. When they returned, Douglas passed on the news that Agnes had arrived home tanned, relatively refreshed, and eager to find a good therapist.

There's really not much of a moral to this story, except that maybe Aunt Agnes was right about the art of conversation being lost on the younger generation. Douglas and I have invited her to dinner many times since the ordeal, but she always replies with a courteous, "No, thank you. I think I'll stay in." I don't blame her.

Before he and Yan left for Calgary, Gregory received death threats after writing a column about how heterosexuals should spend more time worrying about the escalating divorce rate rather than trying to stop same-sex marriages. This prompted him to adopt a pseudonym, Morris Middleton. I still believe that Leon Cuisiné would have been ideal for him. After he finished reviewing all of Calgary's restaurants he started doing book reviews. I got a post card from him telling me maybe Toronto wasn't so bad after all. He closed it off with a pithy 'Oh well,' and a post script that simply read: 'Salt is NOT a spice.'

Burt quit the magazine and tried his luck doing stand-up comedy. It didn't last long. Three shows, in fact. Within a few weeks he was hired back at the magazine, but in a different position: mine. By that time I had received the demotion I had always wanted, to Food and Lifestyle Director. My first column, "Dinner Guests and Just Desserts" caused a sensation when it ran. The article was about the perils of throwing dinner parties and the responsibilities of the guests in making it a success. I mailed a copy of it to Nora and Alexandra. They're still together, but I haven't seen them since that night. Oh yes, and they never returned our dinner invitation. I guess that's fine with me. How good a host can a bad guest be?

Douglas is still with the restaurant and seems happy enough. We bought a new white tablecloth when Uncle Trip's blood stain could not be removed. It cost a lot of money. We couldn't afford it, but it looks fabulous. I threatened to send the bill to Aunt Agnes, but decorum stopped me. Instead, I stole the money from the magazine. All the other partners were embezzling funds, so who would notice? We maintain hope that one day Aunt Stabby will accept one of our invitations—to lunch—at a restaurant.

I'LL WAIT HERE

Abel enters quickly, kicks the muck off his shoes at the doorway but does not take them off. It's dark in my apartment so I can't see the streaks and stains he leaves on the floor as he moves in to the room toward me. I will see them in the morning. The one on the couch with his head cupped in his hands is me, watching nonsense on television and wondering why things, people, plans collapse. Impermanence is the new malaise. I don't think I can adjust to it, all the uncertainty. And then there's Abel.

If all the problems and imperfections that might prevent a person from loving someone else were rolled up into one big hulking, lumbering man, it would be Abel. He's a walking, talking billboard for one night stands: distant, unemotional, disinterested—at least while clothed. I'm sure he does something well—other than fucking—I'm just having a hard time remembering what it is, and what it means that I forget. We've been having sex for a few months. I'm not sure what that makes him, if anything. Boyfriend? No. Fuck buddy? Perhaps. Maybe a little more than that… Probably not.

Wisely, he sits adjacent to me on the love seat, the cushions sucking down and inward beneath his weight. He lights a cigarette, drops the burnt-out match on the coffee table. Deep inside I shake my head.

My cat Maurice skulks past my feet, shooting me an accusing glance and pausing to rub his head against my shin. I hear a muted purring. Abel blows clouds of smoke into the room. He has an air of casualness I envy and manners I despise.

"So," he says, cigarette bouncing between his lips as he speaks. Flakes of ash fall downward onto his pants. "What's up man?"

"They fired me."

"Fuck!"

Perfect response, I think to myself. Because that's probably what he wants to do. And probably what he thinks will make me feel better. He wouldn't be entirely wrong, but given the circumstances, it's not what I want. Right now, anyway.

What I want is to have somebody who knows me so well that they could just look at me and words would be obsolete. His glance would say it all. But until he shows up, how can you tell if the person you're just fucking is even capable of that kind of intimacy without uttering the dreaded word *date*? Or *like*. Or *overnight*. Or *yes*. Or *more*.

"Are you all right for money for a while?" Abel asks, shifting forward on the love seat and turning on the floor lamp.

His question takes me by surprise. It's not because it's invasive, but rather because it's not what I expect from him. It's a detail of my life that he wants, and it means something more than just fucking. I am not sure how this makes me feel. I look at him and... Shouldn't I feel something? Anything?

"Yes, I'm not worried about that right now," I lie.

"Okay, good."

Leaning back, relieved, I'm probably asking too much of him to sit and talk with me fully clothed. To throw my financial concerns into the conversation would cause one—if not both—of us to short circuit.

When I was twenty-one and new to the scene, a friend I encountered regularly at the bars told me that there was an etiquette to "All of this," he said after tequila shots, the cheap kind that requires lime and salt and makes grown men grimace. "Never tell someone you're fucking that you love him, no matter how much you think it's true. You will always, always regret it."

"Okay, noted." I replied, wiping remnants of salt from the skin between my thumb and index finger.

"And never lend them money. Buy them drinks, bum a smoke, loan them CDs. But never lend money. Oh, and no matter what anyone tells you, wear a condom."

He flashed a look at the bartender, wearing only a jock strap. Then he looked back at me. "And if you have to tell him you love him, make sure you're wearing a condom when you say it."

"You got an ashtray?" Abel asks, pulling the cigarette from his mouth. Ashes flutter from it, fall to the cushions of the love seat.

"Just grab a small dish or a saucer from the kitchen cupboard," I say. And he moves to the kitchen, does as he's told. He never stops to question why, after months of fucking, I've never asked him anything personal. Not his last name. Or job. Or status. Do I need to know? He always wears condoms, he told me, thereby pre-empting that particular conversation.

I feel his large hands on my shoulders. He presses down and in between my shoulder blades, tries to massage me. "Don't worry," he says from behind. "You'll find yourself a better job and probably make more money too."

"Did you eat yet?" I ask him.

"No, not yet. You?"

"Just some cheese puffs."

"That'll rot your insides."

"Faster than smoking?"

He drags on the cigarette, now barely a stub, and exhales the smoke up into the air as he says, "So." I turn and face him. "Do you wanna go out somewhere and celebrate?"

"Celebrate what?"

"Your chance to get a better job of course! Some people would never think that being fired is like being given a second chance at success."

He has a point.

"Wow," I say. "I thought you were going to be all judgmental about me getting fired."

"Why would I?"

Good question. The unspoken answer is: Because you don't know me and I don't know you.

"Go jump in the shower," he says, moving back to the love seat and stubbing the cigarette out into the saucer.

"Are you gonna join me?" I ask, almost hopeful now that he will.

"No, I had one before I left. You go ahead. I'll wait here."

SMOKING

A need, an urge, crawls upward inside of me, surfaces from the layers of mess and meat and bone, like giant-size blisters of gas in a can of soda waiting to be released. Intuitively I sense it rising and scan the clutter of my desk: two empty coffee cups, a salt shaker, a printout of an angry e-mail from a former friend seething with her Chopra-styled observations about me, paper clips, USB cables, countless packs of matches bearing the logos of disreputable establishments, and there, beneath this carpet of confusion, lies my trusty sabre.

I reach for the thin, pressed paper package and flip open the top, disregarding the bold warnings of fatal lung disease, addiction and toxic second-hand emissions that will kill my nonexistent children. I remove the thin cylinder and raise it to my lips. A match scratches against a deep brown strip and ignites, throwing a small wave of flame. I tense, move the lighted match and inhale. Then, magically, momentarily, the clutter around me disappears. The din diminishes. My lungs scream quietly and tighten. And in the grey cloud I exhale float the broken-down particles of a healthier, more whole self.

THREE WORDS AWAY

I remember you—vividly. I remember the way you walked, the cut and colour of the clothes you wore, your thick mop of blonde hair. I remember how you gazed into my eyes when you talked to me, the way your neck craned upwards to kiss me when we were having sex, the warm, wet caress of your lips and your hands gripping me, pulling me closer to your smooth body. I remember you well. The memory of you haunts me, stops me in my tracks when I think I've moved on, past you, but you're still here. Your name ricochets off the walls of my mind; the echoes an inescapable reminder of how wrong I was, how frightened and unknowing. How did I get from there to here?

I'm not expecting it to be you I see through the front window of a restaurant, but even from across the street I can tell it's you. To be perfectly honest, I'd rather not go through this. I'd rather walk past, oblivious, but as I step closer, I can tell by the rock in my stomach that it is you. The feeling itself is a reminder, thick and heavy. I pass the Celestial Gardens Szechuan Restaurant thinking, *how appropriate, how spicy.* I'm going to get hot all over again.

I still have the letter you wrote me. It came tucked inside a greeting card with a forlorn-looking clown crying on the front and, on the inside, in your bold handwriting in black ink you wrote: *Sorry. I really am. X O. Danny.* I pull it out of my filing cabinet and read it whenever I need a reminder that somebody went out of their way to get through to me, to show me they loved me.

I was already in the process of running away from you when you wrote me that letter; it was the only way I knew how to respond. I was frightened by your intensity and capacity to love. Do you remember? I'm sure you do, but you've probably changed in the meantime, become wiser. I am still very much like you remember me but I'm in a different place today. I'm searching for love, the very thing that used to frighten me. And now it sees me coming and in turn and runs from me. What terrible irony I have earned in my adult life, and shame.

And so I pass by your restaurant and I don't acknowledge you in spite of what I know and remember and feel. My response to you is muted, layered. It is one of thwarted good intentions and realizations that have come too late, like searing pain on flesh, dulled by time. What good is the ache without the intensity? I can't tell you I'm sorry because I'm sorry isn't enough, but I can tell you for the first time that I love you. I did.

I've walked past your restaurant twenty times in the past five days and haven't seen you since Monday morning. The city is a bitter, icy blast, anguished and frozen. The brutal concrete beneath my feet feels like it's on the verge of cracking open as I pace up and down Jarvis Street. By the time I approach the Celestial Gardens Szechuan Restaurant my heart is racing ahead of me, anxious, anticipatory, pushing and pulling. I've got soothing music playing in my headphones; pan flutes blowing above the sound of waves gently lapping an unpolluted shore and women softly singing, *You are one, You are love, You are the spirit and everything* and other calming clichés. I play it in an attempt to maintain some sense of peace, but it only reminds me of how stupid and helpless I feel, and how lonely and desperate I am. Just by trying to feel better I end up remembering all the stupid things I've done that lead to this; watching you dancing at Rock 'N Roll Fag Bar, the eye contact in the darkness, the nervous hello, shots, letting you take my hand, our fingers entwined, the kisses from your plump lips, and taking you home with me after you were obviously drunk but seemed only to need one thing—to be with me. So you said. I'm just walking, thinking about what kind of world we live in that you and I aren't together now, and that of all the mistakes I have made, you are the most obvious and uncomplicated one I wish I could undo. And then, all of a sudden, Danny!

There you are, across the street. I call your name out, my voice hoarse in the icy air. But you've got music playing too, so you can't hear me above of what I imagine is Nancy Sinatra singing "These Boots Are Made For Walking," so I run parallel to you and then ahead of you, dodging cars to get to your side of the street, to get your attention. And then at last I swerve, jerk, and land in front of you.

You stand there, a little shocked, probably embarrassed and uncomfortable because you thought I was smart enough to leave you alone, to leave it alone. But I'm not so smart. You just stand there frozen for a moment as I feel warm fear rising from deep inside. You look as though you want to run, as if I was missing an arm and had just asked you for spare change. It isn't as if we meant something to each other some dim moment ago. Yes, I can see that your insides have hardened to match your muscular exterior and, yes, I can't help but wonder if it is really you in there somewhere or whether I just can't see past your pain or your pouting lips or your heavy black boots that were made for walking or your leather jacket and your hair sticking up, so defiant, so guarded, so much product.

I reach forward and pull the earphones off your head. I look into your eyes and they are no longer confused and hurt as I remember them. They are black and unyielding and tell me you couldn't be any less interested in talking to me. I understand. And not only because somebody once did the same thing to me. There are many reasons why I've followed you and why I can't help the fear and the tenderness and yearning I feel, or forget the many faces and names and nights alone since you. It's important to grab onto what is in front of me now: you. And you don't have to be nice to me because we're not at your restaurant. You could just push me to the side and walk away, kick me, punch me, scream at me, do it all Danny, because I deserve it, I really do. But you could also listen—suspiciously at first, all right. You could try. Oh, how I wish you would listen to me. I would tell you I'm sorry, that I love you, that I hate myself for letting you go, and I'd tell you how afraid I am of losing you over and over again, although haven't I already lost you, and for good? But dare I speak when there is no arc to follow, no climax or resolution? Just a million plot points exploding in my mind and the cold silence of your eyes revealing nothing. How did you get so big? So hard? Is it because of me? The one who is sorry.

This is what I do as I roam up and down the streets. I think thoughts about you that most people would consider sad, if not perverted. My synapses keep firing to continue the thin thread that stretches between then and now. There's not enough to grab hold of, but enough to keep me grasping, in my mind; frayed tendrils leading from lust to oblivion. I don't want to be here without you. Shit.

The truth is I haven't bumped into you in the street. I haven't chased after you or called the restaurant, hoping to hear your voice. I haven't gone in for dinner or even told my friends that I'm obsessing about you again. I'm standing here alone around the corner from the Celestial Gardens Szechuan Restaurant, wishing I was God for one hour so I could know how you feel. But what do I know? *What if* and *sorry*, and they don't make for a life of warmth and tenderness, a passionate hug and kiss when I come home after a shitty day. What if doesn't caulk in the cracks of my loneliness and sorry doesn't erase the pain. Maybe I'm supposed to stay three words away from what I need the most. I could say them now, Danny, really. I love you. But...

Wait a minute. This is bullshit.

Okay, I'm sorry that it didn't work out between us. All right? I treated you badly. I was young and inexperienced and, most of all, afraid. I can apologize to you, sure, but when do we move on? When do you acknowledge me in public again? When do you nod discreetly as we pass or maybe smile or even say hello? Will you ever get over it? Grow up? Go around it? Move on?

Do I just keep getting fucked up over you every couple of years until I have to move to another country just to get away from the possibility of running into you? Would you like me to move so you can stop avoiding me?

Well I won't leave. No way.

One day, a man is going kiss me, hard and wet, and he's going to really mean it. And I won't have to run all over the city to find out who he is, where he lives and if he's single or even gay for that matter. This guy is gonna love me and when we have sex it'll last for hours and we'll get all sweaty and we'll cum at the same time and I'll be able to look back at my little fling with you, at those few exaggerated, tender, wonderful moments of insanity and I will... What will I do? Laugh, I guess. I'll have to.

Because you'll still be a waiter somewhere and I'll be this humpy, famous writer that you once went out with and I might not even recognize you. What are the odds? I mean, it's been so long. Why would I remember you? Really. By then I'll have lost all that extra weight and found a haircut that suits me and I'll have learned how to dress myself in something other than jeans and shirts on sale at the Bay. I'll be out to lunch with a pack of other famous writers and you'll be serving us our overpriced, preciously garnished food, trying to squeeze past everyone's agents, bodyguards and stylists. You'll gasp and tell the other waiters who I am and how you know me. You'll bring me a free glass of wine—a tepid Canadian hybrid Chardonnay—ignore my guests and ask me to autograph a napkin and want me to call you because I'm somebody now, because I mean something suddenly. You'll be more than happy to acknowledge me then, won't you, Danny?

Well fuck you!

I never really liked you that much in the first place.

HIDE EVERYTHING

His eyes open slowly, revealing blurred, elongated shapes and exaggerated figures in the room. He struggles to pull himself upwards but is too weak to move. For a moment he hears a rushing sound but it quickly fades into a gaping silence. He can't feel the burn of pain in his arms, bandaged and limp beside him, or the weight of the two eyes staring at him.

He feels as though he is strapped to a mattress and suspended in a haze of thick clouds, plummeting downwards, backwards, out of control. His mind processes things slowly, randomly, so that what he perceives is nonsensical. This results in an immediate acceleration of his heart rate, a film of sweat appearing on his brow, a tightness in his chest, the urge to vomit. Something arises nearby, above the sound and physical sensation of his heart racing and the discernible buzz of vaguely green fluorescent light coming from above, and the tick-ticking of something metallic in the distance: a voice. *Here, there and everywhere,* is what he thinks he hears, *but that doesn't make any sense. Where am I?*

Green light. Another wave of pain ripples, this time through his wrists and hands but stops at his fingers—he can't feel them. He looks down. His body tightens, arms swollen and pulsing. A low moan. Tom turns to where the voice came from, tries to focus his vision, but perceives only blurred and twisted shapes in the faint gauze of green light from above. A hand on his chest.

"There, there, honey." It's a woman's voice, kind and throaty.

She moves from beside him to the end of the bed and back, then places a cloth on his forehead, dabbing the moisture there. He closes his eyes and lets his head fall back down to the pillow. He looks up and sees shimmering green light, frosty green. Tiny, iridescent pin pricks of light like a thin cloud of gas hovering over him. *Coming from the wall,* he thinks. *Maybe.* He senses that he should get away from it somehow, but he cannot grasp precisely why. His awareness of his confusion sends another wave of fear through him. The drugs aren't working.

The voice sounds again but he is unable to discern the words. A pressure has built up inside his head. And in his body, more pressure building up, squishing his guts into unusual shapes and places. He goes under, away. When he wakes, she is sitting in the chair he cannot see, beside the bed where he lies. The rushing sound again, the sound of something slicing through the air at great speed.

He looks up. An enormous steel structure, silver and gleaming with a sharp edge, reflecting flashes of light as it hurtles down upon him. Tom opens his mouth to scream but no sound escapes. He throws his arms up to ward off the blow, but the blade slashes through his hands, rips into his skull and tears him into two glistening halves. Blood gushes. He can see what's happening to him from somewhere else. He sees it all happening but cannot feel the pain. Horrified, frozen, removed from the sensation of the gory spectacle but mesmerized by it nonetheless. Something to remember.

He opens his eyes. The room is a little darker than before, but he can focus now. The haze of green light above him comes from a thin fluorescent light bulb, housed inside an old fashioned fixture that looks antique but, at the same time, not old.

"You all right?" asks the voice.

Tom turns his head to the side, looks and sees a woman sitting in a chair beside his bed. She has olive skin and dark penetrating eyes. He struggles to sit up but feels the pull of something stuck to his arm. He looks. Sticky tape. An intravenous tube attached to his forearm leading to a coupling of clear plastic bags that drip liquid slowly, making the muted tick-tock of a clock, only slower, like half speed, his breath anxious with every drop. *What?*

He notices his lower arms and hands wrapped in bandages. To his right he sees a table with a few cards on it and a bouquet of flowers; daisies, some baby's breath, a lilac or two and a red rose. The woman follows his gaze for a moment before rising and speaking.

"The flowers are from Raymond," she says. "So is one of the cards." She walks slowly back and forth at the end of the bed with one hand in the pocket of her lab coat and the other by her side. The coat is immaculate and white. "The other one is from your friends at work."

He looks at her with a puzzled expression. She comes around to his side and edges slightly toward him, leans in, notices his confusion and softens. "Do you know where you are?"

He shakes his head from side to side, a grimace of fear and apprehension growing on his face.

"You're in the hospital, Tom..." She continues speaking but the words disintegrate before they register. He can't hear her over the throb of his pulse, redundant feelings and other, discernible sounds. She senses his panic and stops.

His reality shifts, blurs, becomes something else; a train or plane of thought caught in a life-size horizontal glitch, repeating, repeating. He closes his eyes as he feels the weight of sadness and remorse pushing out from within him and, at the same time, pushing down on the cells in his body, making him feel heavy, leaden, swollen.

"Don't you worry, now. Everything's going to be all right."

He looks down at his torso. A plain white sheet. Yesterday evening the sheet had had smudges of red on it.

"Who are you?" he asks, his voice a slow dry croak. It cracks when he utters the word *you*.

"My name is Bonita Correll. I'm here to help you. Can you understand me?" He nods his head. "Good." She takes a deliberately long breath in and then smiles.

Tom cranes his neck forward an inch or so. He sees a bed pan lying on the edge of the sink counter across the room. Eyes on Bonita. Eyes to his lap.

"You're in St. Michael's Hospital, Tom. Yesterday afternoon you tried to take your own life. You cut your wrists. Thankfully you weren't successful."

Something in him closes off, snaps shut. He focuses on the sensation of the tape on his forearm. His throat is dry. He closes his eyes, sinks back onto the bed. *Later, later,* he thinks. Bonita picks up a clipboard and eyes Tom in bed while she pretends to read. He spends the rest of the day in and out of consciousness, sometimes sleeping, something lying still with his eyes closed and his mind racing, trying to trace the events leading up to now, but there's a gap in his timeline. He can't think of what happened or why. He can only think, *Raymond*.

The next morning Bonita arrives with his breakfast on a trolley. She manoeuvres it carefully so that it hovers directly over his lap. She shows him how to raise the bed so that he can eat.

"What's going to happen to me?" he asks her.

"You're being transferred to the psychiatric ward in an hour or so for observation. They'll probably release you after a couple of days if they're convinced you're not a danger to yourself."

"Psych ward," is all he says.

"It's procedure. Raymond has come and gone twice, by the way. You were asleep."

"Good. I don't want him to see me like this."

"That's okay. It's going to take a while before you feel normal again and I'm here to help you until you do. If you let me," she says. And suddenly her voice is cheery, almost a melody.

"Normal," he says.

"Yes, and in order to do that, I'm going to need you to do me a few favours if you can, okay? Will you try?"

"Yes," he says with growing impatience. "If you stop talking to me like a baby."

"I'm sorry," she smiles. "Not my intention. It's just that a lot of times when people wake up, they panic because they don't know what's going on. It's like a blackout, so..." She sits down in the chair and looks at him intently. "Now that I know you're alert, I'll talk to you like an adult. How's that?"

He nods.

"Good." She takes a breath. "Tom, you attempted suicide by cutting your wrists. And you came very close to succeeding. When your partner Raymond found you, you had already lost a lot of blood. That was two days ago. Today is Friday. Your condition has stabilized somewhat and we know you are going to be all right." She moves her head forward. "Physically. So, how do you *feel*?"

His purses his lips tight together and shakes his head slowly from side to side, fighting off something. There is a tightening in his chest like a hand gripping tight and he knows, he just knows, it will kill him. He has to stop it. Block it out.

"That's okay. That's okay. Don't worry if you don't have words or answers. Just take a breath. In. Out. Like me, okay? In. Out. And in and out. All right? We're going to look after you."

The next morning she comes again. Her arrival coincides with that of his breakfast: a Del Monte fruit cup, powdered eggs, cold toast, tea—in a clunky metal teapot. The lid doesn't fit properly. The water is tepid. He doesn't like tea. *Who told them I like tea?* He pushes the tray away gingerly with his elbow. The bed's wheels squeak when he does this. He draws a sharp breath in, winces.

"Yeah, you're going to be tender for some time," she says. Her voice is soft, cautionary, and... *What is that other thing? Parental? No.*

"You must have had some pretty good reasons to try to end your life," she says to him after feeding him tidbits of fruit salad. It was all he would eat. "I'm just glad Raymond found you when he did," she says looking at the remains of his breakfast tray. "I saw him last night," her voice almost a question. "He wants to see you, but I explained to him that you wanted to be out of, well, here. So he wants you to call him."

"Are you a nurse?"

Bonita stands up and walks around the rolling bed-top table and opens the curtains a crack, letting a sliver of light into the room. Then she moves back toward him and sits at the edge of the bed.

"In a way, I am a nurse, yes. But not a medical one, although that's part of the training of course. I'm going to be your emotional nurse. If you let me, that is. And in order to do that you're going to have to learn to trust me. It's an important thing, knowing how to trust someone. My instinct tells me that giving your trust has ended up hurting you. I hope we can change that. I hope you'll try with me so we can both make sure you end up in a better place than this." He is silent for a moment. She wants a response from him. "Okay? Tom?"

He nods his head, senses something climbing up from the depths of his consciousness, a little off track but rising, an air bubble under water during an earthquake. A name. *Raymond*.

Where is Raymond?

Tom feels an icy chill spread up his spine as he walks through the apartment toward the back patio. When he steps outside, unseasonably warm May air caresses his face and takes the edge off his anxiety. He reaches into his pocket and removes a pack of cigarettes, takes one out and raises it to his mouth. He feels the skin of his fingers tingling and blood pulsing through the veins in his wrist, like a muted drumbeat. Before he lights the match, he hears the sound of his breathing in his head, short quick breaths drawn in and pushed out again, almost like wheezing, but not quite. Not quite out of breath. Just like when his mother would roll up her sleeves.

He pushes that memory down. It rises up every now and then and is followed by an urge to run. But running doesn't work, so he pushes the memory down hard, deep, where he thinks it belongs, where he thinks he can control it. *I will run. Just not now.*

He tastes the smoke as it courses down his throat and into his lungs: he is calmed. He closes his eyes and is hurtling through darkness. When he reopens his eyes he is safe, on the lawn chair, sitting still—not falling—in the late afternoon sun, not darkness. The Mount Pleasant Cemetery spreads out before him beyond the rusty railing of the balcony. Tree greens and headstone greys and blacks and browns melt together to create an out-of-focus greeting card in his mind. *Dear Tom, having a ball. Wish you were here. See you soon.* Privately he's always liked the idea of Spanish, Mexican, Cuban graves. The elaborate decorations and ceremonies. Rituals. The day of the dead. The dead and their decorations. *Christmas and Hallowe'en together at last.*

After he finishes his cigarette, Tom goes inside to the bathroom and brushes his teeth for five minutes. Then, with his toothbrush and some toothpaste, he scrubs his index and middle fingers—his smoking fingers he calls them. He rinses with mouthwash and sprays cologne on his hand just to be sure, and then rinses his hand under the faucet. He feels confident that Raymond won't be able to tell he's been smoking. Where is Raymond?

Tom glances at his watch. It's still early. He has at least half an hour before Raymond gets home. Enough time to go to the store.

When he returns and sees Raymond's shoes inside the front door, Tom tucks the small package he's bought into his jacket pocket and rushes upstairs to find Raymond in the shower. Tom quickly disrobes and joins him, kissing him, tasting coffee on his breath. Tom gets on his knees beneath the warm spray and takes Raymond's hardening cock in his mouth. Steam rises around the two of them, their bodies pressed together, hands and fingers touching in the cascades of warm water. Tom shudders and hesitates. The water envelopes them as they writhe and breathe deeply, loudly together, their bodies in an intense embrace. Tom's emotions are lost in steam and water.

The two men move to the bedroom, still wet from the shower. In an hour they are almost asleep, still slightly damp and craving more of each other, craving more; a distraction—at least for Tom.

"I'm so glad you came home to get better, Tom," his mother says. Her voice is self-regulating, self-aware; it gives nothing away. No emotion. No intention except to elude. "Back in your old room, momma's little sick boy." His stomach churns at that. "I'm going to make some coffee and have a smoke, so I'll be in the kitchen. Knock on the wall if you need something." She pauses at the doorway, a dramatic effect. "Aww, it's just like when you were home sick from school. Remember?" She smiles her sickly-sweet smile at him and turns and is gone. He closes his eyes trying to push her out of his mind, block her out, but all his efforts are in vain. *She just keeps coming. Why won't she stop?*

He makes his way slowly to the bathroom and looks at himself in the mirror, noticing the blue shower curtain behind him. *New.* It was a different colour when he was young. He remembers her saying that it matched his eyes. How old was he then, when it started? Eight?

"That's why I bought it honey," she says. "It matches your eyes."

She takes a step toward him. His brow tightens. Wrinkles form. The muscles around his mouth pull downwards. She stares between his legs, at the blue corduroy pants that are bunched down around his ankles, partially covering his North Star running shoes. His feet can touch the floor now. It won't be long before the training wheels come off his bicycle. She gets closer. He squirms, sees her face looming in, all lipstick and pointy-at-the-sides glasses and rolls of hair piled on top of it all.

"Going to the toilie?" she asks in that voice.

He barely nods. She kneels down in front of him and places her hands on his knees. She feels him shaking and she thinks he's excited too. He reaches his hand out and presses it against her shoulder. She sweeps it out of the way with her hand. Her smile intensifies. It's all he can see, her hard smile.

No.

The sun shines in his eyes and pulls him out of another night of troubled sleep. He wrestles with the covers, trying to free his hands. Then the pain comes and he remembers everything. Reality snowballs, almost knocks the wind out of him. He focuses on his arms, like logs beside him, heavy and unmoving. He manages to pull himself into a sitting position and then looks at the plastic Marilyn Monroe clock beside the bed. The telephone rings. He hears it through the wall.

Tom looks around the room, his old room. The phone rings again. Footsteps crossing the kitchen floor on the other side of the bedroom wall.

"Hello?" It's her.

He leans over and presses his ear to the wall.

"Yes he is. May I ask who is calling, please?" Muffled, but still he can hear it in her tone, her phone voice—high pitched, full of pretence and polite condescension. "No Peter, I'm sorry he cannot take any calls just yet. He's had a most serious accident and can't talk to anyone. Right now he's asleep. How do you know him, may I ask? I beg your pardon? I'm his mother. Who are you? Oh, I see. Yes. Yes I can. Certainly, Peter, I'll tell him that you called. Yes, just as soon as he gets up. Thank you for calling. Goodbye."

Footsteps sound from the kitchen. Painted wooden cupboards open and close. A chair squeaks. A metallic sound chimes as a spoon is stirred inside a cup. The telephone receiver is lifted out of its cradle. Tom hears the phone being dialled. He can't believe that his parents still have a phone with a rotary dial. *It's 1997 for crying out loud!*

He notices as he looks through his room that things have changed since he moved out. Posters have been taken down. Some books have disappeared from the bookcase. The walls have been painted a darker shade of blue. The blinds have been removed and replaced by a light see-through curtain. The neighbours can see into his room now. *They can see everything.*

The walls press in on him. Tom looks down at his arms, wonders how he's going to masturbate with his hands buried beneath layers of gauze and bandages, heavy and without feeling. *How long till they come off?* A noise sounds from behind him. He turns around and sees his mother standing in the doorway.

"How are you feeling?" It sounds like an accusation.

He shrugs, "Tired."

She knits her eyebrows together, spreading lines across her forehead. This is all familiar to him. He wishes it weren't. The urge to say no fights against everything he knows. They did not teach him no.

"After all the sleeping you've been doing?"

And there it is. His stomach tightens. *I'm bad and stupid and can't talk back.*

She steps forward into the room and looks about at the walls with a contented smile.

"Who was on the phone?"

"Oh, just then?" She looks away from him, past his pain, and out the window where the sun is shining, a warm spring wind is blowing and the neighbour's dog is yapping. "Nobody." She looks back at him. "Do you need anything?"

He shakes his head and lies back down as she turns and walks out the door.

Through the hallway he walks, toward the bedroom door. He pushes it open and moves to the closet, sliding the door open and pushing a row of adorned hangers to the left. Tom leans forward and pulls the dark grey suit from the rack and holds it before him. The funeral suit. He lays it down on the bed and fumbles with the jacket, pulling it open and reaching inside the right breast pocket to reveal a package no larger than a box of wooden matches. He takes the package in his right hand and places the suit back in the closet.

How many times did she do it, he wonders, but not in thoughts. The question manifests as a heaviness in his body. He can only feel the weight of it, the intensity, not the words or their meanings. Squirming inside and out. Twenty? Two hundred? Perhaps so many times that it seems like one long tortured moment. How long did that moment last? How many years?

"Come on, then, let me see, Tommy." He remains still. "Let mommy see what you've done." That smile. He worries that if she opened her mouth, a snake or maybe lightning would come out. He looks down at the floor; light beige tiles with gold sparkles, the thin strip of grout between them discoloured.

"I haven't done it yet," he says in a meek voice. Tears soon. He is... How old?

She moves in closer. He wriggles back, feels the toilet seat lid pressing into his back. He can feel her breath on his face, see a smudge of red lipstick on one of her teeth. So close.

The bathroom door opens. Tom peers over his mother's curls and sees his father's stern face regarding them from the doorway. He says nothing and, after a moment of silent admonishment, walks away, pipe in hand. Tom takes on the situation as a punishment. He has learned to accept what is given to him.

How old was he when it started? Seven? Eight? It started before that, with him being forced to urinate in front of her, not being allowed to close the bathroom door behind him, the day the lock on the door was removed, not being allowed to flush after he finished, always having everything he left behind examined. In puberty it got worse. In addition to documenting the onset and growth rate of his pubic and underarm hair, stool charts were kept, sizes and consistencies categorized and given names. Enemas were administered every other week. It was as if she wanted to know everything that was inside him by analyzing what came out of him. If he ever broke wind in her presence—which he did his utmost to avoid whenever possible—he could see the strains on her face as she tried to detect which gases of digested foods were being expelled. In the kitchen, in the cupboard above the fridge, she kept a binder with details of all the meals she had prepared for the family.

Wednesday, June 26, 1976. Dinner: liver, mashed potatoes, creamed corn. Milk.

Often, after she had called them to dinner, young Tom would amble in to the kitchen and find her writing in the binder and then gingerly place it back in the cupboard.

The phone beeps, pulling him out of his memory. He lifts the cordless receiver and with the push of a button, breathes a quiet hello into the mouthpiece.

"Hi, Tom, it's your mother calling. How are you dear?"

There is a slight crackling over the line. Tom moves closer to the window and wraps his right hand tightly around the small package.

"I was just thinking about you."

"Pleasant thoughts." Not a question.

He laughs quickly and quietly. *I am bad.*

"Well, Tommy, the reason I called was to cancel our dinner for Sunday night. Your father just can't get used to the idea of you living with that man. Well, any man. And to be quite honest, dear, it sickens me too."

He gulps down air. *I am bad.*

"So maybe we should just forget about it, all right?"

I am stupid.

"And not talk about it."

And can't talk back.

"We'd be more than happy if you came, though. Alone."

He shakes his head in disbelief. *Is it me or her?* "Look mom, I can't really talk right now. It's not a good time."

"Oh, really? What's wrong?"

"Everything. Look, I've got to go. Call me if you change your mind."

"Don't hold your breath."

"I won't."

"Goodbye, Tom."

He clicks the button and places the phone on the dresser across from the bed. He puts the tiny package in his pants pocket, not noticing the red marks the edges have left on his palm from squeezing it.

In the kitchen he lights a cigarette and sits at the table, flicking the ashes into a saucer in front of him. He edges the lighted end of the cigarette toward his left wrist until he can feel the heat on his skin, sharp and pulsating, sending little warning shocks to his brain. Tight smile. Closer and closer it comes, colouring the surrounding skin with a dull orange glow. Then he stabs the cigarette out in the saucer and looks out the window at the graveyard in the distance. After a moment, Tom recognizes the dull scent of old coffee. He looks across the room and sees that the coffee maker has been left on.

He approaches the counter and takes the pot by its plastic handle and lifts it from the heating element, smelling the burnt liquid and seeing the glass pot lined with a thick, black ooze. With his other hand he flips on the faucet and lets the water run for a second before moving the smoking decanter under the flow.

There is an instant crack. Tom jumps backward with the pot still in his hand. He examines it, seeing a thick jagged line across the width of the glass. He raises the pot in the air and hurls it to the ground. It shatters into pieces large and small. They scatter on the tiled floor. Tom walks across the path of broken glass and makes his way upstairs to the bathroom.

"Now who would have thought that I'd have to look after my son again after all these years?"

She's on the phone again. Her voice pulls Tom out of the haze of sleep. "It's funny, Pat, that a family that seems so distant from one another can be brought so close together by an accident. In a way it's like turning the clock back twenty-five years and having a little boy all over again. He's so dependent, you know, so helpless. It's adorable."

He has the feeling that he's being pulled backward again. He tries to call out to her, but his throat is closed off. He thinks for a moment that it's the Demerol making him feel this way, but surely he's stopped receiving it by now in favour of something milder, less disorienting. He sits up, scans the bedside table for pill bottles but there's only Marilyn showing him the time. Tears well up in his eyes. He is helpless against this feeling rising up in him. He sinks back down onto the bed, not bothering to cover his face to diffuse the sound of his sobs. He wants to hold his teddy bear but he knows that it's long gone, hidden away in some dusty box in the attic or thrown in the garbage along with his Duran Duran posters, muscle magazines, the dog-eared copy of *The Front Runner* he bought on his first trip to Glad Day Bookshop. They put it in a brown paper bag. *Hide everything.*

He falls in and out of sleep, crying most of the afternoon when he's awake—great mournful sobs and their ensuing gasps for air—and fighting with the blankets in fitful bouts of slumber. When shadows appear on the bedroom walls and a thundercloud of activity booms through from the kitchen, Tom knows his father will be home soon. It isn't long before he hears a car approaching in the driveway and then the sound of the front door opening. "Hi dear," he hears his mother say. There is no response. Just the sound of drinks being made, drinks being poured, drinks being drunk.

"Go say hi to him, for God's sake. He's been in there crying all afternoon like a fucking baby. I don't know how much more of this I can stand." No response. In a moment the bedroom door creaks open. Tom closes his eyes and pretends he's asleep.

"You awake, Tom?" his father asks in a hushed voice. The door closes after a moment.

He drifts into a half-sleep, waking again when he hears his mother's voice, shrill and annoyed. "And Raymond keeps calling. I don't want him coming here. One in the house is more than enough. He cries all the time. You don't have to sit and listen to it all day, Hank."

"No, I have to come home and listen to you. I don't know what's worse."

"You poor thing," she says in a voice heavy with sarcasm. "Your own son is practically retarded and you complain about me."

Footsteps on linoleum, some garbled muttering, footsteps leaving the kitchen. The doorbell rings. In a moment there's a knock at his bedroom door.

"Tom, Bonita is here. I'm sending her up to see you."

He rushes to get out of bed, trying to step into a pair of sweat pants but he can't get them past his feet. There's another knock at the door.

"Are you decent?" It's Bonita's voice. Already he is relieved.

"I can't get my pants on." He wants to laugh and cry at the same time. "Come in."

The door opens and Bonita enters. She is wearing a blue print dress and a light blue jacket over top.

"I need help," he says, letting go of his pants.

"Of course, sweetie. Hold still a second."

She gives him a warm smile as she leans down and grabs hold of the waist of his pants, unevenly bunched around his shins. "There you go." She stands up. "How are you feeling today?"

He clenches his teeth and shakes his head from side to side. That twisting, grabbing feeling in his chest. A sound escapes him. Bonita has come to know his pushing down feeling by the delicate trembling of his lips and the way his eyes avoid hers.

"Problems?" No response. "Your parents?" It's a whisper.

"I don't..." His throat is tight. He doesn't know what to say. "I can't do this."

"Do you want to move somewhere else? Is that it?" He nods. "Okay. I think it would be better for you to be somewhere else right now. Especially in light of the things you've discussed in your sessions."

"She just called me retarded."

"What?"

"To my dad, just before you came. She said I'm practically retarded."

An indignant huff from Bonita. She turns to the door, thinks twice, and then looks back at Tom. "You know that's not true, don't you? Tell me you know that."

He nods his head. He knows it's expected of him, *to acquiesce.* He barely questions it anymore. Most of the time he doesn't even notice. She steps closer and embraces him.

He's been at his parent's house for over a week. Bonita comes for counselling sessions every second day. His mother took the first two visits as an excuse for her to leave the house, but as the days wore on, she began to be suspicious of Bonita, and stood outside his bedroom door listening to their conversations. During her second last visit, Bonita left the door open and saw her shadow on the floor, cast from a bright, naked light bulb in the shape of a candle's flame.

Bonita had made no qualms about inviting Tom's mother in to the room that afternoon. She didn't respond. Just the sound of footsteps receding. The squeak of a kitchen chair. The faint odour of cigarette smoke making its way into the bedroom.

"I can't go back to Raymond."

"Why not?"

"I just can't."

"Honey, you've got nothing to be embarrassed about. If that's what this is all about... Raymond cares for you, don't you know that?" He has a blank look on his face. "I think it might be a good idea for you to see him. He is your partner." Tom is silent. "At least think about it. If you could go back to your apartment you'd be better off than here, that's for sure."

"Oh really?" asks a voice from the doorway. Tom turns and sees his mother leaning against the doorframe. Drink in hand. "As if anyone cares about what you think." She steps into the room. Bonita stands up and turns to face her.

"In light of Tom's emotional needs, his desire to recover, and the nature of his troubles, I feel that he should be somewhere else. Not to mention your insensitivity toward him."

"My insensitivity?" she seethes. "Is that so? Well, Miss Psychotherapy, who asked you?"

"Someone who cares about Tom, ma'am." Bonita takes a breath in, takes a step forward. "Apparently your son's partner cares more about his well being than you do."

"Enough to fork out a miniature fortune for your services, I'm sure. You're paid to be here. I'm his mother. Who do you think is better qualified? Who cares more?"

"Can you handle an honest answer?"

"Can you?"

"This is not a contest Mrs.—"

"Isn't it?" She straightens her posture, clears her throat. "Now you listen to me. You have no place here and I don't think I like the influence you're having on my son."

"I wouldn't expect that you would like it or understand it," Bonita says without emotion.

"What does that mean?"

"Never mind. Why don't you just leave us alone so we can talk?"

"Because you're in my house. You think I'll stand for the two of you talking about me behind my back and plotting and scheming?"

The words stop Bonita. She can't think of an appropriate response. She makes mental notes, connects the dots of the bits and pieces Tom has told her, what Raymond has told her. She steels herself, takes a breath in, looks hard at Mrs. Lang. Then the words come. "That's exactly what I've come to expect."

"Meaning?"

"Where's your compassion, woman? Your only son was in so much pain that he tried to end his life and here you are—"

"So this is my fault?" She smiles her cocktail hostess smile. Tom's stomach churns. He shudders.

"You're not listening to what I'm saying," Bonita scolds, her voice unrepentant and brimming with impatience, frustration.

"Ever since Tom had this accident—"

Bonita cuts her off, her voice indignant. "Your son tried to kill himself, Mrs. Lang. It was no accident." Bonita pauses and notices the furious look the woman gives her son.

It is cold outside for Spring. Tom walks awkwardly, his arms stiff.

"I'm sorry," Bonita says.

"That's okay. Where else was I going to go?"

"Raymond..."

They walk in silence for a minute. Bonita tries to imagine what would comfort him. She wraps her arm around his waist.

"Do you ever wonder why some people even have children?" she asks, perhaps more to herself than to Tom.

"Maybe I was an accident."

"There's no such thing."

Tom enters the bathroom and sits down on the toilet. He stares directly ahead, into the mirror in front of him, into his eyes and past them. He pulls a fingernail along the edge of the thin plastic wrapping and opens the small package. He reaches forward and places four razor blades on the counter top. He slides one to the edge of the toilet tank with the tip of his index finger and holds it loosely in his hand. He hears the rain outside and the distant rumbling of thunder. He doesn't hear the words *no* or *don't*. He never learned how to use them. *Whose fault is that? Doesn't matter.*

He rises and takes two steps forward to the counter top where he reaches his hand out, turns on the tap. Hot water. It splashes out of the faucet and swirls around and down the drain. Tom looks at the edge of the blade as it goes down, in and then disappears.

Red rises up and out. It spills into the sink, swirls around the basin, and gurgles down the drain. A cyclone of red, dissipating. He drags the blade across. Sees a white hazy flash. Feels sick to his stomach. He can't fight it anymore. Can't fight.

As he places the blade in the other hand, blood rushes everywhere; across the counter top, down his pant leg, into the sink, onto the floor. He digs the steel into the right wrist. His knees buckle. Muscles in his thighs seize. The blade falls into the basin. Tom extends his left wrist under the tap. He feels a flap of skin being moved around by the flow. He feels the water but not its heat. He just feels it. It's something he can think about, focus on, not remember.

Before he collapses, he catches a glimpse of himself in the mirror. He doesn't think he looks like himself. For a split second he sees somebody else, maybe even her. Horrified, he wonders what his mother will say. He wonders what Raymond will say. *Poor Raymond. Has to find me.* Thoughts are aborted. *Out, out.* The last thing he thinks.

Raymond pushes the front door open, surprised that it isn't locked. Walking into the apartment, he can smell cigarette smoke and hear water running upstairs. He goes to the kitchen and notices the cigarette smell growing stronger. He walks toward the refrigerator and then jumps suddenly, hearing a crunch under his shoe. He looks down at the floor and sees broken glass everywhere. Then he sees the saucer on the table beside him and the cigarette butt.

"Tom?"

He heads up the stairs and stops at the bathroom door. He leans in, listening for a second before he knocks. He hears the water running, can tell it isn't the shower. He knocks twice.

"Tom? Everything okay? There's broken glass all over the kitchen floor. Did you cut yourself?" He waits for a moment for a response but hears only water running. "Are you hurt? Tom?"

Raymond presses his ear to the door before opening it. Immediately his eyes are drawn downwards to Tom on the floor between the toilet and the vanity, covered in blood. The countertop is covered with blood. The white towels are spotted with red and scattered about on the floor. Hunched over beside the toilet, Tom is motionless, a crumpled, broken statue.

Raymond freezes for a second and then rushes in and lifts Tom's head up. His eyes are turned upward. Raymond looks down and sees blood spitting out of the gashes on Tom's wrists. He doesn't hear himself sobbing and calling Tom's name out over and over again.

"Oh no." Moaning between sobs and gasps at air. "Oh no."

He doesn't hear his loud, rapid breathing or the water running in the sink or the floor squeaking beneath him as he tries to lift up his bleeding lover, or the rain outside or the boom of thunder so close, so close.

He follows the gurney and the ambulance attendants out through the lobby of the building, not realizing that people are standing around watching beneath umbrellas.

He huddles in the back of the ambulance and watches Tom nervously as they are driven furiously through the wet city streets. He can't hear the siren wailing above his confusion and shock. He can't see Tom's chest moving slightly, slowly. He sits off to the side of the stretcher, shivering and crying quietly, looking down occasionally at his shirt and rubbing at the blood stains on it.

Tom's face is covered with an oxygen mask; clear, pliable plastic tinged with the light fog of his shallow breathing. Raymond's sobs grow louder. One of the attendants turns to him and offers him a tissue. The man says something that he doesn't hear. Raymond cowers against the inside wall of the ambulance, shivering and shaking his head in disbelief, trying to swallow his surroundings and wanting to return to the way it was yesterday or the day before.

STALKING HAROLD GREENBAUM

Sylvia Elder pulls the compact out of her purse, opens it and lifts it up in front of her face. Not normally the sort to flaunt her vanities in public, she checks her appearance methodically on her return back to her office for a reason; she knows that someone will be there and has convinced herself that he will be looking at her.

Critically self-aware, she observes her behaviour, watching for any signs of the eccentricities and lapses in reason of someone whose better judgment has been compromised by the passage of time, time spent alone, the sudden dips and swells of hormones and a litany of older, best-forgotten indulgences. At fifty-seven Sylvia had already been married and divorced, experimented with marijuana, gone through a woman's change—her mother called it that—but, unlike her mother, whose condition escalated to the point of histrionics, Sylvia took what she thought was a radical approach to her situation; she cut back on cosmetics purchases, thinking, *What's the point?* Without a husband or partner, she saw no good reason for keeping up. But that was before a new employee was hired at Invigro, an accountant who sat at a desk not far from Sylvia's. It occurred to her then that her physical appearance was not merely something she could use to further the enticement and acquisition of something highly valued—in this case, a man, *the* man—she thought it might be fun to use it as a weapon and then sort through the results and regroup, restart, if necessary. But she didn't know how. She didn't know where to start. She needed a nudge. A guide.

The people crammed into the elevator around her take no notice of Sylvia until the muted click of her compact opening. Her eyes dart quickly left and right, over the upper oval rim of the compact, and then back again at the small round mirror, flecked with a dusting of foundation—colour: fair, *for porcelain skin with pink undertones,* the packaging read. She gazes into the tiny mirror and lets out a gasp. There on the left side of her nose are three aggravated pimples forming a rather menacing-looking triangle. The woman beside her glances over her magazine. Sylvia catches her look, snaps the compact shut and clears her throat.

"I knew they were coming last night," she says to the stranger, as if an apology or explanation were due, "But I didn't think they were gonna be this big." The woman offers only a puzzled look. Sylvia interprets it as judgmental. "Or that they would group together like that." Her voice wanes to a sigh.

I did it again. What the hell is the matter with me?

The electronic whirr of the elevator ascending underlies a moment of uncomfortable silence. Sylvia pushes past the feeling of awkwardness. "It's like they think it's a club or something," she says, confusing the stranger for a friend, and the elevator for Open Mic night at Yuk-Yuk's. "Hey, let's sneak up on her and meet on the nose." *It's too late. Shit! I can't stop myself.*

It's in moments like this that Sylvia wonders, *Who didn't teach me how to leave well enough alone? Is it mom's fault? Dad was never around much to make that kind of impression. It must have been mom. Or Aunt Lilly. Maybe it's my timing. Who didn't teach me about comedic timing?*

"You shouldn't pick at them," the woman comments, then turns back to her magazine.

The elevator comes to a stop. Sylvia peers past the backs and shoulders in front of her and, recognizing the drab office lobby decor, squeezes her way out of the elevator. She turns around, locks eyes with the woman inside and says, "My mother used to say don't pick at them—"

An electronic pulse sounds and the elevator doors close swiftly, cutting her off.

Sylvia turns to face the office. Clutching a brown paper take-away bag, she makes her way through the reception area. She grimaces politely at the receptionist as she passes. *Whore.* Sylvia allows a smirk to crack her solemn face as she pushes the glass doors open and enters the inner office, a darker shade of beige. *Those tits should be illegal. She must have a good chiropractor. And some hefty bras.*

Tinny, reverberant strains of "Girls On Film" echo through the office, but it's not the version Sylvia knows. It's a girl singing, she notes, badly. And Auto-tuned. *Who wants robots to sing to them? Is that sexy now? This is what we are given these days? Auto-tuned robot chatter?* She bisects the office, passing Helen's desk: empty. *It's Monday. Helen's at the library checking out a new book, probably one of those ditzy romance novels, what they now refer to as chick-lit*. It's a label Sylvia thinks is condescending but not surprising.

The one time she downloaded such a book to her e-reader, she spotted half a dozen spelling mistakes in the first chapter. She took a hard look at the cover art—an extreme close-up of a woman's lipsticked lips, open suggestively and, at the back of her throat, the silhouette of a muscular man, fists clenched and raised up in the air. If she zoomed in, she'd probably have noticed he was holding a gun or a knife. She touch-screened her way to a random page where she came across a paragraph with the word *engorged* in it. She scrolled up and did a search for *engorged*, and, seeing that the word appeared thirty-seven times in the book, Sylvia immediately deleted the title from her library. *Thirty-seven times!* The e-book was one hundred and forty-eight pages long. She can't recall the name of the book, *Although,* she thinks, *"Engorged" would work well as a title, but it probably wouldn't sell to women. Chicks, maybe, but women? And what's with that cover art? Is it saying that inside every woman is an angry man waiting to kill her? Fuck! They should have put one of those skull-and-crossbone warning symbols on the cover or, like cigarette packages, a photograph of a withered spinster sitting in a rocking chair surrounded by cats. This product will lower your I.Q. and distort your romantic ideals.*

Helen Frobisher professes to be old school. She likes the feel of a well-worn paperback in her hands and classy paintings for cover art and titles like *In The Hot Of The Moment* and *Passion Fulfilled, Love Denied*. Every Monday during her lunch break, the librarian at the checkout desk lowers her eyes while scanning Helen's selection. Helen sees the librarian's veiled disdain every Monday but pushes the awareness from her mind. *At least I'm reading,* she says to herself in her own defence. Something in the woman's demeanour makes her sleepy. *I almost died,* she says to herself. *So fuck you. I'll read whatever I like.*

Pinned to Helen's dividing wall, beside her computer screen, is a sign she made herself:

This office isn't big enough for the both of us, so I left my wig at home.

Helen and Sylvia became close when Helen returned to work at Invigro after a successful three-month chemotherapy treatment. They were together at Sears when Helen found the wig Sylvia insisted would help her to reinvent herself, which is what she'd heard many cancer survivors did when faced with the hair issue. She slid into the nearest changing room with the thing in her hand, unwrapped the scarf from around her head and pulled the blonde tresses into place. The act felt strangely intimate to her and, as she noticed her surroundings—the flattering lighting, the immaculately clean mirrors surrounding her on all sides—she thought this process would be better suited to a private bathroom and not the public changing room of a department store. Stepping back to regard herself in the mirror, she was met with a frightening sight: a middle-aged, droopy, unhappy woman. Puffy skin powdery white. Ill, but gaining. Lipstick too red. *I should just buy the Dorothy Hamill one,* she thought, but then she hesitated. *It might be fun to be blonde.*

Fun? What the hell? The illness brought options she never would have contemplated otherwise. *Choices. Money. Time. Fucking cancer.*

Helen's oncologist, a wiry man in his late forties with a prickly demeanour, cautioned her about her negativity and its effects on the immune system.

"Are you trying to say that I made myself sick?" she asked him, feeling outrage rising.

Her doctor made a quiet clucking sound with his tongue, which also seemed inappropriate to her. *Am I a dog?* She decided it was in her best interest not to blow up at him, seeing as he had come highly recommended by c-survivors.ca. *Let him think what he wants,* she thought. *I know I didn't make myself sick.* She decided then to incorporate that phrase into her morning mirror ritual. *I did not make myself sick.* But often, when she repeats the phrase in her mind, she hears the words, *Well then, who did?*

Back at home, Helen pulled the wig out of the Sears bag and shuffled to look at her reflection in a full-length mirror. She tossed her scarf to the floor and tugged the wig over her head. She fought hard against the compulsion to frown and mock herself and set fire to the wig with gasoline and the pack of matches she kept hidden in case she ever decided to smoke the joint her neighbour had given her after her diagnosis. The joint was crammed into the back of her freezer in a Ziploc sandwich bag. She saw it when she threw out all the packaged frozen food she had purchased; she had read somewhere that they were questionable, if not dubious, and that fresh was the way to go. There is a lot of ice in her freezer, made in old-fashioned metal ice cube trays.

If I know and love myself, why should I cave in to the pressure to reinvent myself? Reinvent. I am the real deal.

And so despite buying the wig with great flourish, an act perhaps done more for Sylvia's benefit and not her own, Helen began a tempestuous relationship with the hairpiece. She even considered throwing herself a party—everyone invited would be required to wear a wig in the style of a famous person—but then she thought a tropical vacation would be a better investment—if and when she was capable of travelling again. *Immune system. Note to self: can I even get travel insurance?*

After her treatments had ended and she was officially cancer-free, Helen returned to Invigro half-heartedly and mostly out of boredom but soon found the eight-hour days too long for her to endure, despite taking frequent bathroom breaks. She learned this after falling asleep in the women's washroom one afternoon while Sylvia banged on the door waiting to get in. The awkward awakening that ensued prompted a bond between the two women, based on their shared experiences of pain and suffering and the pride with which they had both endured their circumstances. The only difference between Sylvia's suffering and Helen's pain was that Helen had a rather black sense of humour about hers and Sylvia wrote songs—poems, actually—with titles like "My Sorrow," "I Love You, I Love You, Can't You Hear Me?" and "It Can't Be Over, It'll Never Be Over!" Sylvia imagines them being recorded by Gloria Estefan, Reba McEntire or maybe even Connie Francis, women who understand the hurt. But never Babs. "She doesn't know what pain is." As she's told Helen, "My songs are too deep for Babs."

Sylvia passes a row of adjoined desks, all empty now because their occupants are lined up at the microwave oven in the staff lunchroom, waiting to heat up the previous night's leftovers or store-bought containers of just-add-water Asian splendour, just-cover-and-nuke lasagne or perhaps the perennial favourite, glow-in-the-dark macaroni and cheese. Sylvia looks over her shoulder at the lineup. *Why not just eat plastic?*

She enters the corridor that leads to her workspace and intuitively slows her pace. She opens the top of the paper bag, letting the smell of corned beef escape into the stale office air. Drawing nearer to her desk, she becomes aware that her heart rate has accelerated and that a feeling of anger has surfaced and is gaining momentum. She ignores the urge to examine the anger, to mentally poke it with a stick, and instead focuses on the painting of a moose hanging on the far wall. She glides past *his* workspace and gives the paper bag a little jiggle, hoping that he will look up and—*Oh shoot!*—find her three pimples glaring at him. *Too late to change course. Damn.*

She doesn't need to look to know that he's there eating his lunch, hunched over his desk, probably reading a borrowed book on financial trends. She knows he's there. And when she's passed his desk, a thin sigh of relief escapes her. But the anger lingers just below the surface of her consciousness. She turns left when the moose painting is in plain sight, on the wall beside what is referred to as the dark office where, a decade earlier, someone overdosed with pills, only to be discovered in the wee hours of the morning by a yawning cleaning woman who jammed boxes of pens and staples into her purse before calling the police—but that was when the building was occupied by another tenant. Highly sensitive to the supernatural and prone to losing money on pyramid schemes, Sylvia's boss Arnis kept the dark office locked and unlighted. It was his way of protecting his employees from spiritual danger. After the moose painting Sylvia bisects her department and slips into her workstation.

She slackens her right shoulder, enabling her purse strap to slide down her arm. With a swift motion, she cups her hand, scoops up the purse and places it to her left. Then she pushes her chair back with her right foot and slides down into her seat. For a moment she stares at him. *What bad posture.* She can barely see his head, it's slumped down so far. *Could be sleeping. Or dead.*

She unwraps the sandwich and places it at the edge of her desk, just beyond her reach. Then she proceeds to devour a bag of sour cream and onion potato chips she has hidden in her drawer. She won't touch the sandwich. It's for *him.*

She flips through an old issue of *Weekly World News* from a pile of disintegrating copies she has stashed in a desk drawer and settles on an article called "Amy Fisher's Sex Tips For Married Women." Before long she finds herself moving through a succession of scenarios she creates in her mind, little movies about how she will meet, court, seduce, marry and eventually grow old with Harold Greenbaum, accountant. *Just like one of Helen's racy novels…*

Overcome by the aroma of the corned beef, Harold Greenbaum, tired of his white bread tuna fish monotony, will happen by Sylvia's workspace and, noticing the neglected sandwich, will query, "Is something wrong with your sandwich?"

Sylvia, shocked by his forwardness and his brazen, insinuating eyebrows, responds with a coy, "Why, no. It's just that there's mayonnaise on top and mustard on the bottom and I'm not particularly fond of either. I think the man at the deli gave me the wrong sandwich. Would you like to have it?"

Would he like to have it?

She's followed him countless times on weeknights and Saturday afternoons into delicatessens where he ordered and ate the same thing every time: a double thick corned beef sandwich, medium-rare, on rye bread, with mayonnaise on top and mustard on the bottom. She's even overheard him placing the order, but for some reason Harold Greenbaum, accountant, never has corned beef for lunch at work. So every day, in her attempt to feed and seduce him, Sylvia runs out to the deli across the street and orders a corned beef sandwich, medium rare, on rye bread, with mayonnaise on top and mustard on the bottom. And every day she parades it past his workstation, giving the open paper bag a jiggle, in the hopes that he will be attracted by the aroma and end up falling madly in love with her. But every day the sandwich sits at the corner of her desk waiting for Harold Greenbaum to smell, stare, enquire and consume. And every day at approximately three-fifteen in the afternoon, Sylvia sweeps the hardened sandwich into the garbage can with a crestfallen sigh. *Maybe tomorrow.* Every day.

One grim afternoon as the Christmas holidays approached Sylvia had pulled the calculator from her desk drawer and estimated that she had spent twenty dollars and sixty-four cents (including tax) every week on corned beef sandwiches for Harold Greenbaum. (She thought at the very least he would be impressed with her calculations.) This meant that she had spent five hundred and seventy-seven dollars and ninety-two cents on sandwiches that year, tax included. The year before that, eight hundred and three dollars and thirty-nine cents. Of course, she was buying the large sandwiches back then, with sides of potato and macaroni salads, beets and pickles. The spread looked nice on her desk, but none of it was ever eaten. She had learned a valuable lesson in enconomising soon enough and, after the first year, cut out the side orders. After that, her New Year's resolution—prompted by the unmistakable eye rolling of nearby co-workers at lunchtime—was to switch from a large sandwich to a small. And now, three years after Harold's arrival in the office, Sylvia's choices are even more limited than ever before: *Should I even bother…?*

When Helen returns from the library, she hurries over to Sylvia's workspace with her book.

"Oh, *Passionate Torment*. Again?"

"Uh-huh," Helen grunts, turning the book around to take in its cover: a woman laid out on a beach in the shadow of a man looming over her.

"Must be good if you're reading it a second time."

Helen nods and adjusts the scarf wrapped around her head. She has the trace of a devious smile on her face as she leans up against Sylvia's desk. "It's okay, if you like power plays," she says, her voice gravel. "The main character wears power suits all the time and you know that there's going to be a scene in it where all the buttons come popping off and there's, you know, a pair of hairy, thick hands doing the popping."

"So, like, predictable, you know?" Sylvia notices she speaks differently when she's around Helen. *Like*? *You know? What the hell?*

"Yeah, but I got it for you. I thought you might pick up some ideas on what to do about you know who 'cause, you know, the sandwiches are just stopping you from taking a vacation. I know how much you hate winter. And you give all that up every day when you go to that fucking deli. Anyway, listen to the description on the back...

"'Love doesn't die... People do, as we learn from Reginald Patter's chilling love story, *Passionate Torment*. An epic tale of lust and compulsion, *Passionate Torment* follows the journey of a quiet health care worker who undergoes radical plastic surgery and French lessons to win the love of an old childhood sweetheart, driven by a... *Passionate Torment*. But, disillusioned by his sudden interest in her, she hungrily seduces him and then carelessly casts him aside. And now he seeks to capture her love... Forever. Set in the torrid heat of the Virgin Islands, *Passionate Torment* is a story of obsession that never ends.'"

"Yeah," Sylvia interjects. "Never ends well."

"It's just like you to be pessimistic." Helen tosses the book down on Sylvia's desk. It spins for a moment, almost colliding with the neglected sandwich.

"Watch it!" Sylvia hisses. "All I'd need is for him to come over here after you've knocked his sandwich on the floor."

"All right, all right, don't yell. Enough negativity."

"Sorry," Sylvia mumbles. "It's just that... The sandwich... Is..."

"Yours, Sylvia. Until he comes and takes it, that is."

"That's a technicality, dear. The sandwich is—"

"Hard. Touch it. It's hard. And if it isn't now, it will be in an hour. Maybe you'd like something else to be hard, if you know what I mean." She fumbles with her scarf. "Can you loosen the knot there? Oh, forget it." She pulls the scar over the top of her head, blinking as it slides away.

Sylvia blushes; she tries to. Helen offers her a maternal smile that comes across as medicinal. Sylvia is perplexed.

"And that's why I got you the book," Helen continues. "You know, I figured you'd be able to maybe use some of the character's techniques to help get your man." She is unaware that she is toying with the scarf, pulling it between both hands, stretching the material until it is about to tear. "Everybody could use a little help, if you know what I mean."

"Thanks Helen, but I don't think I'm up for plastic surgery just yet."

"Radical plastic surgery," Helen corrects her. "With all the money you've spent on corned beef sandwiches over the years, you could have had two lifts by now. Maybe more."

"Ha!" *Enough now. Go away.*

"I've gotta go heat up my yam and arugula casserole. You want any, or you got chips today?"

"Chips."

"Yeah? What flavour?" Helen leans in closer.

"Sour cream and onion. But they're gone."

"Gone or eaten?"

"Both."

Helen's mouth forms a straight line. She keeps her focus on Sylvia's cluster of pimples. "Well, I'll see you later then."

Helen walks away but then stops suddenly. She turns and points discreetly at Harold Greenbaum, still slumped over at his desk. "Don't worry about the pimples. He can't see them from his angle anyway," she says in a far-too-loud whisper.

Sylvia pulls the edge of her index fingernail over the surface of one of the pimples and presses down on it. She smiles when she sees the bloody milky smudge on her finger.

Sylvia spends several hours at the small café across the street from Harold Greenbaum's apartment building. She stares outside and up at a curtained window on the ninth floor. The curtains are mint green lace—perhaps an odd choice for a man, but she has figured all factors into the Harold equation: *He could be subletting.* With the lights on in the apartment, the window has a misty green glow to it.

His name catches in her mind like a stutter. *Harold Greenbaum, Harold Greenbaum. Harold... Green. Harold. Greenbaum... Harold. Harold.* As many times as she repeats it and hears the sound of it in her mind it never loses its power, never becomes senseless or numbing. It calms her and sends her pulse racing at the same time. Greenbaum... *Baum. What is baum? What's it mean in English?* She wants to look him in the eyes when he penetrates her. That's when she'll whisper his name into his ear, right when he is fully inside her. *Only a real soul mate would do that. That's what we are, soul mates.*

Staring at the faint green light without blinking, waiting to see a shadow—his shadow—moving past the window, Sylvia is so focused that she doesn't see the object of her affection walk past the café with a small brown paper bag in his right hand. She looks down at the cover of *Passionate Torment*, lying face-up on the table beside her coffee cup. She sees the woman reclining invitingly on the beach, partially obscured by the shadow of the hulking man. She imagines him a Fabio clone with long flowing dark hair, a major dimple and a wild look in his eyes. Probably holding a really big butcher knife. *Ridiculous,* she thinks. *You can't force somebody to love you. That's not love.*

She reluctantly picks up the tattered paperback and opens it to a random page.

Anne decided that the best way to meet Doug Craven would be to have it happen naturally—or at least it should appear that way to him. He was the district supervisor in charge of seven hospitals, one of which employed Anne. In the few days leading up to the first Monday of every month—the day he came to Hillcrest Memorial Hospital for inspection and meetings with the chief of staff and board of directors—Anne made a point of offering up her unit for his inspection.

Marlene Hill, the chief of staff, was surprised at Anne's offer and said that as soon as Mr. Craven requested a burn unit for inspection hers would be the first they came to. Anne smiled, nodded and walked away, knowing that hers was the only burn unit in the hospital and that it was only a matter of time before Doug Craven showed up to inspect it.

When the day finally came, however, Anne was not prepared. Five months had passed since she had approached the chief of staff with her offer. Five months. She had gone to a plastic surgeon's office and received a thorough consultation, estimate, and information on recovery time. Though she could arrange for the time off work, she couldn't afford the surgery. It would have to wait. But when an almost-forgotten aunt died and left her a tidy sum, Anne booked the surgery and time off work for recovery and spent the ensuing months strengthening her resolve. She would not give up. She spent the down time mentally shuffling her cards, but that did not mean the impending inspection had become unimportant to her. The wait made her more determined. Her new face and body were anxious for their reveal. She repeated her mantra, the three Ps: poise, patience, pilates.

Through the hospital's computer, Anne dug up information about Doug Craven: where he lived, his telephone number, his age and social security number. And although she hadn't touched his skin or kissed his mouth, Anne felt closer to Doug. Much closer, now that she knew more about him. She cherished him. And so when he did finally walk into her burn unit, unannounced and accompanied by

Marlene Hill and another of the hospital's directors, the newly renamed, tightly sculpted and spray-tanned Angelique was behind the main desk, typing a love poem into the computer.

She flew out from behind the desk, tripped on a chair leg and fell at Doug's feet.

"Excuse me," Angelique said with a meticulous Parisian accent. She stood up and straightened her uniform evenly with her hands. "It's a privilege to meet you Mr. Craven. I'm so honoured to have you here. We are..."

"Thank you Mrs. Door," he said, straining his eyes to look at her name tag.

"Miss," she corrected him.

"Oh. Miss," he repeated.

"And it's D'Or," she quickly added, disappointed he didn't know better. "Like gold." She pressed her finger to her name tag and then touched his hand lightly, a nice, feminine touch, she thought, and then moved her hand to rub the back of her neck, at the scar there, hidden by her now-blonde hair. She moved sideways and gestured with her hand to indicate the rest of the unit behind them. "Please, call me Angelique," she said. "I'm glad you've come to see the centre. It isn't the largest in your jurisdiction, I believe, but I think you'll find that it's one of the most cost-effective. The nurses all work really hard to keep up the reputation. I make sure of that." A smile. She moved toward the entrance to the burn centre. "Won't you please follow me?"

Doug followed a few steps behind Angelique as they pushed through a doorway and into the main hallway. He looked at the back of Angelique's head, at her hair knotted up in a bun, as she pointed and talked. He wanted to reach forward and undo the bun, to see her long, blonde hair tumble out so she could flip it around like he had seen done hundreds of times in television commercials for hair conditioner, shampoo, curling irons, make-up, and that *Seka Goes Shopping* DVD he'd bought before his neighbourhood video store went out of business.

Sylvia drains the last bit of coffee out of her cup and closes the book. After paying the bill, she pulls her coat over her shoulders and walks out the door. She ambles slowly until she is past Harold's building. In a few moments she is home.

Several months back, she moved half a block away from Harold Greenbaum's apartment building. Compared to her old place, her new apartment is more spacious, the building newer and cleaner and the rent cheaper. *Who knew?* Although she has yet to see him around the neighbourhood, from her balcony, Sylvia can see the green glow of Harold's window and can identify him clearly, with her set of binoculars, when he comes and goes, sometimes the light and the green curtains billowing reveal his figure which, she imagines, is naked and waiting. For her.

Tonight she steps out onto the balcony and looks at Harold's building. She imagines herself unbuttoning his heavily starched white work shirt and then removing—very delicately—the white undershirt beneath it. She can almost feel his damp chest hair between her fingers. She can taste the smell of corned beef on his breath, the lingering notes of mustard and mayonnaise. She wants to run her hands over his almost-bald head, to lie naked beneath his masculine, musky body, to be trapped—taken.

A faint electronic monotone beeps from the alarm clock in her bedroom. Time for *Roseanne*. Sylvia turns inside and closes the balcony door behind her.

Later that night, she pulls the worn paperback from her briefcase and reads herself to sleep, every so often lifting her hand to finger the three red bumps on her nose. She's swabbed them with witch-hazel and tea tree oil, but it doesn't seem to be helping. She lifts her fingers to her nose and breathes in the pungent scent of the oil. *Something about France*, she thinks as she drifts off to sleep. *Something about French.*

> "I love you," Henri said in an even tone. "Je t'aime. Répétez."
>
> "Je tam," Angelique mimicked.
>
> "Non, non," the tutor said, controlling his anger. "T'aime. Pronounce it like you're saying the number ten but with an M instead of the N and then you'll have it. Try it again. Je t'aime."
>
> "Je t'aime," Angelique said.
>
> "Good, good. Very good, Angelique. Now the next phrase is—"
>
> "How do you ask someone to have sex with you?" she interrupted.
>
> Henri blushed and cleared his throat. "Well, uh, let's see. I'm sure there's a number of ways you

could say it, but, uh, the best, I suppose would be... Do you remember that song from the seventies called 'Lady Marmalade?'"

"No," she lied, eager to hear him say the words. "Do I look eighty?"

"Repeat after me..."

He worked with her, going over every syllable and nuance of the phrase.

"Voulie voo... uh... moowah?"

"Voolie voo."

"Voolie voo koo... Shit... Ala mowah?"

"Kooshay."

"Ala moowah."

"Close enough. Now put it all together and don't go overboard with the moi, okay? This is not a drag queen kiss." He paused and gave her a look. "Or is it? Never mind. Try it again."

And after five minutes, Angelique said the magic words.

"My work here is done," he smiled.

"So what does it really mean in English?"

"Would you like to sleep with me?"

"No, but thank you for asking." Angelique laughed loudly as the tutor blushed. She pressed her hand against his crotch. He sprang to life at her touch, stretching the fabric of his pants.

He looked at her beseechingly, hoping to find in her eyes her intention, but Angelique only offered a crooked smile, one that left him more confused and engorged.

When Sylvia rises in the morning she feels the soft fleece of her nightgown as the material plays gently across her nipples while she stretches. She lowers her arms, feels an unusual lightness, as if her sleep had erased a terrible burden and now she is fresh and ready for a new life.

While the coffee brews, she sits and searches the Internet for a dermatologist, wishing she knew someone who could give her a recommendation instead of having to walk in to an office unknowingly.

I'm not going to be shut in anymore, she vows to herself. *I am going to take control of this situation, get these ugly pimples lanced or whatever and get a referral to a good plastic surgeon. Today. Period. Simple as that.*

Sylvia passes Helen's empty workspace. She pauses and glances at the collage of photos and clippings her friend has arranged on her dividing wall: Tammy Wynette, Marcia Wallace, Tina Turner, Gloria Estefan, Olivia Newton-John, Kate Jackson, Julie Harris, and then there are a handful of snapshots of Helen in the hospital, and several blowups of photos taken at various staff functions, of Helen and Sylvia together, laughing, smiling, lifting glasses in the air to make a toast. Sylvia's eyes linger on a photo of her and Helen in which Sylvia points at someone off camera and Helen rests her turbaned head on her shoulder, a relaxed smile on her face. Sylvia can't remember when the photo was taken. She feels a heaviness creep into her chest. Her stomach turns sour.

The electronic pulse of the elevator door sounds behind her and pulls her from her reverie. Sylvia briskly moves toward her desk, half-nodding at the dark office and the moose painting. She does not notice that this is the first morning since Harold Greenbaum began working at the firm that she hasn't imagined—or hoped—that he had left an enormous bouquet of flowers in her workstation. But when she drops her purse down on her desk and her chair heaves a sigh beneath her weight, the sight of her empty desktop confirms it. *Again no flowers.* An angry voice wells up inside her: *Fuck that*. Out of nowhere. A firm, commanding and prescient voice. For a split second it makes her feel comforted. Then weird. *Really weird.* She shrugs her jacket onto the curve of her chair back and pries off her shoes. *Maybe I should buy myself flowers instead of... fucking sandwiches. What if I made a mistake? What if he's turned... Vegetarian?*

Later, at lunch, after Sylvia has lied to Helen about having extra work to do on her lunch break, Sylvia sits reading *Passionate Torment* at her desk. She's fixated on the flashback chapter where she learns all about Angelique's troubled past, her inability to articulate her desires and take action on her dreams, and the jarring, life-altering car accident that made her realize that she was the only force in the universe preventing her from getting what she wanted. *Clear as a bell*, Sylvia thinks, flipping the pages eagerly. *Clear as a bell ringing right in my ears! But*, she interrupts herself, *I'm not going to have to have a car accident, am I? I'd have to buy a car first.*

"Hello. My name is Sylvia Elder and I'd like to make an appointment please. No, I am a new patient. No, I don't have a referral. My doctor had me using something that didn't work and basically told me tough luck if it didn't. So that's why I'm calling. When is your earliest opening, please? Oh. Wow. That's... Just my luck. Thank you! That's only half an hour from now. I'd better get a move on."

The doctor examines Sylvia's nose under what seems like an oversized magnifying glass and then proceeds with what he calls an extraction. And soon the three cumbersome pimples on her nose have been excavated, cleaned, wiped, sprayed and bandaged. The doctor gives Sylvia a prescription and some hints for preventing break-outs and flare-ups. As she thanks the man, Sylvia finds her heart beating faster. She knows she is at a crossroads. *The time is now*, she thinks as she hesitates at the door, staring at the doctor's name tag pinned to his white lab coat. *L. Melendez.*

"I'm thinking of having some plastic surgery done," Sylvia says evenly. "Do you know of anyone you can recommend for an initial consultation?"

A strange, ambling warmth spreads through her torso.

Helen gasps when Sylvia waltzes through the office with gauze covering her nose. She shuffles away from her desk and follows Sylvia to her workspace.

"What happened? Did they get infected?"

Sylvia snorts, sending a flap of the gauze flying upward. "Why are you so interested in my pimples, Helen? Seems a little perverse to me, if you know what I mean."

Helen stops dead in her tracks, an infantile look of shame on her face. "Uh," is all she can utter. It isn't a big shock to her, but she notices it, and will remember it later on, as Sylvia's behaviour becomes more abrupt, removed and condescending.

Later that day Helen saunters over to Sylvia's desk to find her drinking bottled water and eating something brown from a plastic container.

"What's that?"

"Quinoa salad with balsamic vinaigrette."

"Oh. So no chips today?"

"Or ever again. Do you know what's in those things? Chemicals! It's no wonder I was breaking out all the time. The dermatologist set me straight though."

Helen sniffs the air. Something is out of place. She scans Sylvia's desk: no sandwich.

"Where's the—?"

"Don't ask."

A sly smile spreads across Helen's face. "Are you thinking about a tropical vacation?"

Sylvia looks up at her co-worker. An even, patient smile is her answer.

"I changed my name to Angelique Demure,"

she said to the immaculately dressed receptionist. "I guess my insurance company hasn't updated their files yet. I have all the documents here if you need them."

The woman, mummified inside her Armani suit, stared at her but did not respond. After a long pause, she closed the file folder in front of her and looked directly into Angelique's eyes. "The doctor will see you now," she said.

"Thank you."

The receptionist smiled wanly as Angelique passed the office and disappeared down a hallway.

"Angelique Demure," Sylvia hisses and places the book face down on her lap. But within seconds she's reading again, imagining her lungs filling with the soft clinical scent of the plastic surgeon's office.

"Everything. I want everything changed." She paused and glared at the doctor, expecting him to protest. He didn't. A telephone rang in the outer office. Angelique wondered if the doctor has ever had relations with his secretary. In the same reclining chair she was sitting in.

It can't hurt that much, Angelique thought. *Seems like everybody's doing it.*

"Everything? Hmmm," the doctor said, not really expecting a response.

"Yes. Doctor, I don't know if you've ever had to live your life in the shadow of yourself or of other people who don't accurately reflect you. I have. I've spent my life running away from things I truly wanted because I believed I didn't suit them. But now I feel differently, doctor. And I also believe that it's time for me to reveal my needs and desires and for me to reflect those qualities with every breath I take and every movement I make. I've already started taking French lessons and... Oh, my goodness. Am I making sense?"

She wanted him to pull her blouse open, for buttons to fly, their small pings ringing out as they hit the wall and bounce to the floor as their feet shuffled together, pants jammed down around his shoes and he unzipped her skirt in one fluid movement. *Magic hands. All over me. Down there. Oh, yes!*

Helen scoffs at Sylvia's Armani suit when she strides through the office one Tuesday morning after a long weekend. *Oh no,* she thinks. *Power suit.* Helen experiences Sylvia's entrance in slow motion, everything alive with detail. Beams of light from an open office door spill out into the corridor, illuminating the suit with an even pattern of light and shadows. Sylvia passes through the corridor, her heels making distorted sounds as they make contact with the floor, her blonde hair bouncing slightly as she walks. Things speed back to normal after she has passed the moose painting without so much as a nod to her friend.

"Where'd you get *that*?" Helen asks as she scuttles over to Sylvia's desk.

"At a store," Sylvia answers curtly, avoiding eye contact. It's not easy for her to treat her Helen this way, especially since she's so lonely and pathetic, but these are the exact reasons she feels she has to draw the line. *Onward and upward,* she thinks, cracking a bit of a smile, oblivious to its inauthenticity. Helen notices though.

"You must be really getting into that book. Hey, wanna have lunch today? There's a two for one at Larry's. They got cottage cheese and veggie platters for your diet."

"I'm not—" Sylvia stops herself when she hears the severity in her voice, the impatience and aggravation. She rises from her desk, manages a flash of eye contact before angling away from Helen. "I'm not on a diet. Just eating well. And exercising."

"Oh," Helen says, staring at Sylvia's hips. "It's working." Sylvia smiles. "You get a prescription for those zits yet? I heard toothpaste at night works."

"Yes, and you get it all over your sheets and pillowcases," she says, grabbing her water bottle and walking away.

"Put a towel down," Helen bleats.

"And the towel gets ruined."

"So?" She swallows hard, trying to think of something to say to keep the exchange going. "Buy some at the dollar store!"

"Oh, I would never be caught dead there." Sylvia turns the corner with a hand gesture that comes across as dismissive.

Moments later Helen walks into the women's washroom and finds Sylvia washing her hands.

"Hey! I asked you if you were going for lunch."

"I can't. I've got an appointment."

"Oh. Okay."

"Bye."

Helen pushes thoughts around in her mind to steer clear of the stinging feeling in her gut. *Fuck.*

Sylvia wonders when Helen is going to clue in and leave her alone. *Fuck!*

The bathroom door closes. As the distance between the two women increases, they both think, *Harold Greenbaum*, and then, *Passionate Torment.*

When Sylvia returns from her appointment with the plastic surgeon, she glides past Helen's desk without a word.

Helen cranes her neck forward, feeling disappointment all through her body, an unconscious reaction to Sylvia's power suit, or so she thinks. But moments later, when she not only knows something is wrong but feels it as well, she smells the air. Her olfactory system is in overdrive. Not corned beef; perfume, a kind she doesn't recognize except that it smells snooty. *Rich old lady perfume.* Helen puts her book down on her desk, pushes her chair back and rises. She moves slowly but deliberately along the aisle, past the dark office and the moose in the painting staring at her, and stops just short of Sylvia's desk.

Sylvia looks up from her bottle of water and stares glumly at Helen.

"What?"

"Nothing," Helen says in a hushed voice, staring at the virtually empty desktop. Just a bottle of Vita-O! oxygenated mineral water. "I just thought..."

"What?"

Why are you doing this?

Two weeks later, Helen leaves her desk at two thirty for a meeting with Human Resources. Located in the basement of the office tower, with low ceilings and glaring fluorescent lighting, Helen sits in the waiting room wishing she had worn sunglasses.

"So, Helen, what can I help you with?" Sherrie Sondergaard asks her when she is finally admitted to the inner office.

"Well—"

"Oh! Ohmygawd I can't believe I forgot to ask how your treatment went. Everything okay?"

"Yes, it is," Helen says with a smile. "That was over a year ago. I'm cancer-free now and—"

"Oh that's such good news. You know, I should be more on top of things but with a staff of over four hundred it's sometimes difficult, as I'm sure you can well imagine."

"Yeah," Helen says, smile lingering. "I don't know how you manage it. But I was cancer-free when I came back."

"So how are you finding the hours?"

"Tough. But so am I, so..."

"Good. Oh, good. That's so good to hear."

A lull. Sherrie flips through some pages in an open file folder in front of her.

"The reason I came was to see if there might be any openings in any of the other departments that I'm qualified for."

"Oh. Well that shouldn't be too tough to manage. Not happy?"

"No. It's not that. It's a... It's a personal—no, private thing. I just want to be somewhere else."

"I see. Well, Helen, there's nothing available right now," she says, scanning a document on her computer screen. "And from what I can see here, not much of anything on the horizon for at least another month. But things change suddenly. Tell you what, I'll put your name on my short list and will send you an e-mail message as soon as I hear of anything opening up. How's that?"

"I guess that's all you can do."

"It is." A smile of mostly gums and tiny niblet teeth. Sherrie juts her hand out and waits for Helen to shake it.

"You should think about getting rid of this harsh lighting," Helen says as an afterthought. "Maybe a coat of paint. With colour. Some fuchsia maybe. The beige everywhere is oppressive. It deadens the eye... not to mention the soul."

Sherrie looks around her quickly, then back at Helen. "Huh?"

"It's not good for the visual palette. Makes people sleepy. Beige everywhere. You need to break it up, you know? Make a change."

"Oh," Sherrie says dismissively.

"Might not be so depressing down here," she says, moving to the door and waiting. "It's like being in a cage."

Sherrie offers a curt grin and presses a button on her desk to unlock the office door. A loud buzzer sounds, and then a click.

"You take care now," Sherrie says. "And eat lots of greens. I hear that's good for you."

"You too," Helen says, turning and pushing the door open in front of her. "Thanks."

Idiot.

She wrestles with the urge to feel disappointed, telling herself that it was her first visit. *I don't have to stay here. I could work anywhere, doing almost anything,* she thinks, pushing through a heavy steel door. She passes through to the waiting room where she almost trips over Sylvia's feet. She's sitting cross-legged in one of the uncomfortable chairs reading *Vogue. Expensive shoes,* Helen notices. *Really expensive shoes. They look like they hurt. Good.*

"Hi."

Sylvia knows the voice even without looking up from her magazine, which she does gingerly.

"Hello."

"Having an intervention?"

"No," Sylvia says, a deliberate lowering of her voice so she has a deeper, throatier sound.

Now she thinks she's Miss hoity-toity.

Helen waits for Sylvia to say something, but there's only silence. After a moment, Sylvia lowers her eyes and returns to *Vogue*. Helen steps toward the door. As she clasps the doorknob, Sylvia's voice rings out—at least an octave higher than her last words.

"Helen. Look, this isn't easy for me to say, but..."

"What? You can tell me anything. I'm your—"

"I'm here to deliver this paperwork to Human Resources. I've legally changed my name and work is the last place I have to make the switch."

"You're changing your name?"

"Changed. Past tense."

"Don't tell me... Ange—"

"Monique."

"Monique Elder?"

"DuMaurier. Monique DuMaurier."

"Like the smokes?"

"The novelist."

"You're stalking him, you know. It's official. And perverse."

"What? Where did that come from?"

"Look it up in the dictionary," Helen says. "Or do an Internet search."

"I know what it means! I'm not stalk—" Monique stops herself when she hears her voice rising, a tidal wave of anger. "I'm not stalking anyone," she says above a whisper. "I'm improving myself."

"Removing is more like it," Helen says.

"Whatever you say."

"You can come in now," a disembodied voice calls out from a metallic speaker on the wall. The harsh sound of a buzzer. The mechanism of a door lock snaps open.

"I'm not sure how the company will handle this, but I would appreciate it if you would leave Sylvia Elder to rest."

"Oh."

"She's dead."

"And you didn't invite her best friend to the funeral."

Helen doesn't have to physically feel the mucous thinning and moving through her sinus cavity to know it's coming. *Why doesn't she just stick a knife in my back? Monique DuMaurier.* She presses a finger to her upper lip, swivels abruptly and hurries out of the waiting room.

That's the last draw. Straw. Whatever. How can she...? What did I do to bring this on? Was I too clingy? Too needy? Too depressing? Is it the way I talk or dress or look or everything? Am I too identified with the cancer? But I almost died! And she's embarrassed by me?! Ashamed to be seen with me! Like I have an infectious disease. Oh well, in that case, I guess I do! It's called REAL. I am real. As real as they come. Stupid skinny acne-faced mean rotten bitch! And now with expensive taste in clothes. And a fake French name. Dolores DeBourgignon, might as well be. Fuck, I'm so mad I could eat a whole cake. Or just... Or just punch her face into smithereens. Fuck you, Monique DuMaurier!

Monique looks in the mirror after making a cappuccino with the milk frother she bought on her Sears card. *Sylvia no more. Monique. Monique DuMaurier. I need to step things up,* she thinks, after watching dozens of episodes of *Sesame Street* in French and still only being able to understand a fraction of what was said.

Sipping her cappuccino and writing out her goals on a pad of paper, Monique knows she has to learn how to speak two languages: French and l'amour. *Maybe, if I'm lucky, I'll find someone who can teach me both and one will enhance the other. Just like Angelique! Why didn't I think of it before? I need to get a copy of that book again.*

Monique finds Jacques, a twenty-six-year-old exchange student from Québec. He responds to her ad in *NOW* and meets her—on time—at the designated place. He also pays for their cafés au lait.

"I need a crash course," she says breathlessly, examining the lines in the crotch of his pants as they sit down across from one another. *Is he... Intact?*

"How much, uh, do you want to know?"

"Everything. How often can you meet?"

After two weeks of three-hour-long sessions every Monday, Wednesday, Friday and Sunday, Jacques arrives at Monique's apartment. She answers the door in a long, flowing, semi-opaque robe. He steps inside, gives Monique the up and down and feels himself getting hard. Monique notices the slight tenting in his pants and says that perhaps he might like to try teaching her how to French kiss. She pretends not to notice that he closes his eyes when they are in bed, so much sweating and French sex talk she doesn't understand because it wasn't covered on *Sesame Street*. Jacques has seemingly unlimited sexual energy and even though she would never love him the way she loves Harold Greenbaum, she is glad she chose him as her teacher. Later on, as she stands alone before her bathroom mirror, Monique practices smiling, trying to concentrate on the space inside her that only minutes before Jacques had occupied.

I'm happy. I'm fulfilled. Smile!

Weeks turn into months. Monique is comfortable and confident speaking French and having sex even though in the back of her mind she feels as if she's cheating on Harold. But she shooes these thoughts away by telling herself that she is doing it for him. She buys an MP3 player and listens to Piaf, Charles Aznavour, Higelin, and a variety of French lessons as she walks around the city. She follows Harold Greenbaum through the streets every Saturday afternoon. One weekend he ducks into a pornographic magazine shop as Charles Aznavour sings "No Je N'ai Rien Oublié," but Monique doesn't feel safe or comfortable following him inside. Another weekend she pursues him from across the street and slightly behind and watches as he drops a bottle of wine on the sidewalk and, hunched over, seems to cry, his shoulders making small convulsive movements. Monique watches him sobbing from the other side of the street, her hands trembling as Celine Dion sings "L'Amour Existe Encore." A short man bumps against her as he passes and pulls her from her stare.

"You don't just stop in the middle of a busy sidewalk," he jeers. "Get out of the way, narcissist!"

Mon dieu, she says to herself. *Qu'est ce que je fais? Suis-je folle de lui? Je pense que oui. I am crazy.*

She lingers there, blocking pedestrian traffic until Harold has picked up the broken glass and moved on. Only then does she cross the street to examine the remaining pieces of the bottle, hoping to catch the aroma from the spilt wine, but all she can smell is exhaust from the cars that pass and the stench of garbage rotting in the sun.

To love you once, and at any price...

By the time of the staff Christmas party, Helen has grown used to the situation and makes no attempts to speak with her former friend. With a noisy Bing Crosby remix playing over the PA system, she catches a glimpse of Monique in the crowd, standing with a small cluster of people from upper management. Monique smiles and talks about her upcoming vacation plans when she spies Harold Greenbaum crossing the room to go speak with Helen, sporting a new wig that makes her think of Connie Chung in a windstorm. It takes all her willpower to stand still and not rush over and rip the wig off Helen's head. Reason amubushes her. *Why do I care,* she thinks, *about this ridiculous woman?*

"Varadero," she says, unaware that she has already told the group where she would be going for the holidays. "It's quiet there. So I've heard. Read, actually. I think I'm too old for belly shots."

Someone in the group looks at her and speaks. "My brother and I..." But Monique tunes everything else out except the sight of Harold Greenbaum talking to Helen. She glares at his back and smiles when he makes small gestures with his left hand, a plastic cup with red wine in his right. She can't see Helen's face; only that wig.

Suddenly Harold's body rocks with laughter. His right hand jolts, sending red wine down his right pant leg. Monique wonders if he will cry this time. She wonders how he would react if she called out, "Please, Harold, I just want you inside me!" She turns her attention back to the hushed conversation about cheese sandwiches, diarrhea and mojitos, and makes a mental note to buy travel packs of Pepto Bismol and Immodium before her trip.

Just then, Helen leans forward and stares at Monique. Helen mouths the words, *You're stalking,* and then discreetly points her finger at Harold Greenbaum.

"Are you travelling by yourself?" someone asks, laughing, aware that Monique isn't listening. The crowd around her disperses. Helen smiles when she sees this, but deep inside all she wants to do is hug her friend. Really hard.

Alone in her hotel room in Varadero, Monique puts on her sheer nightgown and climbs in bed with the new copy of *Passionate Torment* she bought from amazon.ca.

> Doug Craven entered the room, basking in a white flowing robe, his sun-torched skin glowing golden. She could tell from the sudden hush that had fallen over the room that others at the party had noticed him. Surely he knew it, too. And yet instead of responding with his characteristic gloating, he turned and focussed on her.
>
> She watched as his head turned. The room's lighting brought out the contours of his deeply

sculpted face: the slightly jutting jaw, the exquisite cheek bones, the curve of his lips, the arc of his dark eyebrows. For a second her heart stopped. Was that a sigh of release or an indignant rush of breath that escaped her lips? Surely she could control her heartbeat. Surely she could turn away and feign indifference. She could have done many things to spur Doug on. But it was far too late for that.

Instead, with a chilled grace she raised her champagne flute to her lips and took an elegant sip, her eyes searching the room, from face to face, and then she stared at him. She set the champagne flute down on a waist-high marble column, trying to figure out the theme of the party.

She watched as a waiter approached Doug and offered him a glass from his tray of drinks. He waved the costumed server away, keeping his glance fixed on Angelique. They eyed each other from across the room, in between clusters of people dressed up and partially naked. "You Rascal You" played over loudspeakers. It's as though Disney remade *Eyes Wide Shut*.

She dipped her index finger into the glass of golden bubbly and looked at the crotch of his pants, the angled lines of material stretching out to allow for his superfluous package. He shifted his weight and struck a godlike pose. Angelique broke out in an uproarious shriek of laughter. His posture withered; the imploded outline of a man. But he quickly regained his composure and heaved his chest out as he strode toward her. She had already turned away and was walking in the opposite direction when he barrelled up behind her, his hands on her shoulders, his heavy, black-haired, thick-wristed hands. She gasped and spun around, attempting mild shock.

"What do you think you're doing?" he asked. "Are you trying to make me mad?" She wished he had an accent, Mediterranean perhaps. And before another word passed between them they were in her suite spread out on the king-size bed pouring champagne and warmed chocolate over one another while a mild tropical breeze blew in, creating dancing shadows from the billowing curtains. *Oh my,* she thought with a devilish smile. *This is like that vampire movie with David Bowie.*

When he was on top of her, inside her, she didn't feel his thick, masculine hands moving adoringly over her body—or on any other part of her for that matter. As he thrust into her with increasing intensity she could not feel his hips against hers or his lips at her earlobes licking away any remnants of chocolate, champagne and perfume. There was no sensation of his heated skin or the beads of sweat that collected on the hair that fanned out between the cheeks of his hard buttocks as they gyrated rhythmically, his body against hers. She was somewhere else, far away, in a box, a small black box. Nobody knew she was there. Nobody would ever find her as she writhed and wriggled in small movements, constrained as she was. *More,* she thought, again with a devilish smile. *More!*

The moment he had reached his climax and had pulled himself out and from off of her, she shifted her weight, moved to the edge of the mattress and stared up at the ceiling. He motioned toward her but she stopped him with her hands and pushed him back slightly.

"Time to go," she said, her voice heavy with ennui. She thought it was better than asking for more. *I can't let him actually give me what I want. That would be stupid.*

"But I wasn't finished," he protested. She let loose a snort of air through her nostrils and a throaty jab of a laugh. He turned to his side and looked at her adoringly.

"Two of my fingers are more satisfying than you," she said quietly—more to herself, but yet hoping he would hear. "Just go."

"I don't—" he attempted before she interrupted him.

"Go." She had to struggle to keep the bored look on her face as she stared at him, hoping to see an expression of embarrassment or humiliation on his handsome face. She wanted to make him feel the way she had felt for wanting him: foolish, dead inside. All the money, time, pain, French lessons: It all made her weak when she thought about what she'd done to herself to get him. She wanted to appear strong, statuesque, like women in a Fellini film, *Without the unintelligible nattering,* she thought.

Monique's eyes grow wild with desire as she closes the book and places it on the bedside table. *I couldn't... I can't.* She ignores the tightness of her nipples and reaches to turn out the light. In the moments before sleep she imagines Harold Greenbaum on top of her in the throes of passion amidst the sun and sand of the Virgin Islands. She imagines the beads of sweat forming and shimmering on his hairless head as he thrusts into her over and over again. She wouldn't do anything as bold as asking him to leave after their lovemaking. Rather, she would simply, delicately fall asleep in the middle of it.

Just as she is about to drift off, a name, a face and a physical sensation enter her consciousness: Jacques.

Jacques?!

Tom Avery wakes Helen up in the morning. On the radio. She's been following his career since his informative television mini-show about the entertainment world on the now-defunct EntertaiNetwork. He has since moved on to a country radio station, doing the morning news mini-program. Helen loves the sound of his voice, authorative and caring, an idealized father over the airwaves.

Her bathroom sink is too low. Below it, water drips into a kitty litter box. Her cat Loopy stares up at her as she crouches down to pee. Loopy is annoyed by the dripping water. Helen looks in the mirror and sees past the lines and folds of skin and smiles at who she has become. *No reinvention for me, no way. I am how I am.*

On the train into town Helen looks up from her book, *The Women's Room* by Marilyn French. She thought it sounded like a torrid washroom confessional, but she's having a hard time getting through it. She notices an attractive man at the opposite end of the subway car thumbing through a newspaper. He sees her watching him and sends a confused look her way. He can't figure out whether she's flirting, out on a day pass, or just being friendly. She goes back to her book wondering why people choose to be so complicated. *A look is just a look. Unless it is more than a look. In which case... Never mind.*

On her way into the office tower she stops at the coffee shop on the ground floor and buys a small cup of decaf.

She eases her way into the elevator. The ride up is silent except for the muted woosh of the car ascending. She fingers the lid of her coffee cup, looks forward to the first sip. She knows she could save money by having coffee at home, but her morning ritual is already so time consuming. She never budgets properly and often ends up having to cab it to the subway.

When the elevator stops on her floor, a short pudgy woman pushes past her as the doors open, preceded by an electronic pulse. The woman's thick nylon-wrapped legs move quickly, her heels clicking on the tiled floor, the sound of extravagant feminine things, nails in Helen's ears. The sound of memories. *Of Monique.* Helen stands on the outside of the elevator as its doors swish quietly closed behind her. She watches as the short woman struggles to keep up her pace, obviously late for a meeting, an impressive bundle of file folders, binders and books jammed into her side and held together by her thick arm. *If I were walking beside her I would have to trip her and hope the fall breaks those fucking heels. Why don't I have any important meetings? Oh. I'm a drone.*

As she walks through the corridor, a quick glance up at the oversized clock tells her it's eight-fifty. A procession of women brandishing empty coffee mugs and miniature kettles brimming with cold water passes her on the way to the staff kitchenette to perk, brew, pour and begin the daily consumption of mood-altering beverages. *I'll just stick to my decaf and have a calm morning,* Helen thinks. *And maybe at lunch I can skip down to George Brown and check out their courses on interior design. Just for shits and giggles.*

"Good morning staff and management of Invigro. Have a wonderful Wednesday." The receptionist clears her throat over the public address system and continues with the morning announcements. She reads it like someone would read a poorly translated user manual for a product they're unfamiliar with. "Pam MacKenna report to your desk please. That's, Pam MacKenna report to your desk." She repeats everything twice. *Are people that stupid?*

Helen's recently appointed supervisor calls her over to her workstation to inform her that her productivity levels have fallen in the last two months. Helen swallows hard and lies that she has been worried about a *recurrence*. She says the word in a harsh whisper. The emphasis of the hard C gives her a subtle thrill. She looks beseechingly at the woman who nervously scribbles something on a notepad before offering a tight smile, her body language telling Helen that she is not comfortable—with this tidbit of information, with her job, hairstyle, mode of dress, probably the decor of her home as well. *I could fix that. If...*

"I'm very sorry to hear that," the supervisor says, standing up and lowering her clipboard to her side.

Helen doesn't have the nerve to tell the truth, that Sylvia—

no, Monique now—has thrown her off course. *My best friend has decided to completely reinvent herself and I don't know what to do about it. So it's no wonder that my productivity levels have fallen,* she'd like to say. But that sharing would be inappropriate. She wonders what others in the office think of Sylvia's transformation. The supervisor concludes their conversation with a speech about teamwork. *Upper-management brainwashing techniques to subdue the independent.*

Before she gets back to her desk, the receptionist is on the P.A. system again.

"May I have your attention, please? The staff committee members will be selling raffle tickets between ten-fifteen and three o'clock today. The grand prize is a dinner for two at Gino's Pizzeria. Staff committee members will be selling raffle tickets between ten-fifteen and three o'clock today. The grand prize is a dinner for two at Gino's Pizzeria. Will Pam MacKenna please return to your desk? Pam MacKenna."

Helen pulls the lid off her coffee and breathes in the aroma before taking her first sip. *Delicious. Maybe if this doesn't work out here I could go work at a Starbucks.*

On the other side of her dividing wall, the Q and A girls field phone calls from angry, confused and belligerent customers. Sometimes they argue stoically with the callers. Even when they are screamed and cursed at, these girls remain calm. *They should be waitresses,* she thinks. *In Yorkville, where people who have the appearance of money go through the motions of appearing to eat and drink.* Of course, Helen's random samples usually exclude anyone and anything that might challenge her observations, enabling her to keep her world view intact, so that she feels she knows who she is, and who everyone else is around her. However, in light of Sylvia's transformation, Helen has tried to avoid making too many observations about people; these observations have ramifications and teeth, especially when it comes to Sylvia. *Too much. Too much to think about. Shitty. Shitty, shitty, shitty. Bitch. So... Don't think. About that... woman.*

She looks down at the pile of paperwork in front of her and clicks on Notepad and begins to type out a poem. She calls it "Where To Go From Here."

Out of the blue
And into the dark
I will not stumble and fall
Even though you're not there to walk beside me...

You fucking bitch

She presses her index finger on the delete button and erases her masterwork. She closes the program and takes a sip of coffee, feels the urge to urinate. She takes the coffee cup with her and sits quietly in the stall, remembering the time when she had just returned to work and how her bathroom breaks were the only thing that got her through the day, apart from Sylvia, her company and her sympathy. By the time she finishes in the bathroom, the first jolts of caffeine have entered her bloodstream and Helen is aching to talk. She returns to her desk, adjusts the pictures on her dividing wall, deciding that today's survivor of the day is going to be Jacklyn Smith. But the photo of Jacklyn is tattered and faded. Helen rips it from the dividing wall, the push pins making tiny sounds as they land on her desk. Plink, plink. She looks down at the stack of paperwork, spins around in her chair, stares at her coffee cup. She lifts it to her nose and inhales. *Omigawd I'm high. She gave me real coffee! With caffeine!*

She takes her fifteen-minute break and pops downstairs to berate the coffee shop girl about the coffee. The girl looks at her as if she were insane.

"So, like, what do you want me to do? I didn't do it on purpose."

"Yeah, but you should be more careful. What if I had an allergy or a condition, you know? I could have died!" *I almost did once!*

The girl's face distorts. "It was like an accident, okay? De-stress."

"I would if I didn't have caffeine flowing through my veins."

"You want me to call the manager? He'll have to come in from Vaughan."

"Yeah, call the manager and tell them your incompetence just lost them a longtime customer." *Or better yet, wake up, listen, do your job properly and, most of all, don't poison people! Yeah, that'll do it. I feel much better now. Sometimes it feels good to be honest. Even though... Forget it.*

Helen hurries back upstairs with a Rice Krispie square, the coffee girl's attempt at conflict resolution. She drinks cups of water, trying to flush the caffeine out of her system. She writes another poem, this one about the last man she dated, Marcus, from an over-forties website who talked about his divorces, children, financial woes and, strangely, Chinese herbs. "Marcus, Who I Don't Want To Talk About." *Maybe writing this poem will flush him out of my system. Like caffeine. And Sylvia/Monique. There's not enough water in the world for that.*

She gets through the next two hours and manages to complete

half of the work on her desk, but mostly she exchanges quips with the crooked-teeth girl at the workstation beside hers who introduces herself as a name Helen can neither pronounce nor remember mere moments after she hears it. She smiles and nods at the girl's teeth, wishing she had the gumption to storm over to Monique's desk and punch her in the nose, but she remembers that she's still on vacation. Instead, Helen picks up the telephone and dials her own number, pretending to have an animated conversation. She talks over the beep of her answering message and cackles at an untold joke. "Hilarious," she laughs into the receiver. "You're so twisted!" After the phone call, she gets up and walks down the far aisle, tempting fate, past the dark office and then, at the moose painting, she pauses and looks into the department to see if she can see Monique. An oversized fern blocks her view. Then she remembers again that Monique is away. Helen turns left and grabs a box of pencils from the supply room.

"Pam MacKenna return to your desk, please. Pam MacKenna return to your desk."

Who the fuck is Pam MacKenna and what the hell are her productivity lessons like? She's never at her desk!

When she gets back to her workstation, the crooked-teeth girl looks up at her, asks her for a couple of pencils. "You mind?"

"'Course not. I had a feeling someone might need them," she grins, rolling her chair over to the girl's desk and dropping several pencils into her open hand.

At twelve o'clock Helen retrieves her lunch from the staff room refrigerator and brings it back to her desk. She's reading *Surrender The Pink* now; *The Women's Room* was just not up to her standards. Out of the corner of her eye she senses movement. She looks up and sees Harold Greenbaum standing in front of her, looking down at the floor.

"Hi," she says.

"Hey," he says, scuffing the toe of his right shoe on the floor.

"What can I do you for?"

"I noticed you were reading that book and was wondering if it was any good."

"Did you read *Postcards from the Edge*?"

"Yeah. Is it as good as that?"

"It's different. But funnier. And more twisted."

"Okay, great," he says, his demeanour lightened by her appraisal of the book. "Thank you."

She smiles warmly. He has a nice, uncomplicated voice.

"Any time," she says. "I bought it on E-bay so if you want to borrow it when I'm done, just let me know."

"That would be great. If you don't mind."

"Happy to do it."

If only, if only, if only. If I could only have a picture of this. If only I had a picture... I'd blow it up and mail it to that bitch. Her and her fucking power suits and clicky heels and I'm-so-much-better-than-you-now attitude. Rotten, pretentious, mean, devious bitch!

"I'm Helen Frobisher," she says with a genuine smile while extending her hand.

He takes it and gives it a gentle shake. "Harold—"

"Greenbaum," she interrupts. "I know. Accounting, right?"

"Yes."

"We chatted at the Christmas party, remember?"

"That's right, that's right," he says.

"Okay then Harold. Nice to officially meet you. I'll let you know when I'm finished the book."

One week passes after Monique's return from Cuba. It is only when she steps out of the shower on a Friday morning that she realizes Helen hasn't tried to visit, call or e-mail her. *Good,* she thinks, at first.

Helen, however, has seen—and heard—Monique's arrivals in the mornings, but either looked away or down, or lifted her head just enough to take in her collage of survivors, anything to block out the flood of physical upset that spreads through her joints and muscles, brings that familiar heaviness inside her body whenever Monique enters her thoughts. But today Helen gets a nagging feeling that something might be wrong. *Something else.* She has the awareness that she could—and should—possibly focus on something productive and positive, if only she could step around what Monique has become to her. *There is something else. I know it. I just don't know what it is yet.*

Monique has grown accustomed to what she now calls cleansing, the planned purging of unwanted things from her life, as well as the lolling hangover feeling that accompanies the newly opened space. Only occasionally does she look in the mirror and think about who she used to be. Or Helen. Or... Jacques!

"Allo, Jacques?"

"Oui, c'est Jacques. Is that you, Monique?"

"Yes, it's me. How are you? How have you been?" She is not

aware that she sounds like an inexperienced party planner at her first wedding—a Vegan one.

"I am well, thank you, Monique." Clinical tone, removed. "How are you? I haven't seen you since—"

"I know, I'm sorry," Monique says with a moan she hopes will soothe him into listening to her. "I wish I could tell you... I don't know if you'd understand, but I thought about you so many times. You were very good for me. I wanted to be sure you knew that."

"Good for you?"

"Yes."

"I was in love with you. You pulled me in so close and then just dropped it all without any warning."

I know. It worked perfectly. "I hope you're not mad." *And I don't really care if you are.*

He snorts into the receiver. "So what do you want? Why have you called me after disappearing and not returning my phone calls?"

"I don't know. I guess I just..."

"You want me to come over and fuck?"

"Well..."

"You want to use me again?"

"Use?" Monique is on the brink of laughter. "I *paid* you." A deliberate pause for dramatic effect is followed by heady gales of laughter.

"You paid me for French lessons," he blurts. "The fucking was free. I'm not a gigolo."

"You get what you pay for," she says, although she's not sure what she means by it, but it sounds harsh. Or she hopes she sounds harsh when she says it.

"What?"

"Nothing. Never mind. Look, obviously you're upset. Maybe this wasn't a good idea."

"The only bad idea was how you ended it. A child could have done it better."

"And what does that mean?" She hopes she sounds indignant.

"It means you've got no conscience," he says, his voice rising. "People have feelings."

"You mean you, don't you? You have feelings."

"Yes, I do."

"But I told you from the beginning—"

"Monique, if that's really your name, I don't care to hear your excuses and rationalization of your bad behaviour. I am not coming over for fucking or French lessons. Buy a vibrator. Ne me rappelle plus, salope! Look it up!"

Monique hears the line go dead after a precise click through the earpiece.

Class dismissed.

She knows she's changed when she mentally glides past his rejection. There is no emotional response at all except for the appearance of a thin smile on her face. She's practiced this one before and is glad it comes in handy, even if no one can see it. She makes a mental note not to be near a mirror when she smiles this way.

> Angelique squirmed helplessly as Doug loomed above her, slowly unbuttoning his tight-fitting shirt and revealing the tanned expanse of his immaculately trimmed chest. Nipples round as quarters, tight and erect, he drew an index finger against one as a tightness gripped the muscles between his legs. His sinewy thighs tensed as he crouched toward her; she watched as he touched himself and noticed the swelling in his thin, ultra white underpants, the form of his manhood showing through the bleached material. *Oh God*, she thought. *He's perfect. I hate him.* She closed her eyes for a second and forgot the hard rope that bound her hands and ankles together and imagined him the way she wanted him: tied up, humiliated, helpless and begging for mercy. And yet somehow, strangely enough, she was in that very same position, with him in control. Angelique, tied up, frightened and completely at his mercy. This, more than anything else, exhausted and defeated her. It wasn't supposed to be this way. *It wasn't supposed to be this way.*
>
> She should have been hovering over him, scantily clad, stimulating herself with one hand and brandishing an enormous, shiny butcher's knife in the other. *Sex death. Death sex. Sex. Death.*
>
> She struggled, trying to kick upwards and rupture his perfect engorged manhood restrained by the stretch of thin white material of his underwear, but the ropes prevented her from moving her legs more than a few inches. She lay impotent on the bed beneath him. He gasped. Not in shock or in response to her, but in response to himself. His left hand trailed slowly down his rippled stomach. He slid two fingers under the waistband and pulled it down

ever so slightly, revealing a cluster of curly pubic hair and the foreskin-enclosed tip of his penis. Out of the thin folds of skin a glistening drop of excitement appeared. He lowered the knife dangerously close to her belly. She trembled, more angry than fearful. Light from a candle reflected on the blade of the knife as he drew it toward his torso and tore through his underpants. Folds of white cotton fell away, allowing a clear view of his curved erection.

And still, bound and helpless, beneath her hatred and fear, trapped beneath this hot, breathing, hard animal, she remembered what brought her here in the first place—to see him like this, naked, hard, excited, glistening wet and, yes, helpless. And she knew that, despite her shackles, she was in charge. This was all her doing. She brought him here, to this. She had willed it and it came about, although ever so slightly differently than she had envisioned it. The awareness thrilled her, caused a stirring in her. She closed her eyes and imagined herself sliding up and down on top of him with his hard curve inside her wetness. But... Disappointment crept into her fantasy, slowly eating away at her pleasure. She yawned. *Damn it, no!* She thought it would feel better than this. Maybe it wasn't enough to know she was somehow still in control. Perhaps it wasn't enough to know that she was right and that he should be made to suffer and was indeed suffering. Maybe, just maybe, he wasn't enough for her. He couldn't love her the way she needed no matter how hard he tried, no matter how long or hard or curved his masculine flesh was, no matter how delicious the sound of it was as it sprung upwards and bounced against his belly, no matter... It was a fantasy she had created, and one he hadn't lived up to. *So it's his fault. Of course.*

A spot of wetness landed on her cheek. She opened her eyes again. He was still on top of her but things had changed. He had dropped the knife, his penis had drooped and become enclosed in its protective covering and tears were rolling down his face.

"I'm sorry," he managed in a whisper between sobs. "I didn't want to hurt you, my darling. I only

> wanted to be with you." His voice tapered off. He untied the ropes that bound her and watched as she dressed and then walked to the door with a withered look on her face. It wasn't until after she had closed the door behind her that he spoke the words, "I love you." And surely, had she heard the words, she would never have understood them.

Helen pulls herself up from off of the couch and removes the DVD from the tray of her DVD player. *Beaches*. She has no idea how many times she's watched it. *This'll be the last time*, she thinks. *Bitches, they should have called it. Why make a movie about unlikeable people? And this was supposed to be a chick flick.*

Helen reaches for the telephone without thinking, grabs hold of the receiver and jabs at the keypad. It isn't until the fifth number that she remembers, the past few months of memories cascading through and flooding the wiring of her brain with misery and despair. She finishes punching in the phone number as though her fingers had a different response to the memory; more determined, less frightened, seeking resolution, closure, justice. She stands up straight, looks out the window, sees the city outside her apartment as the telephone rings. After the third ring there is a click. She sees the skyline, Scotiabank, BMO, the pointy-bulbous CN Tower—*what an ugly skyline!*—and then hears Sylvia's pretend voice over the line.

"Hello. This is Monique. I'm not available to take your call right this moment. I'm so sorry to have missed you. Please leave me a message."

Beep.

"It's Helen. I'm sure you know that and you're sitting by your phone not answering on purpose and I forgot that I'm not very high on your list of priorities right now when I dialled your number. Old habits." An awkward laugh. She cuts it off. A flash of regret is obliterated by her need to communicate, have friends, feel better, level the playing field. She pushes the regret down. It mixes in with the base layer of anger she's felt since Sylvia first wore that Armani suit in to work. She swallows and continues, despite thinking she should know better.

"So I was thinking about movie nights. How many times did we watch *Beaches*? Like ten? Twelve? Anyway, I just finished watching it again tonight and you know what? I think it sucks. I used to love that movie and now it just leaves me cold. In fact, I hate it. Can you imagine why? Anyway... I e-mailed my notice in this morning to the office. I found another job and it's a step up for me so I took it. So you won't have to ignore me at the office. I won't be there in two weeks. You know, I keep thinking that I did something to fail you, like I didn't stand by you or didn't help as much as I could, but I did. I tried really hard. I think I was a great friend to you and I can't keep on like this, Mo—Sylvia. I can't cry anymore because life isn't worth living when all you do is look behind you. Know what I mean? You have to have something to look ahead to, to keep you moving and I don't want to keep looking back and... Wherever it is you're looking, you don't want to see me. So... Thanks for being my friend. I really mean that and I wish you the best but I hope I never hear from you again 'cause you're one hard, unfeeling, narcissistic bitch and I pity anyone who would want to be around you. Goodbye."

After she hangs up the phone, Helen walks to the window and looks down at the sidewalk below her. *How big a splat? Would traffic be stopped? Would I make the news? Will anyone care, notice, miss me?* And then she remembers she can't open the windows. And there is no balcony. *Well.. I'm not sure how comfortable I am jumping off the roof. It's so high up. What if I changed my mind after I jumped? During the fall.*

When her phone rings, Monique is in bed, practicing her sexual technique with an opaque blue dildo that looks like a set piece from an *Alien* movie. She glances over at the display, recognizes Helen's number and then focuses her attention back between her legs, at her wrist and fingers, back and forth and back and forth. A sound escapes her, quite involuntarily. A surprised gasp, suppressed somewhat. For a moment she expects tears might swell in her eyes, but the expectation washes into the subtle feeling of relaxation and warmth. *Oh. How odd.*

After she has what she's convinced herself is an orgasm, Monique showers, dresses and returns to her desk and the telephone. She lifts the receiver, pushes some buttons and hits 7 when prompted to delete the new message. She does not listen to it.

Monique steps off the elevator, remembering to take tiny girl steps even though nobody is watching. *Damn,* she thinks, *these sweats are clumping in all the wrong places.*

It's a late Saturday morning. The office is seemingly empty. She had hovered at her window earlier, eyes on the entrance to Harold's building, but never saw him leave. After a quick shower, she put on her Chanel sweat pants, a hoodie and sneakers and figured he must have gone in to the office.

She moves into the main office space, the only light coming in from outside through partially closed blinds, and quietly walks toward her workstation. Up ahead she sees a thin shaft of light coming from—*Oh hell, no!*

Helen hears the elevator's electronic pulse and the sound of the doors opening and thinks nothing of it because it is not followed by the familiar clickety-click of heels on the tiled floor. Moments pass. Helen can't take not knowing who is there, so she quietly stands up and moves through the department on her way to Reception.

Monique grits her teeth, briefly considers turning around and leaving quietly, but, *If I keep avoiding her, I'll never be able to move on. It's now or never.* She stops. Breathes.

Helen appears around the corner, the blonde Sears wig uneven on her head, and catches Monique frozen in the hallway. She stares at the enormous double C logo emblazoned across the front of Monique's ill-fitting sweat pants. An uproarious burst of laughter. She tries to cover it with her hand but almost immediately a voice inside her says it's time to let go. She thinks it's time. She relaxes. Somewhat.

"He's not here," Helen says like an accusation.

"Who?"

"Oh, honey," Helen cries, "You *are* stalking him. How can you not see that?"

"I... What are you doing here?"

"I'm getting the last of my things and taking down my collage of survivors. Maybe a better question is, what are you doing in the office on a Saturday?"

Monique turns to go.

"It had to be French."

"What?" Monique pauses.

"I mean you couldn't learn Spanish or Portuguese, could you? It had to be French."

"So?"

"You took that fucking book I gave you and you did exactly what she did. You couldn't… I never—"

"You gave me that book to help," Monique interrupts. "So thank you. It did help, but I did the work, not you. The author and I did the work."

"Stealing isn't working. That's not what I mean. If you steal something it's not really yours. And anyway, look at you! Look at your face! Listen to that awful, awful accent! Do you remember Dick Van Dyke in *Mary Poppins*? You're the Gatineau version. And your outfit! I don't think Salt-N-Pepa are auditioning right now. And your forehead! Don't you recognize plastic when you see it? I mean is there anything about you now that's real? Anything? You don't look younger. You look like a desperate fifty-eight year old who caved in and had some work done. Welcome to everyone else who doesn't feel they belong. Are you in better company now? Got yourself some *new* friends?"

Monique swallows hard and struggles with how to react, all the while maintaining her outward composure.

"Oh, and by the way, Angelique's plan all along was to hurt the guy because she hated loving someone who didn't love her back. If you do anything to Harold—"

"Oh Helen, your loyalty is so touching. And misplaced. Do you think he likes you? And those ridiculous wigs..."

"I only have one regret," she says, dodging Monique's insult. "And that is if I'd known you were such a rabid cunt, I would have never spoken to you."

"Such language," Monique says above a whisper. "Your roots are showing."

"And you know what you're showing? Fear. Terror. Gut-squashing terror that you're losing—or maybe that you never had—looks worth looking at. Face it, hon, average is average. When you look like we do, you better have some pretty good guts to make it in this world and find someone who can really love you for who and how you are."

"But I don't look like you do."

"You've made that painfully clear to everyone, dear. You'd have been better off saving the money and carrying a big sign around that says desperate for attention! It'd be far more subtle and probably way more effective."

They both take deep breaths.

"You're doing it right now," Helen scolds. "Aren't you?"

"What?

"Thinking of an appropriate response."

Monique's mouth is a tight, straight line.

"So—"

"Just let it out!"

Monique sucks a short breath of air in through her nose and directs her eyes toward the floor. "I will not."

"What?!"

"Give you satisfaction."

"What the hell does that mean? Satisfaction for me would be

you dropping all this bullshit and being my friend again. Why do you think I'm jealous of you? Seriously. What would make you think that, short of a brain hemorrhage? Do you know how unhappy you look? How fucking tortured you look. I'm not jealous! I'm mad! I hate what you turned yourself into! I'm pissed off! Look at yourself. Can you even see?"

"I'm happy," Monique seethes. "And that makes you—"

Helen flings her right arm forward in an abrupt, violent motion. Her hand makes contact with Monique's tiny purse, knocking it to the floor and spilling its meagre contents: tiny lipstick, tiny compact, tiny key ring with keys, and a Sears credit card.

Oh my goodness! Helen is secretly thrilled with the feeling her gesture produced. *Maybe I will join a gym. Or boxing!*

"Poor, awful, mean Sylvia," Monique says in a mock whine. "That's what you tell yourself to make you feel better and sleep at night, isn't it?" Monique asks, her voice unsteady, her eyes scanning the floor, at the spilled contents of her purse. "I think I understand you a little better than you give me credit for." She carefully bends down and collects the lipstick, compact, key ring and credit card. "I gave you lots of credit," she says, stooped over. "Way more than you *ever* deserved and you blew it by being boring and predictable and safe."

"I almost died, you idiot! Do you know what that even means? You don't! Of course you don't. How could you? I'm fucking lucky to be here. I'll take predictable and safe any day over six feet under."

"Careful, too. You forgot that part, now, didn't you?"

"With my health, yes, of course."

"I mean everything. Look at me? Look at you!"

"I do. All the time."

"Good! I hope you like what you see."

"I don't," Helen smiles, staring directly at Monique. "I love it. I love myself. But you? You're going to wake up one day and be so freaked out by all of this," Helen says, worried that she's running out of ammunition and Monique is still unaffected.

"You might think so, Helen, but I... I highly doubt it. I'm cultivating—"

"And by then all the decent people in your life will be with me. In the gutter. I know exactly what you're doing, Sylvia. All along. Don't think I haven't always known."

Monique stands erect and tucks her purse under her left arm. She decides she doesn't have the time or patience to explain herself anymore. To anyone. "Hooray for Helen. I'm leaving."

Helen mocks Monique's last sentence with a scrunched-up face. Monique catches her and gives her a little shrug and a condescending look before she remembers the sign in Helen's workstation.

This office isn't big enough for the both of us, so I left my wig at home.

Just then Sylvia's walls collapse. Reason ambushes her, disarms her like a gale in a wind tunnel, sending everything scattering. For a brief moment in time an element of her pretence diminishes. She looks at her former friend evenly. When she speaks, her voice is calm and soothing. There is no trace of a fake French accent. "I think it's time for us to stop, Helen. Let's just stop. Before security comes and we're both fired."

"Is that seriously all you're worried about?" Helen says, flabbergasted. "Did you forget? Of course you did. I quit!"

Monique turns and slowly begins to walk away. "Good luck," she says before swanning away, her back to the dark office and moose painting, lurching toward the connecting corridor through the dimly lit office.

"Stop!" Helen wails. "Stoooop!!" And then silence.

She's at the elevator now. She's not responding. She's not coming back. Omigawdshesnotcomingback!

A bleat of a sob escapes Helen's lips after she hears the faint electronic pulse of the elevator followed by the muted swish of its doors closing. *She's going down. Fuck! I tried. I tried so hard to stop her but she won't listen. Determined, friendless bitch. She's going down. Oh shit. Oh, no!*

Two Years Later

Despite all of Sylvia's modifications, it was Helen who ended up becoming friends with Harold Greenbaum. Apart from their few interactions at the office, the process involved her sitting at a Caplanski's delicatessen on College Street one Saturday and overhearing a man ordering corned beef sandwich on rye bread, medium-rare, with mayonnaise on top and mustard on the bottom. Helen looked over and saw a man who looked like Harold Greenbaum, but not quite. There was a difference in his energy, a directness, an assertiveness she never saw in Harold. Also, this guy's clothes were incredible. *A real sharp dresser*, she thought. *They must be related. Either that or I'm in an episode of* The Twilight Zone.

She approached the man while she waited for her order. He smiled and shook her hand when she introduced herself and asked if he had a twin brother who worked at Invigro. When he said yes, Helen chuckled quietly and began trying to explain what was so funny. He introduced himself as Herschel Greenbaum.

"I can see you're nothing like your brother," she said.

"Oh, nice of you to notice. I get tired of saying that, like it's some kind of bad excuse that no one believes. He doesn't see it, strange as that sounds. Makes me wonder about his eyesight."

"Well it was lovely to meet you, Herschel. I'll leave you to your sandwich," she said, turning to go. But then she stopped, remembering something. Two things, actually; her business and her book.

She reached into her purse and pulled out her business card. She leaned in toward him, extending her hand. He took the card and looked at it.

"Helen Frobisher Designs. Nice to meet you."

"Your brother borrowed a book from me and I never got it back. Not his fault, of course. I left Invigro while he was still reading it, but I would like it back." She smiled warmly. He smiled back at her and rocked a bit, back and forth, standing in place.

"Oh, well now I can put him in touch with you. It must have been a great book."

"It is," she said. "But if he doesn't still have it, well, it's not the end of the world." *I know. I've been there.* "Take care now."

He gave her a bit of a wave as she returned to the counter to pick up her order. As she left the deli she slowed her pace and took one quick look back at Herschel. *What lovely, soft hands he has.*

When she climbed in to bed that night, Helen thought about Sylvia and the clickety-click of those lethal high heels on the office floor. The image of a centipede with hundreds of tiny knives attached to its tiny feet sprung into her mind's eye. It made her smile. Helen fell asleep shortly thereafter. She dreamt of robin's egg blue skies as she flew through them. And in the morning, as her coffee maker sputtered and chugged, Helen looked in the mirror and she smiled at her reflection, and at the small pile of paperwork on her desk at the top of which was a three-page contract to remodel the Human Resources office at Invigro, and she knew beyond the shadow of a doubt that she had made the right choices.

THIS FUNCTIONAL FAMILY

She has an aura that precedes her. Like a pungent perfume liberally applied, I can sense Jessie's presence even before she is anywhere near. From the kitchen table where I sit waiting for the roof to cave in on our hastily organized family reunion, I can feel her approaching. It's a rumbling in my stomach, a nervous twitch, an imbalance in my walk, the tendency to glance sideways just before speaking. The feeling is in my body, mostly, but it trickles upward in rivulets to my mind, becomes knowledge there, pure and concrete—Jessie would break that too, probably, given half a chance. She revels in the breaking, always has, a patient, bent smile that reveals the pretence of her innocence in the destruction. The twisting upheaval that delights her to the core fills me with dread. Jessie is a tornado. And even though she has said that she isn't the old Jessie anymore, she's never given me reason to believe her.

She might as well be the old Jessie, the one that bit off my left ear lobe, the one that ruptured one of my testicles as the result of a well-aimed kick when we were kids. The Jessie who was institutionalized and sent weekly post cards from the hospital with *FUCK YOU* written on them in what looked like blood but was really just ketchup. The old Jessie that got kicked out of the house and supposedly got herself straight while I found myself gay. She went to the States to get work and got raped instead. The Jessie that kept the kid, the kid that would never find out why she was kept or how she was conceived but exists nonetheless. Under Jessie's rule.

It was the new Jessie that scraped enough money together to fly her and her two-month-old daughter to England where she would make a new start. What is the difference between the old and the new? About twelve years in total and probably little else. I hate to have to go to the dark side, but in all honesty, I am only being pragmatic. This new Jessie has no precedent so I can only expect that the old one will show up with a new hairstyle, or, in this case, a kid. Old or new, Jessie is coming.

I got the phone call from my father early Monday morning informing me that my stepmother Ruth's condition had taken a turn for the worse. She wasn't going to make it. In my groggy state I didn't make the connections necessary to produce an appropriate response.

Dad always expected more from me than he got. I knew this and did my best to live my own life without feeling like I was driving a stake into his heart. When I grumbled, "Does this mean she'll be in the hospital for a while longer?" I was met with an awkward silence on the line.

I heard Ruth's voice echo in my ears. "Jessie hurts your father and me, but I don't think she means to. She's just bad, you know, with her psychological condition and all. But you, Brian, I think you try to hurt your father on purpose. And you'll see how much you hurt him and then it will be too late. Mark my words. After he dies you'll attend the reading of his will and that'll be a sad day."

"Yes," came the response, my father's tentative voice pulling me from yet another memory meant to shame me. "And that also means that a visit or two if you can afford the time to come up." He was asking me. And as he rarely, if ever, refused me anything, I agreed to visit. For him.

Ruth slid into a coma late the following Thursday night, not long after my one brief appearance at the hospital. "Don't expect anything," she wheezed at me and then lost consciousness. The doctor said it was unlikely that she would come out of it. Dad didn't call to let me know until Monday morning. I suppose he didn't want to ruin Sunday, my day off. I appreciated his consideration, but then wondered if it would really ruin my day off to know that my stepmother was in a coma? Not really, except for my concern for my father. Selfish? Definitely. If Ruth were awake, I'm sure she'd be shaking a finger at me and making that shame-on-you clucking sound with her tongue. I suppose *Don't expect anything* means I'd been cut out of the will. Probably. Maybe I imagine too much. Perhaps she was just being a bitch. So why did Dad wait to make the call? I wouldn't dare ask him. Too many barriers. There's no use in breaking them down, especially since we might not like what we find on the other side.

Dad tracked down Jessie and told her the story, said they had a nice talk. He wired the money for plane tickets to her. A free trip? Of course she would come, the new Jessie. And so would Christine, who I've only ever seen in pictures. There's a few of them on my refrigerator at home. I see the new Jessie in photo-op mode, snuggling baby Christine on my refrigerator door every morning. The new Jessie smiles a mysterious, affected smile that I usually associate with people in mental institutions in foreign horror movies; a muted, plaintive madness that masquerades as rebelliousness, indifference, possession. But make no mistake, it is madness, expertly controlled and intricately disguised. On my refrigerator door Jessie holds Christine, and every morning their faces are the same. Even the new Jessie is old. How it all makes me want to climb into myself and never come out.

Dad decided somewhere along the line that a granddaughter was sufficient grounds to erase Jessie's trail of destruction. I applaud his willingness to forgive, but it stings because I suspect his real motivation was simply desperation to compensate for the way he and our mother responded to Jessie's sociopathic behaviour during her teenage years. But there was no need to. They were lenient, patient, but those qualities can only be stretched so far. I stood back and passively watched Jessie terrorizing our mother, bringing home bad boyfriends—and STDs—stealing clothing and jewellery and a whole litany of major and minor infractions that turned their beautiful house into an awful, excruciating home. And yes, the missing earlobe, the kick to my crotch that resulted in unevenly dangling testicles. I see Jessie as a rather pathetic and empty vessel with only one aim: to be filled, by whatever means. And Dad? It's hard to blame him. A simple man, he only wanted a family. What he got was an ice queen for a wife and two strays: one a sociopath, the other a homosexual who learned very early on that the best way to survive was to be invisible. Can I blame him for wanting to feel less guilty and less alone? My prediction is that Jessie will become the new reigning ice queen and the job of bad guy will be assigned to me. The black sheep dyed pink.

I hear footsteps coming up the front walkway, then swearing. I look up and over to the door and see Jessie, hair straying all over her face, cigarette plugged in her mouth and an overnight bag in one arm. The other arm is wrapped around Christine, shaking her in mid-air. I hurry to the door to greet them.

"Why do you have to make everything so fucking difficult?" Her last word is punctuated by the dropping of the child to the top step. Christine falters, falls.

"Hey!" I shout, lunging forward to grab her flailing arm. I pull her up. She straightens and climbs back to the landing. Mother and daughter eye each other for a second and then stumble into the house as if no time had passed since they'd last been here. Then Jessie turns and glares at me.

"Nice save," is all she says.

"Who is that?" Christine asks in a stubborn British accent. She points at me as she speaks.

Jessie bats her hand down and smacks her behind. "Don't point!"

Christine closes her eyes and has a moment before fixing them on me again. Her mother tugs at her coat, an ugly brown thing with soiled white edges around the cuffs, obviously something she's picked up at a thrift shop and never bothered to wash. A spray of ashes falls from Jessie's cigarette and land on Christine's head.

"That's your uncle Brian, remember? I showed you his picture." She throws Christine's coat on the floor beside the closet and looks to me as she wiggles out of her own. It is as used and neglected as her daughter's. She walks to me and stops several feet away, her eyes on my chest. "When did you get in?" I can tell from the sound of her voice that she doesn't give a shit.

"Monday night."

Jessie sits down at the kitchen table across from me as if the moments preceding this one never happened. There is a momentary flash of eye contact before she moves her head and looks at the wall behind me, then turns away to look anywhere else. "How did Christine deal with the flight?"

"It was long and shitty."

"How did *Christine* deal with the flight?"

"She slept through most of it, with a little help." Jessie says this as she turns to look at Christine who plops her thumb in her mouth and begins sucking. "The plane left two hours late. Fucking nightmare."

Within moments Christine is standing beside her mother, grabbing hold of her leg and then moves behind her. She looks at me suspiciously, as if she knows something horrible about me. But what?

"Do you always swear in front of her like that?"

Jessie laughs and looks at me, and with condescension and disbelief in her voice, utters, "You're kidding."

"No. She's going to end up... How old is she now? Three? Four?"

"Four," Christine interjects, slipping out sideways from behind Jessie. "I'm four, plus."

I bend down to introduce myself, but she pushes herself back further and out of sight behind her mother. Jessie turns and manages to disengage herself from her daughter. Christine looks at me, then at her mother. Jessie walks through the kitchen and into the dining room where she starts to inspect the contents of the china cabinet.

"Do you want me to get you a calculator?" I ask. Christine laughs at this, although I'm not sure why. I should probably focus my attention on where it can do the most good.

"Christine, I'm your uncle Brian. But you can just call me Brian. Will you shake my hand and say hello?"

"Why?" she asks, curious and yet still shy.

"Do it," Jessie barks from the dining room.

I can't help but smile at Christine and this, I believe, relaxes her a bit. I'm not taking her mother's stern voice seriously. I bend over and speak low in her ear. "If someone asks you to do something that makes you feel afraid or nervous, you can just tell them that you don't feel comfortable about it. It's better to be honest and that way the person will understand why you don't want to do it."

"How did that work out for you?" Jessie deadpans, suddenly behind me.

"Right back at you."

Christine looks at me as I stand up. Her eyebrows are furrowed and her lips form a subtle pout.

"That's okay. I don't mind if you don't want to."

But she steps up to me, cracks a shy smile and extends her small hand out. I meet it with my own, feeling her soft fingers against the palm of my hand.

"I sent some toys to you in London. Did you get that Sesame Street Farm for your birthday?"

She nods her head.

"Do you play with it?"

She hesitates. "Sometimes."

"Don't you like it?"

"Mummy doesn't like me making a mess with my toys," she whispers.

I go to the screen door and slide it open, letting the cool fall air circulate around the stifling house. "But that's what toys are for," I tell her. "And that's what four-year-old girls are for. You're supposed to make a mess."

"I don't think mummy would like to hear you say that," she little more than whispers.

"Well, we'll just have to find you some toys so you can make a mess while you're here and I'll help you clean up after. Maybe we could go to the store later on, just you and me. We could pick out a few messy toys for you so you'll have something to play with."

"Maybe," she says, flushing with excitement.

Later in the evening, while Dad is conferring with a lawyer in the den, Jessie and I sit on the back porch, talking about how miserable we think he'll be without Ruth. I'm trying to ferret information from her about her job and life in London, but she's not interested in revealing anything. I wait until we seem to have run out of things to say to each other before opening the floodgates.

"Why are you so brutal with Christine?"

She turns to face me, cigarette smoke trailing out of her nostrils. "What are you talking about?"

"She's just a kid. You treat her like she did something really shitty to you."

"I have a huge scar from the C section. She did that much."

"Forget it," I say, seeing where this is going to go.

"You're jealous."

"Of what?" I laugh, incredulous.

"That I made something of myself."

"Which is...?"

"I'd say being a mother is an important job."

"Oh, cut it. You were raped and were too lazy to get an abortion."

"Lazy," she asks, "Or smart?"

"I get it. You're a martyr. The kid is your meal ticket."

"Fuck you."

"I wouldn't put it past you."

"What do you know about kids anyway?"

"About as much as you, I'd say. Probably more, otherwise we wouldn't be having this conversation."

"I know exactly what I'm doing. As opposed to you, drifting."

"I have a job."

"Playing records is a job now?"

"No dance clubs in England? Or radio stations? Or are you just being a cunt, as always? Spare me the crabs."

The shadow of a smile cracks her face. Or is it a smirk? "Touchy." Jessie is bemused.

"Why did you keep her?" *Touché.*

She stubs her cigarette on the wood floor, not considering the burn mark it will make. She doesn't answer my question, just stares at the house across the street.

"That guy really did fuck you, didn't he?"

Jessie leans toward me as if she's about to reveal a secret. "Listen up. I don't like you. I don't give a shit what you think or say about anything, about me and especially my kid. Got it? Now fuck off and leave us alone."

I guess you could say that was round one. Nobody won, but I left the playing field when I heard the clinical tone of her voice. She wasn't angry. She was stating facts. Her eyes reminded me of photos of the mechanical shark used to make *Jaws*. Black. No emotion. Not hungry, but will go through the motions of devouring you nonetheless because... There is no because. That's just what it does.

I stand up, pick up the cigarette butt from the porch floor and hold it in front of her face.

"Old habits," I say and drop it into her lap.

Later on that night, after everyone is asleep, I go downstairs to have a bite to eat. When I go back upstairs, Jessie's door swings open. I hesitate, lingering in the doorway to my room. Jessie steps into hallway and, looking around, notices me.

"Do you remember when Dad had to put locks on all the doors in the house so you couldn't get in and steal everything?"

Jessie says nothing. I scan all the doors in the upstairs hallway, making a little nod with my head with each lock I see.

"It was like Fort Knox in here. Remember that?"

I move in to my room, making a point of locking the door once I'm inside.

The next morning, after Dad sits down in the living room with a newspaper and Christine beside him, Jessie follows me downstairs into the pantry and asks, rather presumptuously, how long I've been HIV positive. I don't acknowledge her comment, but I return the gesture: "You should have heard some of the things Mom and Dad said about you after they kicked you out of the house. Do you remember the police escort? I had no idea of half the shit you were doing."

"I don't care."

"And when you came home with crabs. Twice. That I know of anyway. How old were you, like twelve?"

"I don't ca—"

"Of course not. You never have." I find a five-pound-bag of potatoes and lift it off the floor.

"Blah, blah, blah."

"These potatoes are all rotting," I say more to myself than to her. She looks at me with bland expectancy. "It's amazing that I can have a more coherent conversation with your four-year-old daughter than with you."

"Yeah, but nobody listens to you because you talk like a girl."

"That's mature. Not to mention misogynist. You can look that up later. I'll show you how to spell it. Hey, how happy do you think Dad would be if he found out you tried to get an abortion at eight months pregnant with money he sent you for rent?" This was one of the last details of her life she had shared with me. Nice. "Oh wait, don't tell me. You don't care."

"You got it."

"The sociopath's credo," I say.

"I should have kicked you harder when I had the chance. But you never had balls anyway."

"Awww. You must have inherited that gift for language from your birth mother." No immediate response. I take it as a green light. "I guess she couldn't afford the hook either. Or maybe she was just like you and didn't give a shit. Either way, nice thing to pass on to your child."

"I'm a good mother."

"You're the poster child for involuntary sterilization."

"What do fags know about raising kids? I'm a good mother."

"You just keep telling yourself that," I say. She doesn't seem to understand, or to care.

"Where are all your friends, Jess? Nobody's called or dropped by. At least not in fifteen years, and even then it was just people whose stuff you had stolen looking to get it back. Sure made Dad feel great. Just after you left... Do you remember the police escort? He told me he was thinking of disowning you. It's a good thing for you he didn't, right? Because then you wouldn't be here raiding the china cabinet and whatever else will fit in the empty suitcase you brought. Anyway, you have your daughter now. Nice burden to put on her shoulders. Oh, and I found a calculator, by the way. In case you need it to figure out what all this is worth."

Silence. Another green light.

"You must have enjoyed it in some way. I mean I can't imagine anyone getting pregnant after being raped and *wanting* to keep the child."

"Shut up."

"Unless they had ulterior motives and wanted to use the child to—"

"Shut up."

"Explain it to me so I can understand about the rape."

"Fuck you. Right up your faggot ass."

I knew that one would get her.

"I don't give two shits about what you say to me, Jess, but I swear, if you drop her or hit her again I'm going to call the Children's Aid and the police and they'll take your meal ticket away. And then it'll just be you, facing criminal charges, without your ticket to ride. I think Dad will have a hard time keeping the pretence going after that. I mean there's a certain point where people realize there's no grounds for hope, right? And right now we're pretty close. *Ominously* close." I wait. Then, "What would you do for money? Dad wouldn't help. The entire extended family, yeah, they all know your history. Every little detail. None of them wants anything to do with you. And they've told Dad he should wash his hands of you, too. Do you ever get Christmas cards from any of them? Phone calls? Birthday presents? Anyone meet you at the airport? Didn't think so. Everyone loathes you and everything you've ever done. You give new meaning to the phrase waste of skin. You know that, right? I mean even with all your mental blocks and your denial and whatever else being a sociopath does to the brain, you should have been able to figure that out. Or are you the only good person in the world? Is that how you see things? You're right and we're all here to be used?"

I turn to go upstairs. Standing there on the landing is Christine, rubbing her eye with one hand and holding an old teddy bear of mine in the other. I don't know how much of the conversation she's heard or if she understood any of it. I pick her up and carry her up to her bedroom and read her a story from an old story book that Dad used to read to us when we were young. After, I go downstairs and see Jessie on the porch, smoking another cigarette.

"Nice catching up," I mutter through the screen door.

I stop at the entrance to the TV room and see my father sitting in his favourite chair, a dazed, passive look on his face. He looks up as I enter the room and gives me a nod. Before I can sit down the telephone rings. I reach over and pick it up. It's Dr. West from the hospital and he wants to speak to my father. Dad closes his eyes for a moment and reaches his hand out slowly for the receiver.

"Yes. All right. Thank you Dr. West. Should I come over there now, then?" Dad flashes me a look and then moves his head so he's staring at the floor. "Okay. Good-bye."

He places the receiver in its cradle and stares at his feet. He has a worn look about him. He shakes his head and then looks over at me.

"Your stepmother's passed away."

"Oh, I'm sorry, Dad."

"About an hour ago."

I don't know what to do. If it were anybody but my father I would rush to them and hug them, try to tell them physically how I feel and try to assuage a bit of the hurt. But he is my father and so I stay put. I catch him looking at me, his dry eyes, his stunned but accepting face. And I can do nothing.

A shadow moves on the wall to my left. I turn to and see Jessie entering through the laundry room door, an even look on her face like our confrontation never took place.

From the kitchen Christine lets out a scream. As it fades I hear footsteps charging closer and see her mop of hair streaking through the hallway and rounding the doorway to the TV room. Christine runs to me and jumps into the space beside me on the couch, clinging to my arm and shaking her head wildly. Jessie stands in front of the television and stares at us.

"What's wrong?" I ask Christine.

"I hurt my thumb."

"You wanna be there every time she does something wrong?" Jessie says in a little more than a whisper, but I hear it.

I wrap my arms around Christine, pull her onto my lap and plant a kiss on the back of her head. "Maybe I will one day. After Child Protection Services gets involved."

"Faggot."

Dad sits there, shell-shocked.

"Jessie, Ruth died about an hour ago," I say. I count to five before I speak again. Timing is everything. "That was the doctor on the phone delivering the news. Is there anything useful you can do to maybe help Dad? I know empathy is not one the sociopath's skills, but maybe you could try? Offer to make him a coffee or get him some juice? Or would you prefer to go upstairs and see what kind of jewellery she left behind that you can *borrow*?"

"Oh, *Dad*." Her voice is saccharine. "Is there anything you need us to do?" I wonder how she learned to approximate empathy. It must take years of practice. Is there a finishing school for sociopaths that helps them pass in the real world?

"No, Jessie, thank you. I'll go to the hospital tomorrow morning and deal with the, uh, paperwork. Perhaps you two could stop fighting long enough to figure out who'll drive me.

"I'll take you," I say. "Are sociopaths allowed to drive?"

"Are neurotic cock suckers?"

"That's enough. Both of you."

"Watch her, will ya? I gotta have a cigarette." Jessie turns to walk away, but then stops and turns back. "Are you sure there's nothing you need me to do?"

"No, thank you, Jessie." He looks at her with a faint smile. Part of me wishes he were senile and didn't recognize her. But then again, who really knows her? "We've been preparing for this for about a little while now. I think everything is in order. I'll make the calls tomorrow."

Jessie nods. "I need a smoke," she says, then. Then, "Okay." She walks back through the laundry room and outside onto the patio, leaving her daughter in my arms and our father's emotions in my hands.

Dad opens his eyes a crack and looks at me while continuing to shake his head. He closes his eyes and breathes a quiet sigh.

"Do you want a drink, a tranquilizer? Someone to yell at?"

He raises his eyebrows a touch and looks away from me. "Maybe I'd be best off if I was alone for a little while."

"Okay."

"Why is grandpa sad?" Christine asks, wiggling about on my lap.

"He's sad because Grandma Ruth died."

"Who's Grandma Ruth?"

"That was the lady who was married to Grandpa. They lived here in this house together and they loved each other very much. Do you know what it means when someone dies?"

She nods her head and looks up at me. But the nod soon turns to a head shake from side to side.

"It's when a person's body stops working. They just stop."

"Why?"

"Do you see that clock over there?" I point to a windup clock on the far wall.

"Yeah?"

"Well, people are just like that clock, Christine. After a while they slow down and eventually they stop ticking."

"Like Ron's dog Lucky?"

"I don't know. What happened to Lucky?"

"He ran on the street and got hit by a car." Christine says. "Did Grandma Ruth get hit by a car?"

"No." I whisper into her ear that maybe she might want to go and sit on her grandfather's lap and give him a hug and a kiss. She moves off my lap without hesitation and goes and squirms her way onto his chair, wrapping her short arms around his chest and offering him an awkward kiss on the cheek.

"I hope you're not gonna stop, Grampa."

Dad puts his hands on her cheeks and smiles at her. I have no idea what he could be thinking, except that maybe he isn't thinking, just hoping instead, that for himself and Christine, everything will turn out all right, despite everything he knows and thinks and remembers. Yes, somehow, as if by magic, everything will be okay and everyone in this house will turn out all right.

I search his face for tears or signs of other emotions, but he stares ahead and into Christine's eyes. Maybe she's the only one of us who can console him the way he needs it, honestly, without reservations or distractions or history. Children can feel. Adults know too much.

At the hospital the next morning, Jessie snaps into simulated attentive daughter mode and does everything she can to subdue me. Having never been a good organizer, I cautiously hang back and watch her, relegated to being Christine's official hand holder.

A woman appears at the end of the hallway where Christine and I sit waiting for Dad and Jessie to sign some papers. As she approaches us, her pace slows.

"Excuse me," she says, stopping beside the bench. "You're Brian, aren't you?"

"Yes."

"I'm Marilyn Veevers. I'm a friend of your father's. He called me last night and told me the news. I'm so sorry about Ruth."

"Nice to meet you Mrs. Veevers." I stand up and offer her my hand, but she's already lit up over Christine.

"And who are you, young lady?" Marilyn says, leaning forward.

"This is my niece, Christine. Christine, this is Mrs. Veevers."

Christine looks at me briefly before sitting up in her chair and offering Mrs. Veevers her hand to shake. "Nice to meet you," she says.

"It's a real pleasure to meet you."

"Ruth stopped," Christine says, with a tone that suggests she's telling Marilyn something she doesn't already know.

"Oh I know, sweetheart. Isn't it sad?"

Marilyn sits down in the empty seat beside Christine.

"How's your dad handling it?"

"You said you're a friend of his?"

"Of course, dear. That's why I came."

Marilyn leans in over top of Christine and whispers in my ear. A pungent slap of her perfume stings my nostrils. I remember growing up, the odd appeal of the smell of ladies' things: lipstick, makeup, excessive perfume.

"Your parents and I go way back. Your father and I have been seeing each other for—" She pauses and takes a breath before continuing on in a loud whisper. "Well, quite some time. He... We... We're special friends," she says. "He has a very large, uh, drive. If you know what I mean."

I try to tell myself this can't be happening. I don't want to know that my father was cheating on his second wife. But this is not about me. I decide that Marilyn is either unbalanced, testing me, or simply a dimwit.

"I hope you don't think I'm a floozy," she whispers and then sits upright with a mock serious look on her face that makes me think of Polly Holliday from *Alice*.

"No, I... I mean I don't know you, so... Really? People still use the word floozy?"

Marilyn laughs heartily and reaches into her purse. She pulls out a billfold and hands Christine a five-dollar bill.

"Christine, do you think that you could walk to the end of the hallway and buy yourself some juice at the store there? We'll be right here waiting for you." Then she turns to me. "Is that okay with you?"

"Yes. Especially now that you said floozy."

"Can I get candy, too?" Christine asks, taking the bill from Marilyn and standing up.

"If they have popcorn," I say. "But no candy."

Christine runs down the hall.

"She's the devil's spawn, isn't she?" Marilyn asks, sliding

closer to me.

"What?"

"Oh, drop the pretence. Your father told me all about your sister. Ruth, bless her heart, was always afraid that Jessie would show up unannounced and want to move back in. I think she watched too many horror movies to tell you the truth, or maybe she just knew your sister better than anyone else. But that's how it was. She had a, uh, female problem and my husband Gerry had been dead for seven years and she just said if your father and I wanted to, you know... then she would look the other way and... You understand?"

"Yes."

"And after Ruth got sick, well, we still, you know."

"Have sex," I say, tiring of the awkward stumbling around the nature of their relationship.

Marilyn smiles. "I knew you'd be okay with it," she says. "Gay men are so forward thinking."

"Think again," I say.

"Why? Are there...?" And she seems to lose her train of thought.

"Gay Republicans? Yes. Sorry. Never mind," I smile. "It's just that it's nice to think that because we're different, we're all perfectly different or differently perfect. Truth is I know more straight together people than gay together people. And I don't mean married together. I mean heads screwed on."

"I'll take your word for it," she says, taking a card out of her purse and handing it to me. I see Christine ambling back down the hallway toward us with a juice box and a bag of popcorn in her hands.

"Look what I got!" she shouts.

"My number's on there if you ever want to talk," Marilyn says. "I know all about your sister. Your dad told me everything."

"Not Ruth?"

"We were never good friends. No, she never had much of a sex drive. I think she was relieved when we finally did it. Not like your father would ever say anything. Ever. To anyone. So for years we've just gone on. Like this."

"I think it's great that you both worked it out without anyone getting hurt."

"Oh, people were hurt, honey," Marilyn says, her voice dropping low. "But from before, way before. We were just trying to make ourselves feel better in unhappy circumstances, and who can blame us for that?"

"Exactly. I hope you're both happy. Satisfied. I mean fulfilled."

"Are you a bottom?"

"What?"

"Never mind. You're not very aggressive though, are you?"

"Depends."

"Not yet," Marilyn smiles and jabs me in the ribs with her elbow. "Get it? Depends? Seventy-four years old?"

"I got it. Wow. Seventy-four. I'm impressed."

Christine plops herself down on the other side of Marilyn and tears open the bag of popcorn. "Thank you," she says.

"Do you want me to get the straw into that box?" Marilyn asks her, positioning her head so she is looking down at the top of Christine's head.

"I can do it," Christine says.

Marilyn turns and whispers in my ear. "Did you check her for lice?"

"No. That's disgusting."

"Ever had lice?"

"Do you know how many times Jessie got crabs before she was fifteen?"

"Yeah. What was it? Five, six times? Your dad told me all about that. About everything. You still have that scar on your neck? Oh! Let me see your ear!"

"He did tell you everything."

"I told you."

"I dated a plastic surgeon and he zapped the scar for me. They couldn't do anything about the ear, so..." I start to think that the conversation might be a bit risqué for Christine, but before I can say anything, Marilyn jumps up from the bench.

"You know what?"

"What?"

"I just realized that it might be highly inappropriate for me to be here."

"But didn't you—"

"No, I didn't ask him. He didn't ask me. I just thought I should come, you know? To be here for him."

"I'm sure he'd really appreciate it if you stayed. They should be back any minute."

"Oh, you're a sweetheart for saying that Brian, but I'm not so sure."

"You don't want to see Jessie, is that it?"

"Maybe. I don't know. Good question."

"Bad answer."

"There's no good answer or bad answer. I always wondered what, I mean how I should insert myself in your father's life and then it dawned on me that if he wanted me to do anything more than what I was already doing, he'd ask."

"I don't know about that. He's pretty passive."

"I know. Do you think you got it from him? Being passive?"

"I don't know. Could be."

Marilyn adjusts the strap of her purse and looks down the hall.

"Are you sure? I think he'd really appreciate seeing you."

"Be that as it may," she says, smiling and looking back and forth between me and Christine, "You just tell him, secretly of course, that I was here and he should call whenever he feels like it."

"Okay, I will."

Marilyn adjusts her posture, lowers her head and looks at Christine.

"And you, young lady, I have something I'd like to tell you."

"Mm-hmm," Christine mumbles, her mouth full of popcorn.

"Always question authority. Any time someone takes charge, you should always ask yourself three questions: What's in it for them? What's in it for them? What's in it for them?"

Christine's eyes bulge slightly in confusion. She looks to me and then back again at Marilyn. "That's one question!" And then gales of laughter.

"The more you ask," Marilyn chimes in, "The more you'll know."

"That was a bit cryptic for a four-year-old," I say.

"Oh," Marilyn says, "Well how about this then? Just because something seems to work, that doesn't mean it's working."

"Better. But still, give her ten years."

"I can't come out and tell her that her mother's an emotional and psychological sinkhole," Marilyn whispers. "Chances are Jessie will destroy her daughter's life just as surely as she's destroyed her own and upset yours and your father's. That's the problem with sociopaths you know," she says, just loud enough for Christine to hear over the sound of crunching popcorn. "They don't see. She just doesn't see. There's no awareness, no consideration of anything outside the self. It's chilling."

"How do you know all this? My dad couldn't have—"

"I'm a psychologist. Was a psychologist," Marilyn says taking a step away from us. "Who do you think diagnosed your sister back in grade school when all the problems started?"

"That was you?"

She nods.

"That's how you know my parents?"

"Yes."

"Is that when the thing with my father started?"

"Goodness no. Not everyone is as calculating as your sister. I hope you remember that. And her, too," Marilyn says, gesturing at Christine. "I was brought in by the school board to assess the situation. I think she would have been in grade five. Anyway, that's how I met your parents. They stayed in touch by phone as her behaviour escalated." She cranes her neck and scans the corridor. "Look, I'm feeling a little nervous about being here now, so I'm going to go. You take care."

"Wait a minute," I say, suddenly anxious to know more. "I have so many questions to ask you. You can't just drop that bomb and walk away."

"It's all in the past. The details won't help you figure out what to do. But know this: the sociopath either directly or indirectly terminates anyone and anything that gets in their way. Never trust a single word she says. And be a witness," she says, "for this little one. She'll need it."

Marilyn walks down the corridor, the sound of footsteps fading into their own reverberations. I scramble to connect the pieces of information, searching for a resolution or something meaningful to hang on to, to guide my behaviour, but all I come up with are the two things Marilyn has just told me: It's all in the past and be a witness.

"My juice box stopped," Christine says.

Cute. "Aren't you going to offer me some of that popcorn?"

"Should I?"

"If I had a bag of popcorn, wouldn't you want me to offer you some?"

"Uh-huh."

A small hand thrusts the black foil bag into my chest.

"My mom says it's good for you."

How dire is it that I forego a sarcastic comment?

PLATFORM

I gape at my image in the mirror. Thin blood-red streaks darken the whites of my eyes. Shocked, I bend in closer for a better look. Shit! The shaded semicircles beneath my eyes look flaky, darker than normal. I look ghoulish. Or is it just the fluorescent light in the bathroom accentuating what I would otherwise dismiss as everyday wear and tear? There is a lesson here: You can't trust economy hotel lighting.

I pull a towel from off of the shower curtain rod and toss it on top of the toilet tank, then turn to the sink. I turn on the tap and splash cool Michigan water on my face, letting it run down my chest, stomach, navel, past the scraped skin of my groin. The dots of razor burn that glare out from the background of pale skin are what I show Him of my weekly ritual. The dried lubricant makes it look shiny, crisp. Crusty. When I was fatter, I thought my shaved pubis made me look like a boy, made my dick seem smaller, dwarfed my sexuality. Now I think I look sleek. I want to get toned, bring out elements of myself only hinted at presently. I have much work to do. He will be pleased that I've set my mind to it. I wonder who will enjoy it more. Him or me? Do I really want to make Him so happy?

Things have been different this visit. I don't know if He notices I've been less emotive, that I have taken tentative steps away from Him and this thing we call a relationship. I am not aloof like I was the last time I thought about severing our ties. But that plan didn't work. Only backfired. Trying to end it made me see how much I wanted to stay in it. At least I thought I did at the time. My attempts at humour came across as nasty jabs. Sex was a challenge, a competition. He won. When I said I still loved Him it wasn't true. I was trying to placate Him. And myself. Now, based on the fact that I am here with Him, I wonder if I've been foolish. Perhaps my attempts to untangle myself from this relationship have been a waste of time. What if I'm supposed to be with Him, work this through? Does either of us have the patience?

It was only two months ago that I'd admitted that He was too important to let go of in favour of an older man, a banker, who lived in the same city as I did, who wanted a settled life, a monogamous one, a man who wanted only me. So he said. It turned out that he wanted to own me as well, although in a less obvious way, and in a less intense way sexually. So he went back to the bank, and I went back to Master. Did He understand why I came back? Did He understand why I wanted to leave in the first place?

This visit He has filled in the missing details of His life, let me inside, more than I am comfortable with. He brings me home to meet His lover, shows me around His town, takes me to His office, has His barber cut my hair. He introduces me to friends even His lover hasn't met. And I am trying to keep my distance, control my joy. This visit He has more focus than I've ever seen before. This visit He tells me He loves me first, and for the first time I try to deflect it—and it's not hard to do. It is diminished by His fifteen-year-old relationship, His house—jointly owned, I'm sure, with the partner he cannot leave or fuck—and the fact that He lives in another city, in another country, and, yes, the fact that I am just a visitor here. I am merely a fleeting, blurred thing that will soon fade from His memory once somebody with bigger muscles comes along and makes Him orgasm more intensely than I can.

But after all these side-steps at deflection, He is still here with me in this hotel room, He is still holding me, and His cock is harder than ever before. So I let His love in, although I've shrunk it down to a size that suits me because, after all, He is married, and I'm not really quite sure what I love about Him. There aren't spreadsheets with lengthy pro and con columns to help me know for sure and, for the first time, I feel as though I don't have to make out a list of reasons why. Isn't it enough that I probably do love Him, even if it is in my own fractured way? Isn't it enough to finally feel some kind of comfort with Him? I don't have anybody else. I have Him—in a way—or at least as much of Him as He is willing to give. But then again, who am I to know about love? Surely I am responsible for accepting less than I am capable of giving, a slave to the concept of idealized love. I will do anything for it, even if it means deluding myself that a doomed love is acceptable. So I am bound to be dissatisfied. I am too impatient to wait. I am the ultimate submissive: finely tuned in to the concept of compromise and well versed at settling.

He has reached inside my terrified, fragile mind and massaged me gently. All the idiosyncrasies melt. He takes me to places where I can step outside myself and focus on somebody else's wants, whims and demands. Part of me hates Him for taming me, for reassuring me, for pointing me in all the right directions. Part of me hates Him because I have yielded to Him. Part of me hates Him because I have grown to love Him. And part of me loves Him because I have grown to accept Him. I don't know how this happened. Perhaps it's my insatiable need to need. Maybe years from now I will look back and forgive us both for what I'm certain are our shared mistakes. But for now, I hang the towel up over the shower curtain rod, check quickly to see what marks He has left on my neck, gargle with mouthwash, and return to Him in bed.

He binds me securely with ropes and cables, weighs me down. He sharpens in bed. His eyes grow wider, focus on me, His face so close. He is all I can see. He kisses me with such power, ability and abandon. I am pulled in, lost in our kisses. So close to endless. He twists my nipples hard, searches my face for signs of pain. I show nothing but pleasure. I take a slow, deep breath in. He groans. I feel his cock grow harder against my thigh. He attaches something to my balls and stretches them out with a cable. He smears more lubricant on me, pushes inside me, stares into my eyes, looking at something I'm not sure I understand, but am good at imitating. It is pleasure, but it isn't pure. Restrictions govern it.

Not long after I had committed to Master, a man in a leather bar told me never to fall in love with an S/M trick. I laughed and said it was too late. He looked me up and down and then led me outside to the patio where he pushed me to my knees, shoved his crotch in my face. The smell of a man. The power of a man's sex leaves me completely weak, vulnerable. I must radiate it like a pheromone, a funk of submission that says, *Take me. Make me feel something. Yes.* I slobbered all over the man's boots as he jacked off, sent his cum streaming hot all over my back. "Good boy," he growled, then walked away. I wiped his mess off my jacket in the washroom and ambled home. I brushed my teeth, stared at my reflection in the bathroom mirror, shrugged.

Master pulls out of me, leaves me gasping, strips off his gloves and pulls a beer out of the small refrigerator in the hotel room's kitchenette. He takes two swigs from the can, moves back toward me in the bed, checks the ropes and cables, gives the one attached to my balls a pull, smiles. He moves down toward me. Sips again from the beer can. Searches for something in my eyes. He leans over, kisses me. He opens His mouth and lets beer drizzle into mine. I swallow hard, feeling the cold liquid soothe my dry throat. "You thirsty, boy?" He asks.

I nod. I'm beyond speech, past the point where words have any meaning. Master tilts the beer can and pours beer all over my face. Some of it goes into my mouth. I don't care about the sheets. I don't care about getting sticky. I am a boy. In school. And these are important lessons. I don't consider the pain or the mess that might be involved. It's sensation I crave. Sensation from His hard hands, His hungry, commanding mouth, His probing cock. I want to be able to say to myself, "We did that. It felt good. Him and me." Nobody else makes me want to do and say these things. Nobody else has ever opened me up like He has, reached deep inside me, aroused so many responses and sensations. It's only Him I want, I think. And then I remember; I don't really *have* Him. Because soon it will be time to leave. Leave Him and this room, and it must be all packaged up neatly and put away so the two of us can continue with our lives. Our other lives that neither of us were supposed to have entered. Is this indicative of our unique connection, or have we just been stupid? Have we made brilliant mistakes by widening the margins of the roles we play, by making room for each other? I don't know. At one point I thought so. But now that everything is under a microscope, things He says and does have alternate meanings. They resonate in my mind, wake me from sleep, make me restless. I become distracted by a mundane paranoia that creeps in whenever I can't make sense of the other things He does, the other people He fucks, the countless hands that touch Him, and the lover for whom He has no sexual passion. I am a sort of surrogate. Supposedly I belong to Him, but what value does that have when it doesn't work the other way around? What about the love we claim we both feel? It isn't glue. It won't hold, will it? No.

At the train station I am evasive, slippery. He tries to hug and hold me, tries to kiss me, out in the open. I skirt the issue, step sideways, look away, apologize. He looks at me with a recriminating glance. He knows something is up, but He persists, kisses me again. I graze His cheek with my mouth. I'm sorry, again. Can't tell Him I sense His need, but I don't understand it. And because He cannot verbalize His need, I can ignore it, or at least hope my awareness of it fades fast. I tell Master that I'm not comfortable being affectionate in this public space. "It's okay," He says, indicating the people waiting up on the train platform. "We have more power than they do." Power.

When I turn to Him and tell Him how much I appreciate all He did for me this weekend, it feels as though my words betray me. I want to mean them, deliver the message as though I do, to be a dutiful, obedient, cherished boy, but there, underneath, swimming in the illogic of it all, is the suspicion that I don't mean any of this—and neither does He. And underneath suspicion there is knowledge and uncertainty in equal measure, but... Sincerity? If we don't mean it, what are we doing? Playing? Pretending? Wishing it were real and the context was real, that what we say and do actually bears weight and reflects our emotions and intentions? What's the most important thing then? To be true. If this is all just an act, put on for show or a notch on the bedpost on a line or two in our sexual resumés, neither of us will win any awards. The truth of the matter is that I don't believe in any of these roles or scenarios, and that my efforts to be with him are simply efforts. I saw him. I wanted him. And the only way to be with him was like this. I am not a boy, cherished or otherwise. I am a man, shaved down, wanting, searching. Only the minor details—clothing, grooming, stance and vocabulary—differentiate him and this from that which I have experienced before.

There is a nagging non-response from him, as if he doesn't want to look at the significance of what he has done, and possibly does not want to see the impact we have on each other. He does not want to gauge the disruption it causes and he cannot properly hold on to more than one thing at a time. So many things to do, so many people to fuck. He must always be juggling. I envy the talent it takes, but not urge that drives it.

At this point I'm convinced he has given up on a good goodbye, which is surely our first since meeting in September of last year. He gets in his car and a familiar cloud rolls into my mind. This is the leaving feeling. I won't have him for another month. I feel sick from wanting more. Of him? I move away from the car as he backs it up. I stop and wave, limbs made lead by the clouds in my head and body telling me, reminding me: no. He shifts gears, drives forward. I walk on, round a corner and wave again, closing the gesture with a peace sign I know he cannot see. I find my footing, welcome the feeling of being alone. It settles in the moment he is out of view.

Who will I go home to? Who will I sleep beside? Who will meet me halfway? Tonight I will see myself home. Tonight somebody else will get the part of Master I know I cannot have, the part I have convinced myself that I want: the rough and impenetrable rock deep inside, buried perhaps, but worth finding—if only because I have a gulf inside me that needs filling. It might have turned out better had I not been prone to question authority or motives, if I didn't care about such trivial things as authenticity. If I didn't have a heart attached to my mind. This will be our last visit, I decide. A moment of sanity ambushes me, tells me that I do not want what I cannot have. Master will have no trouble finding another boy. I don't know if he'll miss me. All these things flood my mind as I make my way up to the crowded platform and wait for my train to pull in.

TINY GRIEVANCES

There is a name and a face and a body and they are history, rippling in my memory, like a photograph under the surface of water; cool, shimmering, distorted and out of reach. Manny. He's been dead for ten years. I wish I could remember him better, because what comes to mind when I do are the gaps and distances, the times we didn't connect, the dates cancelled, years gone now just recollections. Even when Manny was alive I missed him.

Love and laughter, humility and humour, fierce devotion, spontaneity. These are the impressions I had of him from afar. Perhaps those words are etched on his gravestone I have yet to see. I was not close to Manny, but close enough to know that I wanted to be. Has the circle of friends and family that surrounded him all his life collapsed since he left it? Is he remembered?

Sometimes in a crowded bar I want to stand up and tell all the twenty-year-olds that they do not know everything, that they are not infallible or entitled or even special. They are pedestrians with affectations and branded bags carried in place of a personality. And instead of the pull toward integral human connection, they have an insatiable demand to be seen, accommodated and celebrated for reasons only they can understand and justify. I'd like to tell them about things they cannot see; the fractures and silences death has caused in our community and how I see it and feel it reverberating in everything that surrounds me when I go out into the world. But how do you inform a disinterested audience about leaden emptiness, about sorrow and regret and forced separations, the emotion of lost opportunities? How do you make them appreciate how precious life is?

The truth of the matter is I have grown to not care. Life has drawn the caring out of me. Perhaps I've been dancing in the eye of the storm for too long and now it's time to sit one out. So I am on the sidelines, seated at the bar sipping my beer and hoping not to be noticed or pointed at or called Daddy. I've had grey in my beard since I was twenty-three. Things were different then. We had manners, social skills and a vague respect for others. But now, if these kids had guns, I'm sure they just as soon shoot each other as have a conversation. Maybe I exaggerate, but I doubt it.

When did this disgust tinged with complacency settle in? Was it around the time of Manny's death? I heard nothing of the comfort of his friends and family, no whispers of him passing in a painless wash of drugs. I didn't hear anything about the anxiety, the suffering or the release. I missed out on having had the pleasure of blasting relatives dressed in department store suits as they rationed out their condolences and sipped tepid drinks from styrofoam cups.

I never really knew him well...

He's in a better place now...

Coffee whitener just ruins the taste of this Earl Grey.

Yes, but it's not Twinings, so who cares?

Did somebody say that? I don't know. Did someone mumble something homophobic outside during a cigarette, and did a gay man turn his back and ignore it? Probably.

At least it's the end of his suffering.

Yes. There's always something to be grateful for.

Did you hear about Myrna's hyserectomy?

The Donaldsons declared bankruptcy.

These shoes don't fit.

Five dollars and forty-nine cents for a bunch of celery!

The priest needs his outfit pressed.

I wasn't there to witness Manny's funeral guests' tiny grievances. I was too busy transitioning my ailing mother into a care facility. The morning of Manny's funeral, I stood in the lobby of Chesterton Lodge and watched two ambulance attendants wheel my highly agitated mother into her new residence. I didn't get to see Manny's still and silent face, but I do remember my mother's incriminating stare, the wild eyes wide, scanning the lobby as they wheeled her, strapped onto a gurney, toward the elevator, arms flailing as much as they could, restrained as they were. "This is your fault," she said over and over again once she had settled into her room, not knowing fully what she was saying, or perhaps knowing exactly what she was saying. Her suffering, fragmented as it may have been, continued. It wasn't for the best—it was for the absolute worst.

Surely none of this would have surfaced if Manny's brother Martin hadn't suddenly turned up in town. He called a few days ago and invited me to meet him for a drink and a chat. When he arrives at the bar, there's a heaviness to him I don't recognize or like. Was it there all along and I just didn't see it when we were young?

He nods as he crosses the room. I rise to greet him, shake his hand. He scans for a waitress as he settles into the booth.

"It's weird, isn't it?" he says.

"I don't know," I answer honestly. "Not particularly. Are you okay? You don't look—"

"Good afternoon, gentlemen. What can I get you?" A waiter has appeared behind me. Martin orders a double Canadian Club on ice and turns back to face me, meets my glance straight on.

When we were children, all the neighbourhood kids gravitated to Martin. He had this relaxed way about him, a subtle air of acceptance that made everyone feel welcome and wanted. Except for his brother, Manny. Manny always tried to eclipse Martin's charm but never quite succeeded—until we reached puberty and our bodies and personalities changed, neighbourhood cliques splintered. Two years and two grades behind me, Manny disappeared from my radar. My mission was to befriend other boys my age, all of us buying Kiss albums and donning the pretence of machismo but listening to Cat Stevens and Jim Croce behind closed doors. As years passed, Manny took to theatre and cabaret and Martin to engineering. I don't know if Manny ever lost his desire to be more like his older brother, but he was never insecure enough to let it jeopardize their relationship—until... I'm still not sure what happened. Over the years I have heard stories passed on by relatives. Apparently there was a wife, a mortgage, another man and a miscarriage. Perhaps Manny sensed what Martin was going through and tried to intervene. I can only assume that if he did, it blew up in his face. By the time Martin moved back to Toronto, single and broken, Manny was unconscious and covered with KS lesions. There was to be no reconciliation, brotherly or otherwise. Neither one of them was capable.

Martin empties his drink in two gulps and gestures for another. His unflinching gaze holds me as his story unravels over many drinks. He is out of the closet now, with his life and finances in shambles. He is furious with himself for having taken so long, for having hurt people, but mostly for losing Manny. And instead of tucking his awareness under his cap and moving forward, he's stalled, stuck and stewing in his own juices. And he knows it.

"I shut out my own brother trying to hide who I was," he weeps, shoulders trembling, head down.

Oh, fuck, Martin, get a grip, I want to say. I don't want to be mean, but really, this is ten years too late and, compared to the world we live in now, your pain doesn't stand out. It just washes in with the rest of the world's misery. He articulates it with alcohol-fuelled hostility. He is stuck firmly inside of it, has no awareness of his mind and emotions, of other possibilities. In their place is a push-pull dichotomy, dizzying in its scope and intensity; the guise of an identity fashioned from his shortcomings instead of his strengths, occasionally wavering but always returning to woe is me. It's as though he has assumed responsibility for his brother's death. What a spectacular burden. I want to punch him to snap him out of it, but I know he'd only retreat further in. Eventually he'll get to the bottom of it and start climbing out and maybe, once he does, he'll see himself and Manny for who they both are and were: flawed, human, simply complex. I am silent. It's not my job to fix him and he's not paying for my drinks.

Martin tells me how he used to pay someone for sex. It's a nice segue to good-bye, although he is reluctant to disengage. I don't want to hear any more. I don't want to know about his sex life, bank accounts, heartbreaks, carpet stains. I can't take him back in time to fix what he's broken, ease his conscience, offer solace. I cannot save him, help him or offer sage advice. What could anyone possibly say that would shake him into wakefulness? *The world is full of people suffering. Be grateful you're in the majority.* Does that help?

STOPPING QUITTING

Chris folds his arms in front of his chest when he looks in the bathroom mirror, past the dried flecks of matter that have sprung forth while flossing and adhered to the surface, past the remnants of toothpaste and saliva droplets and dust particles—an abstract, somewhat opaque painting blocking him from seeing himself. It's nine thirty-eight in the morning. Normally he wouldn't be up this early but aggressive pigeons have tried to root themselves on his balcony once again and their relentless cooing pulled him from his sleep.

Instead of cursing and siccing his ailing dog on them, Chris puts on a pot of coffee and thinks, I'm going to resurface my face. Scrub, rub, exfoliate, cleanse, tone and oxygenate. But when he gets to the bathroom mirror all he sees is the layer of dreck. He looks down at the sink, at his fingertips now resting at the lip of the white porcelaine bowl. Nails need clipping. Too much work for right now. Never mind the face. I should clean the mirror. Nah. Something isn't right.

He goes to the kitchen and removes the bowl of chick peas that has been soaking overnight in the fridge. The beginning of hummus, a gift for the host of a dinner party he'd been unexpectedly invited to, quite expectedly at the last minute, the gesture reconfirming the sense of separation he feels from those around him. It's not a specific feeling like the mood or vibe one might pick up from an individual person, but rather a general awareness, as when one acknowledges the effects of gravity; ever present and pressing down—a condition that everyone is subjected to, keeps them grounded. I will always be invited last and at the last minute.

Instead of wine, he's bringing hummus. The recipe he'd found online indicated that dried chick peas—when properly soaked and boiled—make for a creamier hummus. He goes back to the bathroom and wipes the mirror with some toilet paper. He sighs at himself in the mirror, at the appearance of a new pimple forming at the very tip of his nose. He fights the urge to squeeze it—that would only mean he'd end up a no-show at the dinner. Sorry, can't come. At home nursing a pimple. Or, in an attempt to put everyone else but himself at ease, he would show up at dinner with a nametag on his chest: Hello, my name is RUDOLPH.

He moves back to the kitchen, unevenly painted and with colours none of his friends could comprehend. Even the clerk in the home decor aisle at the hardware store questioned his choices. Really? the man said, examining Chris' paint swatches. In the same room? Yes, Chris replied. I guess the decorating tips are free. That's what he thought, the sanitized, family hardware store version of his unspoken bitchy response. You must be European. No, but the colour scheme is. Ass. Maybe I should just start saying these things out loud and people will smarten up. Or at least think twice before saying something stupid, insensitive, offensive. How much mental energy do I spend trying not to offend other people? How much does a clerk in the home decor aisle of the local family hardware store make? Why call it a family hardware store? Single people are the new atheists.

He eyes three withering beets on the counter. He had planned to juice them today, along with some ginger, an apple, three carrots, an orange and some kale. But the beets had gone from firm and robust to decrepit and sad overnight as the chick peas soaked. At least the hummus will work. I should probably think about putting the juicer in a bag to protect it from dust.

He picks up two large red peppers and rinses them under the faucet and proceeds to core, seed and slice them. He dons rubber gloves and minces garlic. Four globs of olive oil in the pan, some ground pepper and sea salt, and in go the garlic and peppers. They will roast at 350 degrees for an hour and then be incorporated with the chick peas in the food processor he bought on sale at Canadian Tire five years ago and has only been used twice. He keeps it inside a garbage bag tied off at the top so dust won't settle on it. It sits under the sink. Chris sometimes wonders, if inanimate objects could think or hope or wish, what his food processor might think or say. Consider all the wonderful things I can do, all the delicious, nutritious foods I can make. Think of all the pleasure. And you leave me here inside this bag, hidden under the sink. Such a waste.

He fills an oversized mug with coffee and brown sugar and moves toward his computer at the far end of his apartment, passing the door to his balcony with its little table and an overflowing ashtray and crumpled pack of cigarettes on top, waiting. Calling. Just outside.

Not today. Or ever. I have to stop. I have to. Now what do you think is going to try to stop me?

At twenty-three minutes after ten the apartment has filled with the smell of boiling chick peas and roasting red peppers and garlic. He's hungry now, wishing he had doubled the recipe so he could have some of the hummus for himself. But it's a gift. Surely that's worth something to the host. Maybe not. He makes a mental note to buy a bottle of wine to bring with him in case the hummus is moot. Chris sits down at his computer and turns it on, taking small sips of coffee, a combination of Sumatra and whatever was on sale at the grocery store. He forgets the alarm he feels every time he sets foot in a grocery store; the cost of food escalating is unnerving. Thirteen dollars for a paltry, emaciated chicken. He boils them and shreds the meat afterward to add to his dog's meals.

There's work to do, he tells himself, and makes a point to sit upright in his chair, not slumped forward, spine curving, shoulders jutting. Tomorrow I'll sign up for yoga. Not the hot kind. That's just torture.

He checks his e-mail. There's an alarming number of messages from Twitter. He highlights them all and hits delete. His hydro bill is due. His credit card payment is due. A friend he hasn't spoken to in years has sent him a cautious how-are-you-doing message with *Reaching Out* in the subject field. Fuck you. That's how I am. Delete. Then there are various messages from people wanting favours. I'll favour my way into bankruptcy, he thinks, shutting down the program and noticing a sluggishness in his psyche. A cigarette would take care of that. And send my heart racing. No. Never again. I have to quit. Stop.

What's the difference between stopping and quitting? He considers this. Maybe stopping is an internal process—a final one; it acknowledges a tendency toward something one ought to avoid and logic wins out over irrational urges, however strong they might be. Stopping factors in to it that the person stopping has no emotional attachment to the thing being stopped because a higher, healthier state is sought. Reason kicks in. Stopping is an accomplished intention. Now that he thinks of it, it occurs to Chris that there is no stopping. There is only stopped. It is a completed action. Quitting, on the other hand, is a process, over-compensation for a problem one is likely to wrestle with for some time, a phrase, a notion, a bold statement of intent but without action or a game plan. It is a grand, empty gesture. Outdoor voices in a library. In Chris' case, inaction. The pull might always be there, if...

If I keep giving in, I will only stay put, continuing the ridiculous circle of making bold assertions I do not really mean and panicking when I see I'm down to my last cigarette. I have to decide whether I want to be pulled by irrational urges or to do some of my own pulling. I have to stop. No more quitting. Must stop quitting.

He logs back into his e-mail account, clicks his way to the trash bin and finds his former friend's e-mail. Chris shakes his head as he reads it.

Bridge the gap... move forward... important person... your personal issues... my responses... personality disorder... professional help...

I quit you, he says evenly to the message. No, actually, I stopped.

Like standing at the foot of a mountain. There's a mountain. Stop. It was a ridiculous, unbalanced relationship. I walked away. I did. I'm glad. Isn't it grand when unwanted people, things, thoughts, mountains actually disappear?

There's a tightness in his chest. If he listens closely, Chris can hear a very faint sound when he breathes, his body telling him it's time to have stopped. Cigarettes, among other things.

He pays his bills and prints out the receipts. Throws the receipts in a pile on the floor beside him. An empty moment startles him. He sits, staring straight ahead and through the windows that need cleaning and focuses only on accepting the empty moment. Sounds like new age bullshit but... Surely something will nudge it aside soon and... the negative will stop.

He'd read in a book—Eckhart Tolle's or Shakti Gawain's or Michael A. Singer's—stop arguing, breathe, observe, be aware. There's a gap big enough for him to climb into. He sits back. Opens.

Ten minutes later the oven's timer dings. The peppers and garlic are done. Chris hears the ding, doesn't move. There's a chill. It spreads from his biceps down to his wrists, sending the hair on his arms straight up and goose flesh rising. Tiny reminders. Energy flowing through, surging around, making itself known in this otherwise empty moment. He is still. He focuses on the goose flesh and sticking up hair on his arms, his awareness of them feeding them, encouraging them in a celebratory union. It's like an orchestra playing under the surface of his skin—Phillip Glass or Brian Eno? He catches himself distracted and smiles inwardly. How long can I ride this out? What is actually happening? How can I explain what I'm doing? And why, when I'm doing it, does my awareness of it seem to make it expand? Increase? Is something physically happening or am I making it happen? Is it a trick? Oh, there, look. The peppers.

The moment expires, killed by thought.

His coffee cup is empty. Chris rises from the chair and moves to the kitchen, past the balcony door and cigarettes outside anxious to induce anxiety. I could just have one. Half of one. And then tomorrow I start all over again. And how long have I been doing that? That's quitting.

He was supposed to have quit in December. It's now March. How much money? How much vitality, health, lung power have I lost as a result? Why ask these questions when you know it's all a ruse to keep you smoking? When you know...? Who is saying that and, if it is me, why say you? Those voices in my head are astute. Not at war with each other and yet not quite complimentary, they haggle and... Voices? No, they're just thoughts. And if they're just thoughts, in my head, I am producing them, no? Maybe not. Maybe... Who is the creator and who is the creation? Maybe it's just one big—

He pours the remnants of coffee into his cup. Adds brown sugar. Stirs. He peers inside the oven, at the shrivelled peppers and brown clumps of garlic slathered with greenish oil. Something intensely erotic about that smell. Maybe I should eat something.

Eat something. Toast with peanut butter and honey. Coffee'll rot your stomach unless you pad it, fill it with something else. Thank you. I wish I understood who or what is behind those thoughts. What about the—?

His telephone emits an electronic pulse. A message has arrived. Chris moves to the balcony door and opens it, spies the ashtray and cigarettes in a flood of sunlight. It'd go great with that coffee. Only in that moment though, he thinks. Or he thinks he thinks. Thoughts aren't voices and voices aren't thoughts—although a voice can certainly give voice to a thought. Just fucking smoke one. Stop picking everything apart and light one up. Do it, do it, doitdoitdoitdoit.

Chris leans in toward the sink and splashes water on his face. He is hungover. It's nine twenty-nine a.m. Too much wine at the party. They devoured his hummus and had wanted more. New people. Introductions and hand shakes. How I know him and how they know each other and all the irrelevant, useless information necessary for us to form connections in our brains, to be at ease or, at the very least, to be entertaining. I used the juice of a whole lemon instead of half. I think that makes it brighter. Colour or...? No. Brighter tasting? Yeah.

He had come home early, walked his dog in the park and afterwards cuddled up with him on the couch to watch an episode of Gilmore Girls, but ended up with his thumb on the mute button of his remote control whenever a subordinate character would start ranting. Fifteen minutes in and his thumb was sore. I used to love this show. What the hell happened?

There's a doggie-diaper-pad spread out on the floor in front of the oven in case of an accident. Accident? Blondie says they never happen. Sometimes you just gotta pee. The dog has never used the diaper-pad and Chris isn't convinced it's because it is a bargain brand, bought for three dollars and fifty cents at the Dollarama. Like a dog would know the difference. And yet people do. Everybody—except some people—wants cheap, disposable everything: bookcases, music, sex, food, movies, kitchen appliances, shoes. An inexpensive fix. Is it the object we want or the thrill of acquiring it? Let's examine society's obsession with shopping: hunting and gathering gone haywire. Welcome to your local landfill, brought to you by poorly-made, inexpensive crap you have to replace every few months. It's not cheap at all. A bargain is usually a misnomer. This kind of wrong-thinking has to stop.

He dries his face and leans in to the now-clean mirror. The pimple at the tip of his nose has decided not to come to a full bloom. Good thing you didn't smash the shit out of it, he thinks. Who? You? It's a good thing you didn't smash the shit out of that zit. It's repeating itself. Or: I am? Who is generating these thoughts? Who is hearing them? Hearing? I don't actually hear them. I... I'm aware of them? Okay.

In front of his computer, Chris stares at the monitor as it boots up. No thought. Empty space. Tingling in his bicep slowly trickling downward through his arms. Hairs on end. Goose flesh. There is a non-verbal urge to chatter but something higher up or bigger or stronger has decreed that this moment of emptiness is to be endured. Witnessed even. He holds there, open and semi-focussed. Electricity. Elastic. Esctatic.

The coffee maker beeps five times. Just... Just...

He extracts himself from the moment ten minutes later, like a child fighting his way out of a prickly oversized woolen sweater. It seems to take forever to become untangled. And when he has come out of it, he rises from the chair in front of his computer, walks toward the kitchen, past the balcony door, and does not contemplate the absence of the ashtray on the little table outside, or the empty space on the table where normally a pack of cigarettes would be—unless, of course, it were raining.

INSIDE THE SCAR CIRCLE

Coming Off Drugs

Changing his online profile name to Puff&Stuff probably wasn't the best idea, but then again Guy37, his former handle, didn't really care that much. There was usually no shortage of men eager to see inside his bedroom, and not for the decor. His real name was José and he was always up for a laugh, a joint, sniffing a dirty jock and a pair of feet—sometimes in that order. And it wasn't long afterwards that José became known on phone apps as The Sniffer or, as he preferred to say, "The guy who will."

"I'll do just about anything," he told an acquaintance over a pitcher and fisting videos at the recently renovated Black Eagle, now a thinly disguised danceteria and occasional ground zero for bachelorette parties. Puff was well aware that when he was out in public men would cast curious glances his way and then scramble to look him up on their phones. He was on all of the apps—a busy man, perhaps, but certainly not hard to find.

That's him there...

Oh...

Hmmm...

At least his pic is recent...

It looks like a thick cock to me, at least from here...

Unless it's padded...

You chatted with him?

Not really. Just sent him a dick selfie...

What is with that word? Can't anybody say picture?

Puff&Stuff rarely wore underwear and it surprised him when he was on the receiving end of lewd looks and gestures from passersby on the street. He wasn't street trade—although at times his demeanour and clothing might indicate otherwise. He took it in stride, at times gloating a little for being able to provoke reactions in people he had no intention of meeting—usually. He revealed this nugget of information to his most recent fuck-buddy, Clayton.

Ten years older than Puff, Clayton Miller was a tightly wound ball of sexual energy who, perhaps ironically, called Puff "Daddy" in the thrusts of ecstasy. The irony was lost on Puff, who was more attuned to Clayton's voice and the changes it made while they fucked. Puff knew when Clayton's voice flipped into a connected head register rivalling Mariah Carey on a good day—at least in the early 1990s—that this was his signal to either a) cum or b) take a break. He suspected that Clayton was in love with him—or at least infatuated—and he did his best to discourage him from getting too involved because, "You know, we're just fucking, right?"

Right.

It didn't occur to Puff that Clayton was simply hungry.

If Clayton were being honest with both himself and Puff, he would have confessed to having analyzed each and every phrase uttered between the two of them so that he could feel reassured that his lust for Puff was, in fact, love. Lust was for dirtbags, miscreants and drug addicts, so he had convinced himself. It was now August. His first meeting with Puff had been in October of the previous year; a quickly arranged precautionary introduction at Zipperz that was interrupted by a flash flood during which an alarmingly thin drag queen pleaded with them to participate in her "show," all the while casting nervous glances out the window as debris drifted by in a small river that could not be accommodated by the sewer system. That had been ten months ago. They had fucked approximately twice each month since then, occasionally three times, bringing their total to about twenty-three.

Clayton often wondered where it was headed, and was quietly curious about whether Puff thought about it as well. Clayton wanted a confrontation—other than Puff saying, "That was awesome, man. Like porn star sex"—a confirmation that they were on the same page that he could interpret as an important sign, based on past experiences. He liked it and wanted more. Puff just wanted to get high and fuck for a really long time and then be left alone. Neither one thought they would be married—especially to each other. They would get together, occasionally, whatever that meant and entailed, so long as they both enjoyed it and so long as none of Puff's buttons were pushed.

Clayton had come out of the closet in his twenties, at the onset of the AIDS epidemic, and refused to have sex with men his own age. Instead—and only occasionally—he did so with a select few of the older, lonely, unattractive men who frequented the bar where he worked. Those experiences dulled his sexual appetite, and he poured all of his energy into being a good waiter and amassing an impressive collection of imported twelve-inch singles. In the 1990s, however, a friend dragged him to a bathhouse where he learned that other men found him attractive. He spent the next ten years taking advantage of that fact, but the sex proved to be less about connection and more about ego. So despite feeling he did not fit into the gay scene, these encounters in bathhouse cubicles made it seem as though he belonged, however briefly. But to what?

It was in a bathhouse that Clayton found an unlikely partner, Kevin, and they moved in together a few months after meeting. Within a year they had separated and reconciled, but Kevin died of sudden heart failure. Clayton decided that he was not cut out for relationships, and returned, infrequently, to the bathhouses, hoping to reconfirm his sense of self worth via roving hands and body parts. Through it all, he was removed, robotic, never feeling quite inside himself no matter who was inside him. He hoped that going through the motions would wake him up, make him come alive, or at least give him the same experiences as everyone else around him. That way he would be part of the group. He drifted through the early 2000s this way. As younger and hotter men became the focus of other people's attentions, his visits to the baths decreased, often reduced to perfunctory laps around the dimly lit hallways. By the time he turned fifty, Clayton realized, once again, that he was on the outside fringes and longed for... something. Recognition, connection, understanding, and maybe a bit of empathy. Something more.

It was Puff who had reawakened Clayton's interest in sex; it had waned after his last fuck buddy, Desmond, had refused to do anything to get him hard, and then, strangely, demanded to be serviced. The last time they had been together, Desmond had maneuvered Clayton onto his bed, stuck his ass up in the air and said: "Eat it and fuck me." A selfish, self-centred, pushy bottom with no interest in the pleasure, comfort or interests of his top. Clayton thought it was strange behaviour indeed. It didn't seem psychologically sound to be an aggressive *and* lazy bottom. At the time, however, with the mood ruined, his delusions shattered and his penis flaccid, Clayton pushed Desmond's ass out of his face and stood up. He got dressed, apologized profusely for being abrupt, and left, thinking, *Holy shit, that's work, not sex! He wants me to do all the work! And no paycheque. Where's the pleasure in that?*

They never saw each other again. Less than two months later, Clayton found himself staring out the window at Zipperz, past the emaciated drag queen, wishing the rain would stop so he and Puff could go smoke up and fuck.

He wanted to be naked, to be touched, to be the centre of one man's attention, pushed to the brink of... Whatever that feeling was, he didn't know its name, but he got his wish. Approximately twenty-three times. Even months later, Clayton would never stop to wonder if perhaps his wish was too limited in scope. And as time passed and the sex with Puff had increased in intensity—and, Clayton thought, intimacy—he wondered if perhaps Puff, too, had a secret wish, and if he might play a part in making it come true. But the prospect of a romantic entanglement had been quashed when Puff came over to Clayton's apartment the third time, many months before. Clayton had opened the door, smiled at Puff and stepped aside to allow him to enter. Puff looked directly at Clayton and said, "I'm not looking for a boyfriend." And again, several months later, "nothing romantic" were the words Puff had uttered during a conversation about what he was looking for. *Nothing romantic* reverberated in Clayton's mind whenever they were clothed together. They became his guiding mantra, and he followed that mantra because he did not want to lose what had become so integral in his life. So it came as a surprise to Clayton when Puff said one night while pulling on his track pants, "We could do more than just fuck, you know? Like watch movies or have dinner." Not something to pyrograph onto a wooden plaque to hang in one's home, but something encouraging nonetheless. To Clayton it was.

Occasionally they would eat together and watch movies, their hands sometimes touching in the gap between them on the couch. Clayton offered massages, took yoga classes to improve his flexibility and stamina, bought strong weed to fuel their intense sex, and always felt a nagging semi-loss when Puff would leave his apartment without a kiss, an embrace or even a glance. This led Clayton to begin questioning the importance of their relationship, and he decided not to instigate contact with Puff from then on. He would simply wait, like a professional bottom, for his counterpart to clue in and bridge the gap. But only a few days following Clayton's decision, Puff called him on the telephone and said he was nearby and why didn't they go for a walk. It was a sunny Sunday afternoon. They walked through Cabbagetown, crossed Riverdale Park and sat in an empty baseball dugout where they talked about passivity, vulnerability, body fat, horror movies.

"So what kind of work do you do? Can I ask you that?"

"Yeah," José said flatly. "Hospitality. And I own a bar with my cousin."

"Nice."

"He runs it most of the year and I cover when he's on vacation."

"Nice. Around here?"

"No, back home."

"I work in television."

"Cool."

Clayton recalled their outing as they undressed in his bedroom later. He felt pleased that Puff had suggested the walk and that he wasn't afraid to be seen in public with him, but then remembered his comments on vulnerability. José had said he thought that Clayton was incapable of making decisions and those he had made were mostly bad ones. He should change his behaviour. *It doesn't seem as though he has a very good opinion of me,* he thought, rolling a joint. *So why does he still want to fuck me?* As the marijuana kicked in and his inhibitions gave way to an intense sexual haze, Clayton thought to himself, *I am* strong, *in my own quiet way. And this... This was not a bad decision.*

A few weeks later, forgetting about his pledge not to instigate contact, Clayton sent Puff a text message inviting him for dinner. Three days later Puff responded. Something about it all being too much. Clayton was crestfallen and confused. A small anger grew inside him, but he pushed it down. He resolved once again to not instigate contact with Puff. He would respond, still see him, but he would not instigate contact. The sting of rejection and the awful hangover-like feeling afterwards were too devastating.

He tried to choreograph his life to avoid the feeling. It left him alone much of the time, and lonely, most of the time. He craved José's touch, his body, kisses, the magical sex that the pot facilitated. It wouldn't be easy to cut off contact. *But he's not giving me what I want. At least not everything. But... We're just fucking.*

Things settled back to the way they had been, with Clayton longing and Puff occasionally texting hello or let's-get-together messages, sometimes even calling on the phone. Weeks passed. The dinners and movies stopped, and Clayton figured that this was the new normal, that he'd better adjust to it or he would lose their all-consuming, mind-blowing sex. And then one night as Puff returned from the bathroom after a post-sex shower, the cycle started up again.

"Why don't we watch a movie or something?"

"Okay. But you're not going to get all weird and stand-offish if I invite you over, are you?"

Puff laughed and checked the crotch of his track pants for any evidence of post-cum-haste. "Why would I do that?"

"You mean again?"

"What?"

They had both wanted the sex, but not the lingering afterthoughts it engendered. Try as they had to keep the sex as their focus, the afterthoughts tainted their appetites and kept them both wondering if they were doing the right thing.

"Well, you told me you weren't looking for a boyfriend and I—"

"I'm not. But that doesn't mean we can't..."

"Do things that boyfriends do?"

They were both on the defensive now, both of them unable to articulate what it was they wanted from each other. Clayton couldn't believe he'd actually confronted him. He wished he could take it back, but later he would be proud of his conduct.

"Only boyfriends have dinner and watch movies?"

"No, but—"

"Look, forget it."

"No, don't forget it. I'm just trying to be clear."

"Loud and clear," Puff said, standing and moving to the door. His back was toward Clayton when he heard himself utter a curt, "Gotta go."

"Okay," Clayton relented, thinking, *Passi-vulnerable.*

Puff felt a cooling feeling of relief flooding his system. He didn't wonder why he would feel relief or question the small vacant feeling in the pit of his stomach as he tucked his Che Guevara t-shirt into his track pants or felt that parched, drawn-out tension in his throat, the urge to flee and not look back. *Flee. Free.*

"Thanks," Clayton said simply.

"What are you thanking me for?" José asked, voice like a father.

Because you put your armour on and yet you still show up, Clayton thought. But that's not what he said.

"You're amazing in bed... You know I can't get enough of you sexually... So if you want to hang out and watch a movie or whatever, I guess that's cool."

Hang out? Cool? I don't speak like that!

Their meeting ended with Puff leaving like a stranger and Clayton masturbating in front of his computer, furious that he hadn't said anything about Puff's flip-flop. *Come here. Go Away.* Nobody had ever fucked him like Puff. The sex was spectacular. Nobody had ever grabbed him by the shoulders and demanded he look him in the eye while being penetrated. "Look at me when I fuck you," Puff had said countless times in his gravelly sex voice as sweat ran in rivulets down his face, chest, arms. And so Clayton glared at Puff's brown eyes as his sweat dripped onto his stomach, chest, face. He stared longingly at Puff and wished he could read his mind. *What does he want? Why does he keep coming back?* Clayton squealed and grunted and panted and bucked and Puff would demand: "You like that?"

"Yeah."

"Yeah?"

"Yeah."

"Oh yeah? Who fucks you like me?"

"Nobody, buddy, nobody!" And his voice jumped.

The unfortunate truth, Clayton acknowledged ruefully, was that nobody did fuck him quite like Puff and that unnerved him. He was, after all, a one-buddy man. Experience had proved it, pretty much, although Clayton wondered if he should make the effort to find one or two other lovers so that he wouldn't be placing his entire sexual focus on José, a sort of outlet that would benefit both of them. But he never followed through, *because,* he thought, *I should spend that energy trying to find an actual partner. One who isn't allergic to dating. Someone who understands that* come here *is the opposite of* go away.

This is when Clayton made the leap from the phone apps to guysnearyou.com and found himself fielding the strangest questions from men in faraway places despite the warning in his profile: locals only.

'Do you speak German?' That was the introductory question from K-line in Hamilton, who followed his query with a series of links to excerpts from obscure German films of the 1940s on Youtube. Clayton sped through K-line's profile, amazed that the site had ranked them as ninety-eight percent compatible despite the fact that K-line was twenty-four and Clayton fifty and specified in his profile preferences that he was looking for guys his own age, and: 'Don't call me daddy!'

Then there was the message from Assfault in Little Rock, Arkansas. Assfault's message was a critique of Clayton's profile, with comments on his use of grammar, paragraph structure, and it closed with, 'I would have asked you out on a date except you list *Atlas Shrugged* as one of your favourite books and I could never date anyone who likes Ayn Rand.'

Wow, Clayton thought, scrolling through the message a second time, *the internet really is full of freaks. This guy is actually pre-empting rejection by notifying the men he isn't interested in. Spread that misery around. It would be genius if it weren't so insane. Why not just fucking ignore people? No, this guys wants people to know he's rejecting them. Prejecting.* Clayton deleted the message after he clicked on the 'block user' button. *Arkansas isn't local and... Who calls himself Assfault anyway?*

He tweaked, plucked and pruned his profile, relegated the Ayn Rand comment to the very last line of the last paragraph of his profile where, he was sure, most people never read. The profile didn't last long. After meeting one of the members for coffee, Clayton arrived home to find the man had blocked him on the site. Never a good sign. Back to the phone apps.

One evening, when Puff had cancelled getting together due to a head cold, Clayton offered to take him some Echinacea and Oregano oil. "Why are you so nice to me?" Puff sniffed as the accepted the little white drug store bag from Clayton.

"Why wouldn't I be? What kind of question is that? I was nearby and you're sick and I'm bringing you something for your cold." *That ought to do it,* Clayton thought, clapping himself on the back for giving such a straightforward answer when all along he was thinking: *Because I... Well, for sure I don't love you. That's the appropriate answer, but not the right one.*

A drawn-out, silent look passed between them. Puff stepped back and gestured for Clayton to enter the apartment. Clayton reluctantly stepped inside, making a very grand gesture of it in his mind. *He's inviting me in.* He didn't stay long because he knew that come here eventually leads to go away.

Clayton asked his therapist what he thought it meant that he thought so much of José based on such a thin connection.

"Thin?" the therapist responded. "The way you describe it to me, the situation seems very plump and juicy, if you'll pardon the pun. Have you ever thought of just enjoying it for what it is?"

"I don't think I know how."

"What do you think that means?"

"Do you think I'm choosing situations like this on purpose? To create dis—no, drama?"

"What do you think?"

Clayton shrugged.

"Why not tell him you'd like to see him more often and see how he responds? That is what you want, isn't it?"

"Because he told me he doesn't make plans."

"Ask him to make an exception. Don't you think the situation warrants it?"

That's a good question, Clayton thought. "I guess I'm afraid to rock the boat."

"Why?"

"Uh..."

"Clayton, you know how to swim. You ended it with Desmond. I thought that was very brave of you, considering."

"Considering?"

"Yes, the circumstances."

"Okay, but brave? To stop seeing a fuck buddy?"

"I think he was a little more to you than that," the therapist said, eyes on Clayton.

"A-ha!" Clayton said loudly, shifting forward in his chair. "It's a cycle, isn't it? I'm repeating. The same thing is happening with Puff, except the sex is really good. Both of us are closed off emotionally, but at least Puff leaves the door open a crack... Before he slams it in my face. Thank goodness he's not a bottom. That would be a disaster. I hate using dildos."

The therapist tried not to smile. Clayton caught it, felt good about having entertained the man, and then quickly tucked it away inside his psyche so he could ruminate on it later.

They were at the doorway. Puff had his back to Clayton as he pulled his running shoes on. Clayton combatted the afterglow of their sex and the irresistible urge to wrap himself around Puff physically to prevent him from leaving.

They had smoked up and slipped into the bedroom with a pint glass full of cold water. Rain pelted the bedroom window as Puff pulled off his clothes and Clayton fiddled with his phone, trying to get it to play music over a pair of speakers he had plugged into a wall. Puff patted the empty space beside him in bed. Clayton climbed in beside him as a song came on, randomly selected by the phone's music app. The live version of "En La Ciudad de la Furia" by Soda Stereo played. And then "Everwanting" by Maxwell, followed by "Far From Me," the live version, by Nick Cave and the Bad Seeds. The sex, the intricate, probing, sweat-soaked, passionate exchange went on, seemingly endlessly, two men inches away from getting a glimpse of what it's like to be inside of—or a part of—something outside themselves. So close…When the drug had worked its way out of their systems, they were just two bodies going through the motions. Separate. Neither one climaxed. They simply wore each other out, separated and ejaculated alone.

Clayton stood in the foyer as Puff tied his shoelaces. Clayton looked at the expanse of his back and wondered what Puff would do if he placed his hands there, wrapped his arms around him from behind, enveloped him in a warm embrace and whispered his confession: *I don't know what to call this. It's not love, but I care about you. It's not only sexual, even though it is just sex. I love being with you. I want to do this more.* He knew exactly how he felt but could not articulate it out loud, even to his therapist. He erased the words from his mind, but they would return.

Back to reality, he thought. *Yeah. Much less fun.* Clayton wanted to tell Puff everything; he knew it would make himself feel better, but Puff...?

The trick is to make him not want to leave. But I'm not a magician. How do I make him stay? And what would I do with him if he did stay? I guess eventually we'd have to cum. Eventually I would have to tell him that I care for him, even though, even though... I hardly know him. Maybe this kind of connection is unqualified? Unquantified? Not in reference to anything or anyone outside of the two of us. Would that soften the blow, Puff? And I'm nice because… because I care for you and I show it the best I can, any way I can, usually in my bed. There. I'm done. You can leave now, as I know you will, as I know you want to.

The bolts on the door were unlocked and unfastened. Puff stepped back, pulled the door open and, with his back to Clayton, said, "See ya buddy." And then he disappeared, the diffused light from the hallway creating a hazy aura around his body as he stepped through the threshold of Clayton's apartment and disappeared around the corner. Clayton felt the veil of the high lifting. His focus changed. Things became clearer. *I'm not in love. I'm not.*

He stared at the empty space where, moments before, Puff had stood. The fast, fleeting shape of his body here and gone. Purple tee-shirt. Track pants. Running shoes. No socks. No underwear. And then empty space. Clayton focussed on flashbacks of their sex, their bodies in motion, the wetness, closeness, intensity, thrusting, hard shapes penetrating darkness and bringing light, sighs, eyes gazing and holding fast, cries and oh, yeah. The sweet, probing kisses saying everything and nothing. He concentrated on minutes ago. The present moment offered only reflections of the past. He stepped back when he heard the elevator door opening. Clayton closed the door, fastened the locks and looked at the doorknob, the very one that, moments ago, had been grasped by his fuck buddy's hand. José left and would not come back.

Volver

Clayton's flight arrived at the Gustavo Díaz Ordaz International Airport in Puerto Vallarta at the same time as the majority of the day's international flights arrived, at the peak of rush hour. After grabbing his suitcase and green-lighting his way through customs, he found himself standing outside the terminal in a curving, disorderly lineup for taxis, feeling the force of the sun on his bare arms.

Like many pivotal events in his life, he has been able to cull all the details of that moment into his mind, re-experiencing the hypnotic, ethereal sensations of arriving in a hot climate from a place frozen over with ice and snow. But he wondered whether his attraction to Mexico might be significant of something else; scattered pieces of a previous life, the call of destiny, the land where he would be accepted unconditionally, the one place on earth his ideal man was hidden. Or perhaps he was just grateful that there was some place away from his home in Toronto that was warm and welcoming. In that brief moment after contemplating the possible whys, he considered that perhaps Mexico was just a warm place with friendly people and great food. The thought passed. It was far less intoxicating than the other possibilities. Clayton looked around him and then up to the sky. He closed his eyes as he recalled the snow and ice back home. His chest heaved with a deep breath in, followed by a long exhale. *I'm here. I'm here.*

After checking in at his hotel, Clayton rode the elevator up to the fourth floor and found his room. He closed the door, dropped his suitcase and pulled a magnifying glass out of the side pocket of his carry-on bag. He kneeled at the side of the bed, lifted the blankets and scanned the bedding, mattress and headboard for bedbugs. Finding none, he moved to the chest of drawers and checked there as well. Nothing. Bathed in relief, Clayton unpacked his toiletries, travel documents and cell phone as Spanish-dubbed dialogue from an episode of *The Simpsons* seeped in from the room next door. He figured out how to use the room safe and descended the four flights of stairs to the lobby.

Light danced on the surface of the swimming pool in the back courtyard and laughter echoed off the walls that enclosed it. Children's laughter. He walked through the lobby and stepped out into the courtyard. There was a woman sprawled out on a lounger with a baby nursing at her breast. In the smaller wading pool two children splashed and played. *That's an odd sight,* he thought, *for a gay hotel. Or is my version of gay now defunct?*

He turned back inside and saw a small table with a computer on it. A sign reading *Free Internet* hung on the wall above it. Clayton sat down at the computer and did a search for Cielo de Plata, Puerto Vallarta, Jalisco, Mexico. Various websites came up in the results, most of which referred to Together, a gay hotel in the Romantic Zone.

So the hotel had had an identity crisis. *A sexual identity crisis*, he laughed to himself, and wondered what exactly had been involved in the switch from gay to... not gay. *There had probably been a jilted male lover stewing somewhere on the sidelines with a lawyer on speed dial; both of them using binoculars to keep tabs on things, just in case.*

He left the hotel and ate chicken mole at Tizoc, stopped at Sama Martini Bar only to find it hadn't yet opened, and then returned to his room. Clayton stood out on the balcony. It faced the rear of the hotel and offered an uninspiring view of the back courtyard and swimming pool and provided a few hours of direct sunlight until the light shifted and left the space shaded throughout the rest of the day. He slathered himself with sunblock and laid down on the balcony, pulling the edges of his bathing suit up to match the tan lines he had established in the weeks before his trip.

Within half an hour, the sun disappeared behind the hotel, so Clayton made his way down to the courtyard and listened to Lola Beltran's *Los Grandes de la Música Ranchera* on his MP3 player, his ear buds smeared with a thin layer of Life Brand 50 sunblock and Off spray-on insect repellent. When "Soy Infeliz" came on, Clayton looked up at the sky, saw the sun had moved away and left the pool deck partially in shade. Visual flashbacks from *Mujeres al borde de un ataque de nervios* played in his mind and made him smile: the low angled dolly shot of Carmen Maura's shoes pacing back and forth, the slap in the lawyer's office, and the shot of Maura crumpled on the floor of the recording booth after having fainted, her glasses at her side—an homage to the Hitchcock through-the-glasses shot from *Strangers on a Train*.

I should go to Spain, he thought. *Next year.*

"Quisiera Olvidarme de Tí" played next. Clayton remembered burning his hand on a pot while making Mole Poblano for the first time. Lola was playing in the background then too, and José was rolling a joint on the couch. "I don't like your papers, man," he had said. Clayton had spent almost the entire day cooking, enveloping his apartment in the sweet, earthy aroma of the sauce. The recipe was from mexicoinmykitchen.com and was the third recipe Clayton had tried from their offerings. In preparation for the task, he had taken the streetcar to Perola's Supermarket in Kensington Market and pulled out his list of ingredients. After he had all of the the chiles the recipe required, the woman helping him asked what he was making. "Mole Poblano," he answered. She smiled. Clayton pretended not to notice her turning to the man behind the cash register and the look that passed between them. He knew most of his friends and acquaintances already laughed at his Mexican fixation so what difference would strangers in a grocery store make? *What if it turns out good? Or great?* From then on, whenever Clayton hears "Quisiera Olvidarme de Tí," he still thinks of that day making Mole Poblano, the look on José's face when he ate the meal and then asked for a second helping, the mountain of dirty dishes in the kitchen, and the smell of his own burnt flesh.

He walked the beach for just over an hour in the afternoon with Mercedes Castro on his MP3 player. At four o'clock he headed to The Rec Room with the bear-flag beach towels he had brought for his friend Francisco, who had taught him how to swear in Spanish during his first trip five years before. *¡Toma! Chupe la verga. Me voy a chingar ese culo. ¡Que perras!*

"¡Hey, mi amigo!" Francisco cried when Clayton entered the lounge.

Clayton waited until his friend came out from behind the bar, and then wrapped him in a warm embrace. Francisco growled quietly in his ear as their bodies connected. He was about six feet tall, with dark hair, expressive brown eyes, a flowing beard, and a demeanour that was open and responsive. Francisco had aligned himself with *the bears* and clearly believed that animal sounds, however poorly approximated, were far more expressive than human language. Clayton rubbed Francisco's back and smiled. He was another reason he returned here year after year.

"You're early," Francisco said, disengaging and going back behind the bar. "I'm just getting ready."

"I know. I won't keep you," Clayton answered. "I was trying to get familiar with the streets and thought I'd drop off your towels." He placed a white plastic bag on the bar between them.

"Thank you, thank you!"

Francisco opened the bag and unfurled one of the bear-flag beach towels. A big, wide grin spread across his face. "¡Qué hermosa toalla! I'll be the only one on the beach with these," he said.

"A lot has changed since I was here," Clayton said, looking around at the bar.

"It's been two years?"

"Yeah. What about all those expensive new shops on Lázaro Cárdenas? Holy shit."

"I know. Always empty though. Did you see the pier?"

"Just in passing."

"Where are you staying?"

"Cielo de Plata."

"Together," Francisco grunted as he wrapped the bear-flag towel around his midriff and did a quick spin to show it off. "Grrrr!"

"I was wondering about that. It used to be gay and now it's not."

"I don't know what happened."

"Maybe the owners sent it to aversion therapy."

"I never understand your jokes," Francisco said, crouching down and sliding bottles into the fridge.

"Neither do I."

"Then why make them?"

Clayton shrugged and blushed. "To fill in the gaps, try to be more comfortable."

"Relax," Francisco smirked. "You want a beer, perra?"

That night after dinner—again at Tizoc and with impromptu Spanish lessons from Rafael the waiter—Clayton walked along Amapas, not straying too far from his hotel in case... Just in case. He slid his headphones on to cover up the tumult of a drunken drag show at the Blue Chairs, and still, beneath Melody Gardot's smokey smooth voice in his earbuds, he heard thump thump thump and the disconcerting sound of Kesha's braying reverberating off hotel walls. He decided to walk in a different direction—*away from the gay,* he thought to himself. He headed up Pilitas and within ten minutes was lost.

After a short cab ride back to his hotel, Clayton changed his clothes and brushed his teeth. He paused in front of the mirror and flattened his cowlick with hairspray. *What am I doing here?* he asked himself. This is when he thought, *I am repeating*. And then, curiously, *cigarettes*. After a quick stop at the Oxxo at the corner to buy a pack of Marlboro Blancos and a lighter, Clayton headed straight for Sama Martini Bar. There he drank a tamarind margarita and a Pacifico, sitting inside at the bar, overhearing brief exchanges between the bartender and the waiters. It was something he liked to do for entertainment and to expand his vocabulary. He walked past the noisy stretch of straight bars on Olas Altas and made his way to The Rec Room where he talked with Francisco in the lounge as the younger men corralled on the dance floor in the adjacent room. When the drag show started, Clayton knew it was time to go.

He smoked a cigarette on his balcony when he returned to his room just after one o'clock. He laid down in his bed, almost oblivious to the stiffness of the bedspread, and with enough alcohol in his system to subdue extraneous thought and enable him to fall asleep. Then his phone blipped.

He pulled the blankets back and sat up, reached toward the nightstand and clicked on the bedside lamp. He fumbled for his glasses as the sound of the ceiling fan rocking back and forth in small movements made him wonder about the security of its wiring. He grabbed his phone, touch-screened his way into the Growl'r application. A message from CapNJon.

—Handsome. What are you doing?

Clayton typed in, *Just lying in bed.*

— :-)

CapNJon had nothing else to say. Clayton went back to sleep after turning off his phone.

Jean Harlow Winked

He awoke to the sound of his neighbour's television pouring through the rather generous gap between the floor and their adjoining door. The room's heavy wooden furniture, with the notable absence of a desk at which he could read and write, the fissure of a bathroom and the constant blaring of the neighbour's television prompted Clayton to go downstairs to the front desk and ask to be moved. He tried in Spanish, but found himself tripping over which words were masculine and feminine. He gave up and started over again in English.

"My neighbours have their television on all the time. It's really loud and half the time they aren't even in their room. Is it possible that I move to a different room? Please."

The concierge looked Clayton up and down and then glanced at the hotel register on the desk before him.

"Tengo que trabajar, y necesito tranquila," Clayton added as a buffer, perhaps to legitimize his complaint and request.

The young man smiled mischievously and leaned forward slightly. Heavily tweezed eyebrows. Clayton thought of Jean Harlow and wondered how a man could—

"Sorry they disturb you," the concierge said.

"¿Puedes hablarme en español, por favor? Necesito practicar."

"But how will I practice English?" he answered. Then Jean Harlow winked.

Big silver earrings shone from the young man's drooping earlobes. He stood behind the heavy, oversized wooden reception desk, a fawning child in need of sustenance in an adult world. Clayton immediately felt the weight of what was behind the look: the need, the sprawling, directionless needs of this man. *I can't help you,* he said to himself. *I can barely help myself. I just want—*

"Where did you learn your Spanish?" he asked, smiling, and then looked back at the register.

"Movies," Clayton answered in Spanish. "Pedro Almodóvar's to start."

"Ah! My favourite," the concierge said, looking back up from the desk.

"Classes, friends, books, lovers." *José. Just change my room, please.*

"I have a room on the six floor," he said, "but it isn't, uh... It isn't ready until four o'clock."

"That's great. I'll move my things myself later then," he said. And, "Gracias."

He walked up Rodolfo Gomez to Dee's Coffee Company only to discover that it had closed. He stopped in front of the spot where it had stood two years before and wondered where he would get his coffee. He would have to establish a new morning routine.

He crossed the intersection at Rodolfo Gomez and Olas Altas. Verona Bar, Farmacia Oli and the Applegate Realtor were still closed, but next door to that, Farmacia Olas Altas was open. Clayton looked past the displays of bottled vanilla and rack upon rack of tanning lotions and smiled at the cashier. Ana Gabriel sang "Volver, Volver" on the small radio behind the counter.

"Hello," he said in Spanish to a yawning cashier. "I'm looking for Dee's Coffee Shop. Has it closed?"

"No, señor. It's... to Francisca Rodríguez," she said in a monotone, pointing outside. "You walk there. Next... uh, calle de la izquierda," she said, emphasizing the turn with her left arm and hand. "¿Entiendes?"

"The next street on the left?" he translated.

"Sí, señor. The next street on the left. En frente del Oxxo."

"Gracias," he said, and turned to go. Then he remembered a lingering question.

"Excuse me," he continued in Spanish, indicating the display of vanilla bottles. "Why do all the drug stores here have so much vanilla? Is it true that people use it to get a darker tan?"

The woman laughed. Her right hand moved in an arc and rested on the countertop before her. "No, no. It's not for tanning. It's for cooking," she answered, her left hand indicating the array of bottled vanilla in the storefront display. "It's the best. Pure and cheap."

"Gracias, señorita," he said with a chuckle. "Buen día."

He found Dee's Coffee Company and waited in line for an Americano and a breakfast bagel, sin jitomate. With his coffee and bagel in hand, Clayton left the shop and stopped to look out at the metallic structure that punctuated the pier to his right. It hadn't been there two years ago on his last trip. He made a mental note to take his camera there and get some panoramic shots of Banderas Bay.

Laughter rang out behind him as he stared at the pier. Clayton turned around and saw a man and woman, arms festooned with bags of groceries, talking and laughing as they wrestled with their bags and tried to unlock the small door to a sidewalk taco stand. Immediately his thoughts raced through all the times he had scurried through the streets of the Romantic Zone to get back to his hotel to use the toilet. He wanted so much to eat from a taco stand, yet he did not want to suffer what he was convinced would be the follow-through. The man and woman disappeared inside the stand and closed the door behind them.

Water, he thought. He looked around and realized that he was standing directly in front of an Oxxo store. He walked through the front door and felt a wave of air-conditioned air hit his body. He moved to the refrigerated storage and selected a two litre bottle of Ciel. As he turned, Clayton saw rows of yogurt and yogurt drinks in the adjacent fridge. He paused and pulled the door open. The word *nopale* jumped out at him from the various labels in view. Cactus. He had eaten nopale salad at a Mexican restaurant back home and loved it. Here was a chance to incorporate something new into his diet. He picked up a small container of Activia piña apio y nopal and took his purchases to the checkout counter where two employees laughed and pointed at each other's cell phone screens.

Later in the afternoon, Clayton took a walk on the beach that lead him past Isla Cuale. He spent over an hour looking for the shop where he had bought a Catrina figurine in the likeness of Frida Kahlo on his last trip. But he could find no evidence of the shop, and his attempts to solicit help from nearby store owners were fruitless. Clayton wondered how he would go about finding a Diego Rivera Catrina to keep his Frida company. One store clerk spoke to him in fluent English and told him to go back to the Romantic Zone to look for a storefront near Playa Los Arcos Hotel. But by the time he had walked back, he was too hot and tired to look for the shop and thought, *Frida Catrina will have to fly solo for a while longer. Just like me.* Arriving at the hotel, he got the key to his newly assigned room and quickly packed up his belongings and hauled them up to the sixth floor. The room change meant more walking—the elevator was so slow it tried his patience—but it also, hopefully, meant peace and quiet. He showered quickly and fell asleep on the bed—after inspecting it with the magnifying glass—with the ceiling fan on low and the balcony door open.

He woke at dusk with sharp pangs of hunger in his stomach. In the bathroom he matted down his hair, brushed his teeth and rubbed Aloe gel all over his skin. After dressing and taking money from his wallet in the safe, Clayton tied his black Converse sneakers, grabbed his room key and left for the evening.

Dinner wasn't far away—at Coco's Kitchen, where he had eaten many times over the years. He ordered a glass of red wine and Camaron al Coco. And then a salad. After dinner he headed straight for Sama Martini Bar—it was just up the street and around the corner—and had a Pacifico while absent-mindedly watching dance music videos by no-name auto-tuned pop tarts on the LED screen that hung over the bar. When the bartender announced it was Beyoncé hour, Clayton paid his bill, silently wishing there were places here that American culture hadn't tainted.

It was still early in gay time, so Clayton sauntered back to his hotel, climbed the six flights of stairs to his room and sat down on his bed in the dark, waiting for something to occur to him. *Fuck. Second night and already I'm bored. Fucking bored. I hate that. Why do I keep coming here by myself? The heat? I wonder what José is doing right now. Or who. Puff. What time is it there?*

He turned on the bedside table lamp and grabbed his phone. *Just after eleven here.* He opened Scruff and scanned the profiles in his area. He spotted at least a dozen faces from Toronto, all of whom had *in an open relationship* set as their relationship status. Clayton decided that being in Mexico wasn't a good enough excuse to have sex with a married person. *Besides,* he thought, *why come all this way to have something I could have at home? Eat local.*

He ended up walking to the Rec Room and sat at Francisco's bar for an hour, alternating Pacifico with shots of tequila. No salt, no lime. He chatted with Francisco intermittently, about music, food, and the real Vallarta that most tourists don't see—or choose not to. The lounge wasn't terribly busy, but Clayton did notice that the few who did come to Francisco's bar to order drinks did not stay. They all ended up on the other side of the bar, on the dance floor. He looked over, through the glass partition, and saw two young Mexican men holding up a staggering sixty-year-old drunk gringo. *Shoot me if it ever comes to that.*

"Francisco, what time is it?"

Francisco glanced at his watch and then at Clayton's empty Pacifico bottle. "Twelve thirty," he said, and then, indicating the bottle, "¿Otra?"

"No, gracias. Me voy. ¿Cuanto te debo?"

"One fifty."

"So little? Come on."

"You're going to get lost again going to your hotel?" Francisco asked.

"No, I've figured out everything up to this intersection."

"Mentiroso," Francisco smiled. "I should give you a walking tour, but I think you'd forget it all when you're borracho."

"I'll take a cab."

When he got back to his hotel room, there were messages waiting for him on Scruff. Three, actually, all from someone called cklvr46.

—Handsome guy

—R u there?
—U have been on the grid all night. Were at Garbo's. Join us.

The last message had come in only a few minutes earlier.

—Are you still there? I was out

—Yeah. It says u r steps away. Where r u?

— Cielo de Plata. Thats nearby

—Come join us for drinks. My name is Curt

—Ok. 5 minutes

Clayton pushed the doors open and tentatively stepped inside Garbo's. Doing a quick scan of the establishment, he realized there wasn't anyone under fifty in the place—except for the staff, of course.

It's all sunburned retired men in plaid Costco shorts and Lacoste shirts singing, drinking and flirting pointlessly. Pointlessly? Do people over sixty get laid? Fuck. If I never felt old before, this place will certainly do the trick. Of course, I happen to be staying in a hotel nearby. Maybe they'll renovate it and turn it into a retirement home and this is where I will end my days, walking in limited circles in Puerto Vallarta, moving back and forth between Cielo de Plata and Garbo's. Fuck. Where did my life go? I don't even remember my forties.

"Trana?" A voice interrupted his rumination. A man stood before him, had just uttered Clayton's online profile name. He was in his late forties or early fifties, with a wide smile, green eyes and vacation stubble on his cheeks and neck. Handsome, knowing, perhaps a little devious. This is what he radiated, at least to Clayton. But Clayton was usually wrong about the people he met.

"Yeah, hi. Curt?"

"That's me. What the hell is Trana? Are you a drag queen?"

"No, it's a kind of joke. Some people mispronounce Toronto."

"I thought you were a little weird," Curt grinned widely and threw his arms around him.

"I try," Clayton said, at first embracing Curt, but then stepping back abruptly to let someone pass.

"I'm glad you could make it. Come on with me. My friends are over here."

As they moved through the crowd, Curt confessed he had shown Clayton's profile to his friends and most of them figured that Trana was a drag name and that Clayton was, in fact, a drag queen. "I think they're expecting you in heels," he said.

"I'll change my profile name when I get back to my room."

"Why? You're afraid some methed up guys on Grindr are going to think you're a drag queen? Fuck that!"

"Well you thought I was. Are you methed up?"

"Only if you're lisping," Curt said, and nudged Clayton. Before he had the chance to react, Curt had stopped and stepped sideways, raised his arms in the air and gestured to a group of men seated around a small table behind a large column.

"Trana!" they all cried and, eventually, stood up to be introduced.

"This is Quinn, my partner," Curt said, indicating a handsome man with red hair, a moustache and goatee.

"Nice to meet you," Clayton said, shaking Quinn's hand. "I need a beer."

"And this is Ian," Curt continued. "He's the Blanche of our group. Also a retired physician with a passion for examinations. He brings his own gloves."

"Manners," Ian said evenly to Curt. Ian was very handsome, with a boyish air.

"Hi Ian. I'm Clayton. Good to meet you."

"You too," Ian said. "Manners," he remarked again to Curt.

"You look too young to be retired," Clayton added.

"He's sitting with me, bitches," Ian shouted at the others and pulled Clayton in close to him. "Don't you fucking dare!"

"I need a beer," Clayton repeated, uncomfortable being the centre of attention.

"And this is Preston, our fearless leader."

"You have a leader?"

"No," Curt laughed. "He's just the tallest."

"Nice to meet you, Preston," Clayton said.

"You look like you need a beer," Preston said, shaking Clayton's hand and looking him in the eye. Then he leaned forward, grabbed Clayton by the shoulders and whispered in his ear, "I only drink beer in private. I like the feel of a glass in my hand. Bottles just don't cut it with me." He released Clayton and settled back into his seat. "Also, you never know where they've been."

"Speaking of which... Waiter? Waiter!" Curt shouted into the room. A muscular young man in a tight shirt ambled over to their table, glanced at Curt and then took a step away from him.

"What's that all about?" Curt said, noticing the distance.

"It's your wandering hands, dear," Quinn said.

"Our new friend would like a beer."

"What would you like?" the man asked Clayton.

"Una Pacifico por favor. ¿Tiene tequila El Compadre?"

The waiter grimaced. Clayton looked to Curt, and then the others around him. They all stared back at him. He couldn't tell if he'd mispronounced a word or if El Compadre was an undesirable brand. *Probably both.*

"Apparently I have terrible taste in tequila," he said. "Which should come as no shock since I'm from Canada."

The waiter offered a weak smile.

"We only get about ten brands. Okay. Something reasonably priced," he said to the man. "No muy caro."

"You really know your Spanish," Quinn said. The waiter rolled his eyes and walked away.

Ian chuckled at the waiter, and smiled at Clayton. "Don't you love it when ordering a drink induces trauma? That's why I stick with beer in places like this. Less chance for communication breakdown. Also, I love the way they cut their lime wedges. Check it out when yours comes. There's always some kind of symbol carved into the rind. It's like the beer witch project." He smiled at his own joke.

"Where are you guys all from?"

"Michigan," Curt said.

"Holland," said Ian.

"Beechwood," Preston chimed in.

"Macatawa," said Quinn, pointing at himself and Curt. "All small towns not far from each other."

"So you all planned your trips together? That's smart."

"No, we had no idea each other was coming, actually."

"Really? That's... Kind of odd, don't you think?"

"No. How many people from Trana are here?"

"Oh, don't get me started on that," Clayton said.

"Why? What's wrong with people from Trana?" Ian asked.

Clayton laughed at the continued use of Trana. "Well, it seems they all pack their attitude and bring it down here instead of giving it a vacation as well." Curt's friends exchanged glances. "You pass by people on the beach who live in the same building as you and they look at you and throw their heads up in the air like they're trying to prevent a nosebleed. It's funny. Kind of. Actually, not really. It's disturbing. And I wonder what it means, you know, what's going on inside their minds."

"How big is his cock?" said Preston.

"Fucking queens." Curt nudged Quinn and sat down beside him on the banquette. "It's one of the drawbacks of living in a big city."

"So the city's to blame?" Clayton asked.

"No," Curt stammered. "But you don't really see much of that from small town folks. They're much friendlier. Unless you fuck their boyfriend."

The waiter arrived with Clayton's drinks.

"Gracias," Clayton said, and raised his beer bottle in front of the men around him. "Salud," he said.

"Cheers!" they called out, clinking their glasses and bottles in the air together. Quinn's cracked. He withdrew it quickly as its contents spilled over their table top and chunks of broken glass landed with a muted clink. Quinn's jaw dropped open in surprise as he dropped the remnants of the glass to the floor.

Curt looked at him as if he were a child. "Am I going to have to spank you when we get home?"

"Sunburn," was all Quinn said, bending over to pick up the pieces of broken glass.

"On your ass too?"

"Aloe," Ian said quietly, then cracked a smile. "And poppers."

Las Perras de Puerto Vallarta

The next morning Clayton rose at ten. He stood under the hot spray of his hotel room shower waiting for the steam to shoo away the throbbing in his head. He was unsuccessful. The towels were prickly but smelt good. He made a mental note to himself to ask the concierge at the front desk what detergent they use. *Would they let me take laundry detergent through customs? I could put it in my suitcase...*

The previous afternoon, the concierge stared wide-eyed at his chest when Clayton showed up wearing only a pair of shorts asking for a beach towel. When Clayton saw the man's eyes were focused on his nipples he looked down and offered an embarrassed smile. After a brief and awkward silence—punctuated by the young man's determined stare—Clayton looked back at him curiously, surprised by the attention.

"They're so... Big," the concierge finally said.

Nobody had noticed his nipples before; perhaps because he never took his shirt off in public. He wasn't comfortable having a part of his body segregated and commented upon, but he also acknowledged that it wasn't really in his control what people thought of him. *But that's what happens when you go shirtless. Drawn and quartered.*

After rubbing his skin gently with a bath towel, he smoothed Aloe gel over himself, stopping to look at his reflection in the mirror. *I should stop pulling on them. Or work out. But not both.* When the Aloe had been absorbed into his skin, he pulled last night's aquamarine tee shirt over his head. He leaned down and picked up the pair of khaki shorts he had also worn last night, the pair he was wearing when he had gone to Garbo's to meet Curt and his friends.

The shorts were long enough to cover the birthmark on his left thigh. People would always comment on it when they saw it, often asking if it was a tattoo. *An uneven brown tattoo in the shape of a withering pear?* He wondered what kind of person would mistake his birthmark for a tattoo, and who would get a brown tattoo of a pear—at least on purpose. But then again, the tattoos he's seen on some younger guys were so ugly and randomly placed that it would take a team of experts to uncover their meaning, if there were any. He checked himself in the mirror one last time before grabbing his room key. Moving to the wall safe, he punched in the four-digit code and pulled several bills from his wallet. *My hair.*

He returned to the bathroom and quickly scrunched his hair down with hairspray, although at this hour he did not particularly care how he looked. That's what he told himself. But what would explain the small duffle bag of creams, lotions and toners he had brought with him that now lined the marble mantle of the hotel bathroom? His eyes swept past the row of product, up to his reflection in the mirror, to his gut, protruding, and then to his face and hair. *Looks hurried,* he thought, eyes lolling up and down. *Fuck it. It's morning.*

Clayton's determination to resist peer pressure was one of the many issues he had carried forward from childhood. At fifty, he had asked himself many times when he would embrace adulthood. His therapist often asked him why he thought so much about the pressure to conform. Clayton would shrug and the therapist would jot something down in his notebook. Clayton was obstinate; they both knew it. He never liked easy answers, quick answers or people who talked too much about how little they knew. He had convinced himself that his behaviour was not about conformity or a response to it, but rather that it was an indication of a potentially valuable trait that had not yet been appraised. The therapist suggested that perhaps he just liked to rebel, to question and to make people think, usually about unpleasant subjects. Through the years, Clayton's inability to harness his rebellious nature had fractured almost every important relationship he had had. When his therapist suggested exercising discretion, and to stop to think before speaking, Clayton pouted and lamented, *I want to think less. I'm alone.*

I'm alone, he thought as he looked around the hotel room for ankle socks. His cell phone blipped in the background.

—Where the hell are you? We r on the beach

—Getting dressed

—Green chairs

—B there in 1 hour

Green Chairs was where they were. Clayton would go there, albeit reluctantly, and see how he felt, see if he fit in, with the group he had met last night. *How am I going to remember their names?* He had had his yogurt, coffee and breakfast bagel, and changed into his bathing suit and a bright yellow tee-shirt. He stared at himself in the mirror for a moment, taking a few deep breaths, and then locked his phone and wallet in the room safe. He nodded at the concierge, a different man than yesterday, older, with an unabashed smile, who seemed less likely to comment about his nipples, so Clayton thought.

He walked down Pilitas and stopped where the concrete sidewalk ended and the beach began. He flicked off his sandals and scooped them up in his left hand, his right hand pressed a rolled-up towel with a bottle of fifty SPF wedged inside it up against his side. The sun reflecting on the surface of the ocean before him, the crash of the waves on the shore, sun worshippers straddling a variety of beach chairs, the lack of bite in the air, the din of Spanish from locals in the background, the warmth that welcomed him: this really was a little bit of heaven. *There's a reason I keep coming back here,* he thought to himself, although after five years and six trips to Vallarta, Clayton was unsure of the reason. *Familiarity? Has to be it.*

He recalled his first trip to Vallarta in 2010. Clayton had met up with a former friend who had been spending winters there for several years. He carved out a daily routine in his friend's absences: breakfast alone at Freddy's Tucan, a jog back to the hotel to use the bathroom, followed by a two hour walk up and down the beach, alone, passing the hordes of glistening gay men at the Blue Chairs. He would have the Carpenters' *Gold* album playing on his MP3 player, or *Regarding the Soul* by Dee Carstensen, or a selection of Mexican music he scrambled to put together days before the trip. "El Rey," by José Rafael Jiménez, "Mexico, Lindo y Querido," by Mariachi Arriba Juárez, "Bésame Mucho," by Gigliola Cinquetti y el trio Los Panchos and, of course, Los Panchos' "Lo Dudo," which he had loved ever since he saw Almodóvar's *La ley del deseo* at the Toronto Film Festival in 1987. Since his first visit, Clayton had booked the trips craving warmth, good food, cheap drinks and the opportunity to practice a bit of the Spanish he had been learning. Each of the trips held few surprises and, with the exception of a handful of awkward encounters with his former friend, the vacations unravelled almost precisely the way the ones that preceded it had. *¡Hola! Pacifico. El compadre. ¡Qué perra! Estoy borracho. ¿Dónde está el baño? Pepto Bismol. Rinse. Repeat. Nos vemos el proximo año.*

As he approached the Green Chairs area—officially known as Ritmos Beach Café on Playa Los Muertos, identifiable by row upon row of green beach recliners, just a few dozen yards from the Blue Chairs which had stood for years as the official gay section of the beach—something tugged at Clayton's subconscious. Another memory bubbled up. On that first visit to Vallarta he had stopped in front of the Blue Chairs when his MP3 player fell silent. He fiddled with the device, squinting in the glare of the sun, selected a new playlist and then looked up at the row of chairs to his left.

An older male couple smeared sunscreen on each other's backs as they both gawked at a young man, no older than twenty-one, emerging from the surf and flicking sand from the inside of his bathing suit. A hairy daddy type with everything pierced stood alone smoking a cigar. A few feet behind him, a young skinny boy with sunburned skin waved cigar smoke away from his face. Hard, edgy house music hammered out of speakers located along the beach, something Clayton hated, and not just for aesthetic reasons. Thump thump thump thump. Clayton looked at the sea of men jammed in together on the beach as the bass line from the song hit him in the solar plexus. *These guys would find a way to turn the Grand Canyon into a discotheque. Can't they just sit and look out into the air? There's no room for independent thought in this crowd. We all have to be thinking the same thing at the same time—cock, Madonna, ass, liquor, balls—or we don't belong.*

Fuck, why did I come here?

He had reimagined *Invasion of the Body Snatchers* as a contemporary story about not fitting in to the group to which society dictated you belonged and everyone around you is pointing and hissing and screaming that you should join in, don some attitude, lower your guard and sensibilities. *Acquiesce. Shop, brag, and always carry a designer bag.* A tiny knot had tightened in Clayton's stomach on that trip. It reminded him of home, the gay village he had never felt a part of no matter how hard he tried, the harsh, judgmental looks from clusters of younger gay men and the residual feeling that not only did he not belong, he never had, and he never would. He was not wanted. He was less than invisible. He was fifty. Yes, he could escape the cold and snow, but some things—cliques, clusters and cults—were unavoidable. *It's like Church Street with sand here. Why did I come?*

Each and every time he walked Los Muertos beach on subsequent trips, a knot tightened inside him when he approached the Blue Chairs. To avoid the wave of negativity he would stop when he was in front of the Tropicana Hotel and turn back in the opposite direction to continue his walk. In the intervening years he had tried, with varying degrees of success, to walk past the army of glistening gay boys, gay men, daddies and their ilk. *Isn't this a perverse form of segregation?* he asked himself. *Not if it's voluntary,* was the response in his head. *So what is it? Why do they like it and why do I hate it? They're supposed to be my brothers, according to their lingo. Community this, community that, brothers and sisters, blind. They don't see me. I'm not a part of whatever they are, whatever that is. Mass market gay. I don't belong. So I am a—*

"Clay!" a voice called out above the noise.

Clayton looked up and over, pulled off his sunglasses and peered through the crowd until he saw hands waving. In that moment, without consciously acknowledging what was happening, he dropped his guard and let his issues subside. *It's just a flock of gay men. Nothing more.* His awareness of what had happened—a bit slow to take shape—would come later.

He spotted Ian and Preston among the others who had their backs to him. Making his way between the rows of beach chairs and bodies, Clayton found they had saved him a spot. He draped his towel over the chair and sat down.

The gang had arranged their collapsible green recliners in an uneven circle. Clayton's seat was in the centre, facing the ocean, with row after row of beach chairs and bodies in between. He took off his shirt, wadded it into a ball and dropped it between his feet, making a point to jam his toes into the sand to cover up the missing nails on his baby toes. *What kind of fungus goes only on the baby toes? Is it the fungus or just me, something so innately fucked up about my DNA that I can't even grow a fungus properly on all my toenails?*

He looked up, around. There were new faces in the group, most of them younger; too young to acknowledge as adults. *Ageism is a door that swings both ways. If I were in my twenties, I'd probably have ended that sentence with 'bitches.' Ugh.*

Curt pointed at the man to Clayton's left and introduced him. "This is Hugh. Hugh, Clayton. Clayton, Hugh. He just got in about an hour ago."

"How are you?" Hugh said, looking at Clayton's nipples.

"They're fine, thanks. Are you from Michigan, too?"

"Uh-huh. Wasn't expecting to run into these guys, but glad I did."

"Seriously? You all know each other and are friends and everything but had no idea each other was coming here?"

They all nodded. Preston sucked the remnants from a plastic cup and looked at Clayton.

"What are you having?" His voice was warm and welcoming. His eyes were not focused on Clayton's nipples. "The waiter should be around here somewhere. Tony. Phenomenal calves."

"He's over there," Ian said, pointing with his cup at a man in an orange shirt with long white short pants.

"I always start the day with a Tanqueray and tonic," Preston continued, peering over his sunglasses as Clayton looked down at his own nipples. *They're not that big.* "It's so much better here because of the limes," Preston said. "A fresh lime makes a drink."

"It's too early for me," Clayton said, looking at the deep tan of the approaching waiter's skin, at his handsome face and peaceful expression. *What is it about Mexican men? What colour is that? Burnt caramel? Hazy cinnamon? Bronzed coffee?* He wished he could run his tongue along the man's arms, or legs. Or bury his face in his armpits.

"They're not with us, by the way," Preston said, pointing his straw at the young men at the other side of the circle.

"Hola amigos," the waiter in orange and white said as he approached, flipping through pages on a small pad he held in his hand. "Something to drink?"

He flashed a quick smile at Clayton, or was squinting from the mid-day sun.

"Tell him your name," Preston said. "They'll run you a tab if you give them your name."

"John Trick," said one of the young boys at the edge of their circle. A smattering of girlish laughter was quickly muffled by the sound of the waves pounding on the shore.

Church Street with sand. Clayton shook that thought out of his head and looked at the waiter. He was compact and handsome, with muscular arms and calves that flared out like he'd never seen before. *Straight? Probably. Or somewhere outside of it perhaps? I bet you'll never see a waiter in Mexico refusing to serve a gay or lesbian person. And this country is way more religious. What the fuck is going on in the United States? Idiots in bakeries and pizza parlours and now EMTs wanting to subvert their humanity in favour of their reli— What is it?*, he wondered. *Religious narcissism? Yes, that's what it is. It is. But even more than that. It's religious terrorism. Humanity is hellbound. Why do people refuse to think?*

"I'll have a— What did I have yesterday morning after the gin and tonic?" Preston's deep and resonant voice pulled Clayton away from his thoughts. "Do you remember, Tony?"

Clayton listened to the nuances in Preston's tone, to the subtle suggestions he thought he heard. Even in ordering a cocktail there was an undertone of seduction. *What did I have after the gin and tonic?* might as well have been, *Come wrap your lips around my enormous cock.* At least that's what Clayton heard. And it wasn't just Preston. It seemed to Clayton that gay men had elaborated the double entendre to encompass almost every single syllable they uttered. He wondered why. *The need to cram as much information as possible into every word they speak? The need for attention? The drive to be smarter, better, bitchier, flashier than everyone else—or at least to give an appearance to that effect? This is how I compensate for being looked down upon, shut out, villainized, repressed, hated. We're not all like that,* he protested in his thoughts. *Honestly. But how to convince the world that their version of me is simply that—their version?*

The waiter looked up at the sky. Clayton followed his glance, took in a deep breath, smiled. The man craned his neck back down to look at Clayton as he pondered Preston's cocktail order yesterday mid-morning, and then an awareness showed in his eyes. He smiled and looked over at Preston. "Rum punch," he said.

"Oh, then no," Preston said with a frown. "I don't want that right now. Too strong. That's a mid-afternoon cocktail, I think, not a mid-morning cocktail. How about a strawberry margarita, Tony? Thanks."

The waiter flipped through pages of his notepad and gave a little shrug.

"Preston," said Preston, to clarify.

"Señor Preston," the waiter mumbled, and, finding Preston's page, scribbled on it. "Margarita de fresa," he said to himself and then looked at Clayton. "And for you?"

"Just a bottle of water, please," Clayton said. "My name is Clayton."

"Large or small?"

"Large, thanks. What's your name?"

"Antonio."

Clayton looked at Preston and whispered, "Why are you calling him Tony? His name is Antonio. This isn't Italy."

"Whatever." Emphasis on *what*. It was a real outdoor voice. It perfectly suited Preston. Tall—lumbering one might even say—well built and with really large hands, Clayton was sure that he was popular with the boys.

Antonio looked around the circle. "Okay?"

"Gracias." Preston's voice was like a warm caress. He waved the man away with a flick of his wrist.

Someone yelled behind them. Clayton thought he heard a line of dialogue from *Terms of Endearment*, but wasn't sure. He turned and saw a group of five men in their twenties sitting around a wooden table. On the table were five cell phones, five drinks, an overturned baseball cap and over a dozen bottles of sunblock.

"That's so easy I don't even need to grab my phone," one of the others said. "*The Exorcist*, duh."

"Not duh," another voice called out, prissy and commanding. "*Terms of Endearment*."

Clayton was immediately pulled into a sandstorm of negative thoughts. He cocked his head and looked at the faces of the young men behind them.

"Omigawd," one of them shrieked. "Like, how old are you?" Pronounced *ee-you-wah*.

"Like my grandmother made me watch it, okay? Shut up, bitch."

Clayton frowned listening to the boys' banter. *Where do*

these speech patterns come from? Friends, and friends of friends, and cheap, unscripted, poorly edited television shows. There's not a shred of individuality in their discourse. People are literally cutting and pasting speech patterns in real life. Nobody gives a shit about what they say. The only important thing is that they're heard. Bullshit bullshit bullshit inflection. Hand gesture. Pay attention to my vapidity!

"Yeah like can't we amp this up a bit? Another young voice pleaded.

Clayton turned back to his group. "What are they doing?"

"Re-enacting their high school prom," Ian said, a sly smile on his face.

"Which was three weeks ago, by the look of it," Preston deadpanned.

"You bitches are gonna regret that," one of them cried out. "Whose turn is it?"

"Mine. Pass me the hat so I can get my quote. Oh. Okay. Ready? 'This is the first last time we'll jam together.' Anyone? And... Go!"

Four sets of hands thrust forward, grabbed four cell phones. Fingers furiously jabbed at buttons.

Preston leaned forward and said in a hushed voice, "If you're going to eavesdrop, you'll need an interpreter. They only speak like awesome."

"What's that?" Clayton asked, laughing.

"It's like a new like language, dude," Ian smiled.

"Like awesome, man. It's like like awesome is like awesome."

"Awesome," Hugh sniggered, shaking his head.

There was something in the young guys' voices that got underneath Clayton's skin, left a sour taste. *Too many fucking catch phrases, not enough diversity, too many words. Just like in pop music,* he thought. *The attempt to be cool is ruining the English language and maiming our attempts at communication. Who is responsible? All the lazy, not-cool people.*

Hard stares as they refocused on the young men's game. One of them grunted in frustration.

"Fucking wi-fi sucks on the beach!"

"Get the waiter to call someone."

"Security!" Laughter, shrieking laughter.

"Excuse me, miss!" someone shouted. Giggles. More fingers punching and anxious groans.

"Mine's working!"

"Got it! Oh, wait. What's Farsi?"

"Well, they don't have the skills to actually carry on a conversation," Ian quipped, peering over his sunglasses at the group of young men. "And they can't breathe without their cell phones, so they do this movie quote game. But it only works if they don't know where the quote is from. At least that's what I've gathered so far."

"And they've been doing it for three days," Preston added. "I hope they're not here for two weeks. Imagine not knowing how to end the sentence, 'Luke, I'm your....'?"

"Sex surrogate?" Hugh offered. Preston dipped his index finger into his drink and flicked it at him.

"I still don't get it," said Quinn.

"You're not supposed to." That was Ian.

"Whoever grabs their cell phone and looks up the quotation on the internet first wins."

"Really" Clayton asked, incredulous. "That's a game now? I thought technology was supposed to make people smarter and more effective."

"Keeps them from falling asleep," Preston said. "Or dying of irony."

"What do they win?"

Shrugs around the circle.

"We go by rounds," one of the boys behind Clayton answered in a tone of voice that was as proud as it was uncertain. He leaned forward, his neck craned, eyes on Clayton. "And we all have really good hearing, so like... We can hear you talking about us. Case you were wondering is all. And we know how to hold a conversation."

"Prove it," Preston said under his breath. He turned to Clayton and mouthed the word *awesome*.

Clayton flashed Preston a quick smile, and then returned his glance to the young man who had just spoken. His voice had phrased each statement as though it were a question, with the inflections going up at the end of each sentence. The result made it sound as if he were asking a question or, at the very least, was unsure of what he was saying. Clayton did not know how to process what he was hearing. Statements sounded like questions. *Who has the answers? Who is the authority? Nobody. We are all one massive, unknowing mass. Join us. Join us!*

"*Big Guitar*," Clayton said. "In case you were wondering."

"Oh, a movie buff daddy!"

"Don't call me daddy."

"Well you certainly can't call him buff," Preston muttered.

Curt shifted forward in his chair to listen to the exchange. "Cat fight," he said, grinning.

"Did you like *Llewyn Davis*?

"Yeah," Clayton said. "Except for the colour grading. It's the same as all that rapid-fire editing that induces A.D.D. and draws attention to itself and not the characters or story. It's like hi, I know we're supposed to be having sex but, hey! Why don't you just watch me masturbating instead, everybody? Okay? Look at me masterfully stroking my erect penis! It's not about anything else other than me—"

Clayton heard his own words reverberate in his head. Everyone around him stared in silence.

"Don't we have an opinion about *every*thing?" Preston cracked. "You weren't this talkative last night."

"I wasn't hungover last night."

"So can we expect you to extol the virtues of masturbation every morning or just when you're hungover?"

"Hey, hey," the boy interrupted. "Did you like bring a phone with you?"

"No, but thanks," Clayton said, and then wished he'd worked at least one *awesome* into his response, just to be ironic. Or cunty.

Antonio appeared a few minutes later with their drinks, adjusting his weight and balance to the uneven slope of the beach and the shifting of the sand beneath his feet as he walked, his tray remaining perfectly level all the while. He handed Preston a plastic glass filled with a bright red liquid, and a large bottle of water to Clayton.

Preston tore the paper wrapping off the top of the straw and sucked some of the margarita back. He pushed the straw out of his mouth with his tongue. His lips formed a thin straight line across his face, downward at the ends. "Mealy," he said, smacking his lips and looking at no one in particular.

Clayton smiled, uncapped his water bottle and took a swig.

"So who is here that wasn't there last night?"

"Oh," said Ian, piping to attention. "The kids at the edge there, we don't know them. They just sat with us. Everybody this is Clayton. Clayton this is... Everybody."

Laughter rose up from some of the men Clayton had not yet met.

"I think there's a Paul," Hugh said, lighting a cigarette. "Peter, maybe? I don't know. I just got here, and frankly, I don't give a shit."

Clayton settled in and wondered how long he would last in the sun before he was overcome by the feeling of restlessness, or worse, that awful feeling of his innards boiling that goes hand in hand with being in the sun for prolonged periods while hungover. This was the first time he had actually sat down on the beach in Vallarta. *Six trips*, he thought. Normally he would be at the pool at the Tropicana Hotel where he preferred to stay. Normally...

One of the boys barked out a Meryl Streep line from *Death*

Becomes Her. "Anyone? And... Go!" Clayton turned his head to the side and saw hands grabbing phones. *Death Becomes Her*, he thought to himself. *It should be a feather in Robert Zemeckis' cap. Instead, it's forgotten or dimly remembered as a box-office failure. Stupid people. I hope Scream Factory releases it.*

Clayton scanned the men in the circle around him. When he got to Preston, he noticed two reddish-purple marks on his neck. "I think you got bit," he said quietly, eyes on Preston's neck.

"I wish," was all Preston said. Then suddenly he sat up in his chair and pulled off his sunglasses. "Should we wave Tony down for..." His voice trailed off as he glanced at his watch. "Never mind. It's too early for lunch." He glanced at Clayton and corrected himself. "Antonio."

Clayton scanned the group again. Everyone had a scar, either on their chest or neck. "That's kind of cool," he said. "Or interesting."

"What?" asked Hugh, offering Clayton a cigarette.

"Oh, thanks. I left mine in my room. I was just noticing that everyone has a scar."

"Everyone's over forty," Preston replied.

"Hugh, you're burning," said Ian said, pointing at Hugh's chest.

"I don't wear sunblock," Hugh leaned in to Clayton and offered his explanation as he lit a cigarette.

"He won't wear sunblock," Preston repeated to no one in particular.

"Then you should be wearing a turtleneck," said Clayton, inhaling.

"Or a hazmat suit," Preston said, pulling the straw back into his mouth. "He's afraid the chemicals in sunblock are worse than skin cancer."

"We all end up in the ground anyway," Clayton said.

"Cheery thought," added Quinn.

Everyone in the circle looked at Clayton. The weight of their attention on him would have made his knees buckle had he been standing, but seated, he simply let the familiar feeling of ostracisation settle in. He was used to it, and although he blushed, in the glare of the sun nobody could tell. *These are the things that keep me apart. Fuck.*

"Sometimes I..." He felt the energy diminish as he spoke, knowing full well he didn't know how to defend himself unless it was to say something negative. "Need to remember to lighten the mood, not darken it."

"It's okay, dear," Preston said, wincing as he swallowed the bright red liquid. "You're cute, and no one's listening."

Shrieks rang out from a group of men sitting closest to the shoreline as an enormous wave crashed down and swept up the slope of the beach soaking their feet and legs. A dozen men jumped up from their beach chairs, flailing towels in the air and grabbing at their electronic devices like they were severed appendages.

Clayton was immediately aware that his head was shaking from side to side as he watched the men at the shoreline rearranging their chairs, towels and belongings with the utmost focus and precision, further back from the water. The scenario struck him as very contrived. Foreign, but not quite. *Because it was so familiar? Hmmmm. I am of it, but yet am not in it. Or am I?* He recalled an episode of Kathy Griffin's TV show where she fixed up a school in Puerto Vallarta while on vacation, hoping to out-Oprah Oprah. *I wonder if she's here. Right now. Looking out of her plush condo, looking down on her gays.*

Where are my gays? Clayton wondered. *Where are my authentic gays?* He looked around. *There must be a vacation spot somewhere on the planet where the authentic gay male traveller goes. This is not it. At least not on my budget.* He felt the internal clink of his negative armour clamping tightly shut but it dissipated almost as quickly. That was a surprise—a big one. Normally he would settle in with a negative thought or inner monologue and let it play out. But now he was left with the resounding feeling in his mind and body of something new and liberating—an opening, some free mental space without judgment or negativity. *Oh,* he thought. *That's... What is that?* Years of anger and alienation and the fear of rejection and the anticipation of the sting of rejection fell away and out of his body, through the pores of his skin and trickled down and in between the grains of sand beneath him and down, down into the earth. *I am part of a group. They invited me. They sought me out and invited me into their circle.*

He felt the sun on his skin and the sand between his toes. He breathed deeply, a subtly ecstatic sigh.

"Elastic Heart" played on the speakers nearby.

"This song is following us," Curt said. "How many times did we hear it last night? Nine? Ten?"

"You go out to too many places," Ian observed, and reached for a bottle of sixty SPF.

"And you don't?"

"I'm just saying if you stick to one place you probably won't hear the same song over and over. If the deejay is any good, that is."

"Now where's the fun in that?" Preston said. "That's my sixty, Ian."

"I know," Ian said, opening a tube of lotion.

"I thought you were down to thirty," Curt said, flicking sand at Quinn with his feet.

"I'm feeling my age," Ian smiled and squirted lotion into his cupped palm.

"Who's got the one-fifty SPF?"

"Bitch," Quinn scolded Curt.

"I'll see your bitch and raise you one see you next Tuesday," Preston said with a smirk.

—

Back in his bathroom, after he left the gang at the beach to do some work in his room, Clayton's eyes lingered on the tube of Pepto Bismol To Go. He was grateful that he hadn't needed it so far and hoped that he wouldn't have to resort to taking the pink pills to keep his stomach calm. During previous trips he was always nervous about being too far away from the hotel and the safety—and privacy—of his own bathroom.

Something was happening inside his body this trip, he knew it. He ate mole as soon after he had arrived and unpacked, had a single taco from the taco stand with the balloons on it and churros from the street vendor outside La Santa Cruz church with its beautifully designed windows with small crosses etched into the design of the frosted glass, behind wooden shutters with small cut-outs in the shape of crosses. He had wandered around with Francisco and they had ended up having a snack at Cenadurila Celia, a long sliver of a restaurant on Lázaro Cárdenas run by a family anxious to give Clayton their menu in English, even though he would rather have gone through the Spanish menu and asked for help if he came across something he didn't understand. But there, glaring at him at the bottom of the menu, was Pozole. Sold. In less than forty-eight hours, Clayton had eaten more Mexican food than in all of his previous trips combined. Stomach: unresponsive. To him it was a miracle. He wondered how his stomach could be so sensitive on his trip two years before, regardless of how careful he was about what he ate, and be so quiet this trip? *Is it the yogurt? It must be.*

He sat in the shade of his balcony reading a report on escalating ocean temperatures in Eastern Canada and smoked Mexican-manufactured American cigarettes absent-mindedly. After dinner and a lengthy process to pick out what to wear, Clayton met Quinn, Curt, Preston and Hugh at Macho where they took turns buying rounds until Preston was offered a blowjob by Carl, a drunken frat boy from Columbus. Helping Carl to the bathroom, Preston called out, "I'll meet you guys at Fountain Bar. Ian said he'd meet us there around twelve."

Clayton decided to go home and get some more money, and paid close attention to the directions to Fountain Bar. He got lost anyway, walking in circles and ending up repeatedly in front of Wet Dreams, which he refused to interpret as a sign that he should go inside. He eventually gave up and flagged a cab. When he finally arrived at Fountain Bar, Clayton fell instantly in love with the bartender as he mashed fresh ingredients into a mortar and pestle. He saw the gang seated on stools at the bar. There was one reserved for him.

"Took you long enough," Hugh called out and raised his glass in the air.

"My sense of direction—"

"Yeah, yeah. Try this," Hugh said, offering Clayton a sip of his drink. "You'll love it."

"I already love the bartender. What is it?"

"Prime Mexican beef," Quinn said with a wink.

"Cucumber and jalapeño martini," Hugh answered.

The bartender passed by with two drinks in his hands and stopped to greet Clayton.

"How do you get the cucumber taste so forward in the drink?"

"Put cucumber in it," he answered with a wink. "I'll be back," he said, and turned away and moved along the bar. Clayton noticed his brown eyes, thought of José.

"I keep saying, it's Mexico," Curt shrugged. "Why would anyone use artificial ingredients when the real thing is probably more abundant and way less expensive?"

"Convenience."

"Prep time."

"Tourists. Lots and lots of tourists."

"He sure is handsome," Clayton said to Ian.

Ian pulled his chair closer to Clayton's. "It's the lighting," he said. "Or you've got cataracts."

Hugh piped in to fill Clayton in on the details. "His name is Arturo," he said with a serious tone. "He's single and doesn't sleep around."

Curt made the sound of a wrong-answer buzzer from a television game show. "Next?"

"He runs the bar with his cousin. He's very business oriented and only dates men older than him who are serious about relationships," Hugh continued. "Apparently he's had a hard time finding people to work for him."

"How do you know all this?"

"The place was empty when I got here," Hugh said with a

shrug.

"I should get a job here and that way I could spend the whole winter in P.V." Clayton looked around at the lounge. "You think I could get around the immigration?"

"Or the decor," Quinn monotoned.

"Fuck the decor," Curt said. "How big is his pinga?" He craned his neck to get a glimpse of the bartender's crotch.

"Verga," Clayton corrected him. "Pinga is more Cuba, I think."

"Pollo," said Ian.

"Polla," Clayton said. "Pollo is chicken. It's polla. And more from Spain, I think. Don't confuse dinner with dessert."

"What about South America?"

"I don't know, Quinn. I haven't been yet. It's pija in Argentina, though. Probably most of the Central Americas too. I've also heard pito, palo, pajaro, pene, pajarito."

"In how many languages can you say the word cock?" a deep voice called out behind them. They turned around on their stools and saw Preston standing there.

"That was fast!"

"What happened?"

"Carl turned out to be more of a Carl Jr.," Preston said, pulling an empty chair over to the bar where his friends sat. "Actually, that's not true. Well it could be true. I didn't look."

"I don't believe that for a minute."

"He sucked me off and asked for money for a cab."

"That's putting your money where your mouth is," Curt joked.

"And then he puked all over the floor," Preston concluded as he looked at the contents of his friends' glasses.

"El exorcista del baño," Clayton laughed. Preston cocked his head, lifted one eyebrow.

"Did you give him the money?" Quinn asked.

"No. Just some toilet paper," Preston said, looking bored.

Arturo appeared behind the bar and smiled at Preston. "What can I get for you?" he asked.

"Hand sanitizer?" Clayton offered.

"Stoli on the rocks with lime."

"Aren't we supposed to be boycotting Russian products?" Curt nudged him. "The Olympics, remember?"

"Fuck. I can't get a break tonight," Preston sighed. "Absolut or—no! Grey Goose?"

"Okay," Arturo smiled and looked at Clayton. "And for you, guapo?"

"The cucumber one I think."

Arturo nodded and moved away to make their drinks. When

he returned, Clayton leaned in to Hugh and whispered something in his ear. Hugh smiled and motioned to get Arturo's attention. "This is our new friend Clayton from Canada. I thought a formal introduction was in order."

Arturo wiped his hands on his apron and smiled a small smile at Clayton. "Nice to meet you. Clay?"

"Encantado," Clayton said, extending his right hand. He took Arturo's hand in his, and gave it a gentle squeeze, hoping to tell him all he would need to know to make him comfortable. *For a friendship. For a kiss. For warm nights together without those annoying quizzical, faraway looks in the eyes that always come before the guy dumps you unceremoniously. For forever. Or at least until you ejaculate. On me. Not in me. José never did that, not once. Puff.* Clayton dragged on his cigarette. *If only I could exhale José.*

"I told him all about you, Arturo. He says he wants to come and work here next year. Are you hiring? Do you think you'll still be open?"

"Of course I'll still be open," Arturo said with mock disgust, eyes bulging. "Unless I die, which I'm going to if I don't have a cigarette soon." He slid around the end of the bar, wormed his way in between Clayton and Hugh and wrapped his arms around both men's shoulders. "Can I have one of yours? Do you mind?" He said to Clayton, nestling his head sideways into his neck. Clayton inhaled deeply as his nose grazed the skin of Arturo's neck. He had a clean, earthy aroma. *No cologne. Un milagro.*

Clayton raised the pack of Marlboro Blancos and flicked open the top. Arturo's fingers brushed against Clayton's hand as he pulled a cigarette from the package. Clayton grabbed Hugh's lighter and stared at Arturo's cigarette, watched how he positioned his fingers around it, hoping to see if he was a real smoker or just freelance. He held it like a pro. Clayton's penis stiffened.

"You want to live here?" Arturo asked, exhaling smoke through his nose.

"Yes, but not in summer," Clayton said. "I was here in September once and it just about killed me. Wherever I went people called me el gringo mojado. It was true. Thirty seconds after leaving the hotel room I was soaking wet. By the third day I had gone through all my clothes for the week and had to take everything to the laundry. Never again."

"You're not gringo if you're from Canada," Arturo said.

"That's the nicest thing anyone's said to me all day."

"And you have a beautiful ass."

"Now that's the nicest thing anyone's said to me all week."

"You have very good eyesight," Curt interjected. "It's really dark in here."

"Stand up and let me see," Arturo said, unembracing the two men and goading Clayton to stand up and show his ass. Clayton gave Hugh a look he hoped was just like the one Olivia Newton-John gave Dinah Manoff in *Grease*, at the beginning of "You're The One That I Want," when Olivia didn't know what to do with the cigarette in her mouth.

Hugh pulled on Clayton's arm, helped him to stand up. Clayton felt Arturo's hands moving slowly down his back and resting on the rounds of his ass cheeks. "Mmmm. Qué rico," he said, exhaling smoke at the same time.

Two drinks later—another cucumber and jalapeño martini and a blackberry and basil mojito—they left Fountain Bar and walked Ian and Hugh to the Mercurio Hotel. Clayton, Preston, Curt and Quinn continued on to Sama for a martini but it had already closed up, so they retreated to Garbo's for last call.

They were the only customers left, and sat at the bar and talked with one of the owners. When Clayton had finished his beer, he noticed the bartender wasn't offering more, and figured it was time to go to bed.

Outside on the crooked cobblestone sidewalk they said their goodbyes. Curt grabbed Clayton's ass before turning away. "The bartender at Fountain Bar sure loved your ass," he said, "But I wanna eat it."

"Go home and eat your husband's ass," Preston interjected and then wheeled around to face Clayton. "I'm getting a second wind."

"It's after two."

"I'm going to the sauna," he said with finality. "I go crazy if I don't fuck every three days."

"You've got some kind of alarm system that goes off?"

"Yeah, it's called my big hard dick."

Back in his hotel room, Clayton brushed his teeth and patted his face with Witch Hazel before climbing in to bed. Looking up at the ceiling, he wondered how lame some of his sexual exploits might seem to other gay men, Preston in particular. The late nights doing laps at the local bathhouse, never finding anyone who wanted him or was willing to wear a condom. He thought of the handful of men he had been with over the last few years. Come and gone. *Cum and gone*. He thought of José and the electric, magical sex haze they created together. *Was it him? Puff? Or was it the pot? Maybe I'll never know.* He exhaled loudly and closed his eyes and waited for sleep. *Not everyone finds a mate*, he told himself. *Yes, that's comforting. Sometimes life stops you from finding love. What the fuck am I supposed to find instead?*

Treading Water

Antonio was not their waiter the next morning on the beach. Another forty-something year-old man named Carlos brought them their drinks. Again, Clayton joined the group long after they had rooted themselves in their circle of chairs.

"What happened there?" Hugh said, pointing at the long, jagged scar on Clayton's right shoulder.

"It's the funniest story—" he began to say, but was interrupted by the waiter.

"Señores," Carlos said, sweat dribbling down his cheek, neck and disappearing beneath his shirt collar. Carlos held out a Pacifico for Clayton, a melon margarita for Preston, Rum and Coke for Ian and a large bottle of water for Hugh, who was turning an entirely new shade of red.

"Gracias," Clayton said to the waiter and squeezed a lime segment into the opening of the elongated neck of the beer bottle.

"De nada."

Clayton watched Preston take his first sip.

"Mealy?" he asked.

"No, this one's good. Must have been the strawberry."

"Mealy?" Ian asked. "Mealy O'Hara?"

"Preston's drink wasn't up to his liking yesterday morning. He said it was mealy. I don't think I've ever heard that word used before. Now I can't get it out of my head."

"Whatever happened to Kylie Minogue?" Quinn asked.

Clayton imagined yesterday's phone grabbers clutching their phones and pounding their fingers into the keys to get an update. He turned around and looked behind him. The boys weren't there. "She's still recording and touring," he answered.

"So what happened to your shoulder?" Hugh asked Clayton.

"I slid on a pile of records and knocked myself unconscious."

"No wonder you hate music," Preston mumbled.

"Records?!" Ian said loudly and then broke into a hearty laugh.

"You're old enough to remember," Preston smirked. "When they first came out. Remember? 78s?"

"I fell and landed right there," Clayton said, balling his left hand up and striking it against his right shoulder. "On one of those old fashioned steel packing trunks."

"I hope the records were good."

"Don't ask," Clayton said. "What about your neck there, Preston? You were going to tell me yesterday before we were interrupted by your mealy drink."

"Cancer," he said.

"Are you...?"

"I wouldn't be here baking in the sun if I weren't all right." He glanced at Hugh. "Or would I?"

"Good question," Hugh said, his eyes holding on Preston.

The look that passed between the two of them revealed something shared but sombre. Not secret; intimate. Clayton witnessed it, said nothing.

"I intend to go back a very nice shade of mahogany," Curt said. "Did the doctor say the scar would heal or will you have it forever?"

"Apparently it'll fall off and leave very faintly discoloured skin afterwards. I can live with that."

"Almost didn't," Hugh added.

"Was it horrible?"

"Actually, Clay, it was. I was really sick for a while. Luckily my whateveryouwannacallhim wasn't squeamish and took good care of me, but... I missed two months of work. But it got better. Now I'm here and in May I go back for my follow-up."

"Hmmm," Clayton mused. "Your whateveryouwanna-callhim?"

"Tom," Preston said quietly.

"His cock shrivelled up to the size of a match," Curt said, leaning in and speaking in an exaggerated whisper.

"Have you all slept together?" Clayton asked, not sure he wanted to know the answer.

"No," grinned Curt.

"I'm just not very private about it." That was Preston.

Curt leaned forward. "It's huge," he said in a loud whisper. "We were all worried it wouldn't come back."

"Like Eve Plumb and *The Brady Bunch Variety Hour*?" Clayton asked, thinking his reference would impress them. Nobody caught it.

Preston smiled and shrugged, picked up his drink and sucked from the straw. "It's not like it fell off or anything. I just couldn't use it."

"And your boyfriend was—"

"Not my boyfriend," Preston cut him off. "Very sore spot for me. He is officially my official whateveryouwannacallhim. And he's... Well, let's leave it at that."

Later, after Preston and the others had convinced Clayton that the ocean was safe and that sharks—the standalone variety or the Roger-Corman-styled dinosaur/shark combination, three-headed or otherwise—don't vacation in Vallarta, Preston and Clayton waded through the white caps and into the calmer water to cool off.

"He's married," Preston elaborated. "Four kids under twelve. Still lives with his wife."

"Oh." Clayton was embarrassed. He reproached himself for being nosey, but he liked understanding people's motivations, attractions and dilemmas. So he had to ask.

"Oh is right," Preston said, treading water.

"So despite your voracious sexual appetite, you're a patient man."

"Don't tell anyone," Preston said. "You'll kill my reputation."

Clayton was still nervous about being in the open water. "I saw *Jaws* at too young an age," he had admitted to the group earlier. "Lakes, too. Thank you, Mr. Spielberg, mom and dad." Clayton did not regret revealing his fear of sharks, however irrational it might seem to others. He rarely thought twice about what he should or should not tell people about himself. *I do not self censor.* He was unsure of how proud he should be about this, and it never occurred to him that his openness might simply be an attempt to overwhelm, alienate or, at the very least, keep people guessing as to who he really was. Someone who knew him better might suggest that he was trying to cultivate a more interesting persona. Most people, however, just thought he was weird. This did not translate well into his private life; rarely did a first date lead to a second. *Yet another playing field into which I do not fit.*

"So what's the problem?" Clayton asked, raising his feet out of the water and treading with his hands. "Why call him your whateveryouwannacallhim?"

"Because he's not my boyfriend and he's more than a fuck buddy."

"Oh," Clayton said, and then: "Oh." His groan made Preston laugh. "What's so funny? This whole boyfriend fuck buddy delineation is one of my big push button issues."

"Obviously," Preston sighed with a bit of a laugh. "Is your therapist on speed dial?"

"I choose to ignore that in the hopes that you are just nervous about talking to me about personal subjects. So, fuck buddy... We've got bears and fucking animal names for every fucking body type there is, but have we come up with a good name for someone who falls between the lines of lover and fuck buddy?"

"I guess you couldn't squeeze another fuck into that sentence, could you?"

"Fuck no," Clayton laughed. "And don't say friend and don't say FWB either."

"That's not a gay term anyway," Preston said. "Or it was and the straights stole it and now we don't want anything to do with it."

"Like disco and Madonna after *Ray of Light*," Clayton added.

"Excuse me? Disco? Post-Ray Madge? I could probably spit and hit a hundred gay men who disagree with you. And a hundred bottoms, too," he joked, knowing full well it wasn't far from the truth.

Clayton said: "Spit? Isn't that illegal?"

"Anywaaaaay, you know what I think?"

"What?"

"I think that people are creatures of habit and Tom has his patterns established and I'm just part of a groove he's already familiar with so he goes with it." Preston had it all sewn up into a nice, easy-to-comprehend package. But Clayton saw an opening.

"You mean sexually?"

"No, more than that. The patterns could be vacations, friends, food, you know? Behaviours."

"Like a type you mean," Clayton tried to clarify.

"A situation. You're not getting this."

"You're not explaining it very well." Clayton defended himself swiftly. He paused when he realized this and smiled a bit; it was an unusual thing for him to do.

"Pardon me, madam," Preston laughed. "Look at you being all alpha male."

"I'm not in my element here."

"Huh?"

"The water? Sharks?"

"Oh, oh, got it. Okay, so let me explain it this way: What happens when you go into the grocery store?"

"Uh, I grab a cart, put on my glasses—"

"Right, and where do you go first?"

"Fruit and vegetables."

"Why?"

"Because it's right there."

"Okay, same thing applies. You need groceries, you go to the grocery store and the first thing in front of you is the fruit and vegetable section so you go there first." Clayton looked confused. Preston continued. "I'm trying to explain that I'm the fruit and vegetables in this guy's grocery store. He doesn't *want* to go there first, but he does because it's an established pattern. See?"

"Okay, fuck the vegetables," Clayton said, somewhat exasperated at the analogy. "But what if he just likes you and doesn't know how to integrate you into his life?" he asked. "People aren't that hard to figure out."

"Oh really? You're single, right?" Silence. A forced smile.

Clayton thought about José, thousands of kilometres away, wondered if he thought about the sweat and sex. It distressed him; he felt a tightness in his throat. He pushed the thoughts down, away.

Preston continued, "Thought so. Anyway, I think he's a little too worried about his kids and their attachments."

"Do you have kids?"

"How is that relevant?"

"Walk a mile in another man's shoes."

"Love means never having to say I have bunions." Preston shook his head, made a sour face.

"That was bad."

"That was bad. I think I'm channelling you."

"So what are you trying to get at?" Clayton looked around him, saw a bald man's head surface in the water a few feet away from him. Instantly he tensed, then relaxed when he was sure it wasn't a dorsal fin.

"You'd think he would divorce his wife," Preston said, obviously frustrated.

"You mean *you* think he should," Clayton said, spitting some sea water from his mouth.

"Good point, good point. But then again, most people would say they should divorce based on the fact that he's gay and they aren't really a couple," Preston said.

"Do you have the data to back that up?"

"Don't make fun of me when I'm trying to help you understand this," Preston scolded.

"I thought we were trying to help *you* understand it. Unfortunately I know all about this first hand, so I don't need a tutorial."

"There's a red flag," Preston said.

"Does your theory apply to all couples who don't have sex?" Clayton asked. "Should they all split up? What about love and connections, history, loneliness, benefits? The fear of an empty dance card?"

"Careful, you're dating yourself."

"No one else will."

"Why do you always have to dig at everything? Seriously. I mean I can drown you now if that'll make this conversation end."

"Yes, I always dig," Clayton said. "Sorry. It's the Terrier in me."

"It's all right. Just shut up and let me finish. Some people I've talked to about this think they should just get the divorce over with, explain it to the kids..."

"But most people are stupid and think in bumper stickers. How else can you explain the popularity of—"

"Please don't make this an analogy of what's going on in pop music."

Clayton gasped. "I can't believe you know that about me already." He was genuinely shocked and embarrassed.

"You went on about that the first night at Garbo's. Beyoncé this, Gaga that. And poor Madonna is all I have to say."

"Get out!"

"Of the ocean?"

"I just can't believe I let loose so quickly. Or easily. Must have been the tequila."

"Uh-huh. And you really offended the piano player."

"Did he play that song from *Cats*?"

"Probably."

"He had it coming."

"What is this, our second day together? I could write your biography. And I'll be honest, it won't be a good read."

"Now you're just being mean."

"Sorry. Back to the topic."

"What is the topic? Oh, yeah. There's no need for your sex buddy to divorce his wife."

"You're going to take his side?"

"I'm on the fence," Clayton smiled. "I root for both teams, okay?"

"But you're supposed to be on my side. I want you on my side." Preston splashed Clayton. "I'll defend you from an eight-headed shark attack if you're on my side."

"Okay. I'll be on your side if you do this."

"What?"

"Think about it as a scientific experiment, okay?"

"Is that how you conduct all your affairs?"

"No, come on. Just hear me out. There's no room for emotion, just reason. Got it? Now, describe his relationship with his family, like you're narrating a documentary."

"Well... He's a good man," Preston said evenly, slowly. "Uh... He's honouring his commitments. His wife and him are great friends, and they keep their relationship going because of that and for the sake of their kids, so I guess, yeah, when you look at it that way, there's no reason for a divorce. But."

"What?"

"Well, I think it might actually be hurting the kids, you know what I mean? Setting up a false set of expectations based on the relationship their parents have with each other. 'Cause that's a sort of template for kids, isn't it?"

"I don't know. Are they hiding stuff from the kids?"

"I don't know. Like that he's gay? I haven't met the kids if that's what you mean. I don't think it would be prudent at this point. I mean we're just..." His voice trailed off. "Fuck."

"Oh." Clayton suddenly felt lighter, as if his romantic escapades weren't so heavily weighted when placed beside Preston's. Except for José. Clayton recalled José's body language during their first meeting: arms crossed in front of his chest, body angled slightly away from him, their eyes never meeting. *I should have known it right from the start. But—*

"Anyway, I'm thinking it might be good to look at this as a spiritual kind of quest. You know what I mean? Like what if I'm not really me, but just a generic piece that fits into his jigsaw puzzle of a life?"

Clayton turned and looked at Preston with a broad smile on his face. "That's very passive thinking for a top," he said, and then wondered if he himself were just a piece of the puzzle of José's life. Puff's life.

"You think?"

"Considering we've just met and you insist on writing my biography... Maybe we're all pieces of someone else's jigsaw puzzle... Actually, nah. I don't like that. It's too passive and random."

"Well, if the pieces don't fit, try more lube," Preston said, trying to lighten the mood. But then he relented. "This whole process would be much easier if I knew... If I thought there were grounds for hope. You know what I mean?"

"Grounds for hope," Clayton muttered. He knew it right then: hope is illusory. *It stands on the shaky ground of constructs we build and use to make ourselves feel more in control. So hope, therefore, is irrational. It's a pacifier, a blanket. A photograph. A memory. Clusters of memories. A cell phone. Maybe I should send Puff a text. José. Best sex ever. But there's nothing worse than being chased after by someone you're disinterested in. Actually, no. It's far worse to chase after someone who is ambivalent.*

"Is this why you have so much casual sex? To keep you at a distance?"

"No," Preston said, with a finality to his voice that surprised the both of them. "I was not expecting you to throw that in my face."

"I wasn't throwing anything. I'm treading water. You talk about it all the time."

"That's different."

"How?"

"Look, if you're going to suck all my history out of me, we'll both need plenty of non-mealy cocktails."

"And a stenographer," Clayton added.

"All right. Let's save this until later and go back in. Oh, and that bald guy is cruising you."

"He's cruising my nipples," Clayton said, pushing through the water.

"And you're wondering if it's admiration, shock, or nearsightedness, am I right?"

"I think you absolutely must write my biography."

Preston hummed the theme from *Jaws* as they moved through surf swells toward the beach.

Men Without Subtitles

Fountain Bar wasn't very busy when Hugh and Clayton arrived just after eleven thirty that night, Clayton's fourth in Vallarta. The others, having overdone it in the sun, had slinked back to their hotel rooms for an early night. Except Ian, who had an *appointment.*

"What's going on with that?" Clayton asked Hugh as they sat down at open seats at Arturo's bar. "I mean if he's fucking someone, just say that. Why be coy about it?"

"I don't know who started it," he answered.

"It's precious," said Clayton.

"I know. Don't you love it?"

"No. It's precious. Like suddenly we're in Victorian England. It's 2015. Just call it what it is."

"Desperate, sloppy sex. Feel better?"

Clayton looked at Arturo and felt the familiar sinking feeling in his body. "No. Worse. Sometimes I wonder if I'm actually gay."

"But never while there's a cock in your mouth."

Hugh nodded at Arturo muddling ingredients at the far end of the bar. Mexican pop music played from a ghetto blaster plugged into the wall to the right of Clayton. Around it were scattered brochures for day trips for tourists.

Oh fuck, Clayton thought. *I'm a tourist. People try to sell me cheap crap I don't need. I don't want the tour of rich peoples' houses, or the taco tour, or the tequila tour. I just want—*

"So this isn't your first trip here, is it?" Hugh asked.

"No. Sixth. What about you?"

"First."

"Oh, then welcome!"

Clayton angled himself on his stool to face Hugh. He was actually looking past Hugh and staring at Arturo, who was wearing a green soccer jersey, the material shiny and soft looking, with a big 41 emblazoned in bright yellow on the chest. He could hear Hugh talking in one ear, occasional words popping and sticking with him, above the din of the conversations going on around them and the pulse of the music in his right ear.

Chicos chicos chicos...

The waves pulled my bathing suit right off. I had to...

...awfully expensive for a cocktail.

...quieren estar...

...and it turned out to be an ingrown hair.

...construction on the building next door and I couldn't sleep.

I thought you said Mexico was cheap.

...conmigo...

Look into my eyes when I fuck you. Yeah, that's it, buddy.

They should warn you about things like that when you book.

...esta noche.

Maybe we should do something other than fuck. Like...

"This was a big gay anthem when I was younger," Arturo told him in between some off-key singing.

Clayton recalled Puff singing along with a faded old music video on youtube, Flans' "No Controles." He watched as Arturo carried two drinks out to the floor, delivered them to a couple seated in the lounge, and then stopped behind Clayton when he had finished his sweep of the room.

"Hola Papa," he said. "Are you wearing my favourite pants again tonight?" Even his voice reminded Clayton of José.

"No, it's a different pair."

"Too bad."

"Do you have any specials tonight?"

"Everything is special. Every night."

Hugh leaned over and offered Arturo a cigarette. Arturo smiled, took one, and let Hugh light it. A group of men stood up and made their way outside, leaving the lounge almost empty. Arturo was far more relaxed when he rounded the bar and asked what they would like to have.

"Pacifico for me," Hugh said.

"I haven't had one of your margaritas yet."

"What happened to your Spanish?" Arturo said, looking directly into Clayton's eyes.

"Oh. I haven't learned the past tense yet."

"Forget the past," Arturo said, and straightened his shoulders. "Live in the moment and for the moment."

...estar conmigo.

Arturo put his cigarette down and turned to the bar. Clayton fixed his glance on him as he did. "We can wait until you finish the cigarette," he said.

"Did you think more about coming next year?"

... esta noche.

"Of course! I would love to come and clean your toilets," Clayton said in Spanish, hoping the sarcasm would translate.

"I hope you like to kiss," Arturo said.

"He's very good with his mouth," Hugh said, smiling. "Someone wrote it on the bathroom wall." He made a great, sweeping gesture with his hands. "Right back there. Why do you think he wants to clean it so much?"

Clayton shook his head, embarrassed but clearly enjoying the attention.

Arturo laughed and walked away.

"So why do you keep coming back?" Hugh asked.

"Good question. I have *maybe* answers but I'm not sure how much I believe them."

"What?"

"An answer I think might be right, but probably isn't. Anyway, I think it's because I know the general layout here, so it's not as though I have to learn a new city every year. My sense of direction sucks. Do you think you'll come back?"

"Sure," Hugh said, rummaging for another cigarette. "I don't really care that much about where I go. So long as I have a couple of friends with me to kill the boredom."

"You get bored on vacation?" Clayton regretted asking the question although he wasn't sure why.

"You saw me on the beach. I'm under the umbrella, trying to talk to people. I don't want to nap. I don't want to go snorkelling. I don't want to go on the tour of Vallarta's best taco stands." Clayton laughed. "I just want the warmth and the food."

"I know what you mean," Clayton smiled. "It's like speed dating for lonely tourists. For most of the people, at least. But you can have warmth and food anywhere."

"Except home," Hugh said.

"Right. You're lucky though."

"Why is that?"

"You're here with a group and that opens up a whole new arena in terms of how you spend your time. I know people from home who are here, but..."

"Attitude?"

"That or something I have no word for yet. It's like they're showing off, but what, I don't know. I don't buy it. They're like used car salesmen. 'Hi, my name is Steven and I'm super hot. Wouldn't you like a ride on my really huge cock? I am like so hot.' The act obliterates everything about them that might be authentic. So what happens when—?"

"Just ignore the assholes," Hugh said, exhaling smoke.

"Yeah, I know. I try. And I do love it here. It wouldn't make any sense to keep coming back if I didn't. But, despite the Americanization of it, I... I like the food. I really like Mexican men. I just..."

"What?"

"Oh man, it's so depressing. I hate the thought of leaving, having to go back home to that awful weather and then that shitty waiting period once the snow and ice melt. Everything's brown and dead looking. And it's still cold out."

"I know what you mean," Hugh said. "I call it Marchapril. It's like the groggy feeling when you first wake up in the morning hungover, except it lasts for months."

Arturo approached with their drinks. He placed a Pacifico in front of Hugh and looked into Clayton's eyes as he set the margarita down in front of him.

"Can I buy you a drink?" Clayton asked him.

"Later," he said. "I have to close by myself, remember?"

"Put one on my bill then. Salud," Clayton said, lifting his glass to Hugh's beer bottle.

"Cheers."

Hugh asked Clayton about the health care system in Canada and if it really worked. They talked of politics, movies, Lady Gaga's surprise *Sound of Music* performance at the Academy Awards and all the nominated films neither of them had seen, where they should have dinner tomorrow, finding people to fuck, and people to fall in love with. Clayton looked at Arturo making a drink at the far end of the bar while Hugh decried the absence of reciprocal love between men.

"I find it hard to meet people," he said.

"That's my line."

"I said it first."

"Tonight you did."

"We go way back," Hugh deadpanned.

"It seems like gay men fall into two categories, fucked up and married." Clayton wasn't trying to be funny, but Hugh laughed.

"And the married ones are usually fucked up worse," he added.

"They're invisible to me, except for the little squares they take up on the Scruff grid," Clayton said. "I mean I've been in a relationship before but... Fuck. Forget it. What's the point in criticizing everyone? It's exhausting. I'm trying to have more empathy for people but it's just easier being mean. Anyway... I haven't found the kind of person I would want to be with. Occasionally I sleep with people I want to be with, but...

"I know where this is going," Hugh said. "Same here, unfortunately."

"Ships in the night."

"Shits in the night."

Clayton let out an exaggerated gasp. "Are you into scat?"

Hugh offered a long, expressionless stare. "No, I'm not seeing anyone."

"Me neither," Clayton said quietly, realizing the implications of what he had just said. It was over with Puff, had never really begun. He had never thought that he and José had a connection that bound them together anywhere outside the bedroom. "There was a guy, but he was younger than me and we just never got our signals straight. Or... I don't know. We had this connection but it was mostly sexual, I think. Any time we did anything other than fuck he would disappear afterwards and not respond to me. Like he was ashamed or something."

"It's a virus."

"Well someone find a cure, quick."

"That's why you need lots and lots of friends."

"I think he might be one of those guys who's like a big old fashioned Hollywood musical during sex and then a Scandinavian drama the rest of the time. Without subtitles."

Hugh groaned. "I thought that only happened to me."

"Fuck! How are you supposed to know?"

"Sometimes a Hollywood musical is just a Hollywood musical. Don't expect subtitles."

"Nicely said," Clayton smiled dimly. "And especially upsetting if you're illiterate."

"Or dyslexic. So, what signals were you sending him?" Hugh asked.

"Just one: Come fuck me."

"You? Oh I doubt that. That's pretty direct, don't you think? I mean, you don't seem like the type. No offence. Maybe you scared him."

"Or the sex did. We were high all the time."

"Hmmm."

"We would smoke pot and then have sex or have dinner, watch a movie, or all of the above. I was under the influence and thought that something special was happening."

"That's the pot talking," Hugh monotoned. "And all he wanted probably was to unload."

"And that's *exactly* what I was looking for," Clayton said, practically spitting out the word *exactly* to emphasize the sarcasm in case it were lost on Hugh.

Everything froze except the minute contractions in Clayton's brain. Suddenly—it seemed—he knew what he wanted, what was missing, what bothered him so much about his interactions, sexually and otherwise, with the gay men he encountered. And José. It was so simple, so excruciatingly important, and yet so lacking: a standard of behaviour that enabled all people to recognize and acknowledge another's goodness—greatness, even—even if it only manifests in the ability to kiss or touch or to make another person feel something important, something integral, anything that resonates and is good.

This is why casual sex does not work for me. If the point is... Oh shit. What is the point?

Clayton thought that anonymous sex was like being suspended in outer space where anything and everything can come shooting at you and you're supposed to... What? Love it all? Be grateful? Or maybe casual sex is a furnace that requires only one thing: more fuel. And every person Clayton encountered had none of that to offer—except José, who seemed to have a huge reserve but was insistent on rationing it out, at least to Clayton. And so where did that leave him and what would he do? Would he keep lining up for intensely empty moments with his fuck buddy of the month? Perhaps they were moments of empty intensity. How would he know the right person, the right signals, the right speed, the correct amount of caution? With bravado in spades, men are in motion, coming and going. Very few stand still long enough to even focus on what they're beholding. How can they see? How can they possibly see? And how could José demand that Clayton look at him directly in the eyes while he penetrated him and then disappear? Why ask for something if you don't want it, if it means nothing?

"What?"

"What?"

"You just stopped talking."

"I was just thinking," Clayton said, and glanced over at Arturo.

"Well stop that! You know you probably did scare whoever this guy is, but he's still kind of, you know, drawn to you for some reason and he keeps coming around because he's trying to figure out why."

"Fuck."

"Exactly."

"I just wish..."

"What?"

"I don't know. I wish I had been more clear with him. I wasn't in love."

"Liar."

"No. But I did love the sex."

An hour and several drinks later, Clayton had talked himself out. He had nothing left to offer, pick at, or criticize. He looked at the remnants in his glass and wished he could breathe in Arturo's neck again. And then run his tongue along it and slide it into his ear. Whichever one was closest.

"Do you think it's possible that some people fuck because they need the attention?"

"Duh," Hugh said, raising his arm to get Arturo's attention.

"That's narcissistic," Clayton remarked with a discernible tone of outrage.

"Yeah. And?"

Clayton shrugged.

"Have you got boundary issues?" Hugh asked.

"And mommy issues and invisible father issues and—"

"Tissues as far as the eye can see," Hugh interrupted, gesturing around the bar with his left hand. "Welcome to the buffet of soon-to-be-used tissues. There is no sneeze guard."

Clayton looked at the glowing end of Hugh's cigarette and the few remaining faces and bodies of men seated behind them in the lounge.

"I know you're having a moment," Hugh said quietly. "And I invite you to rejoin me as soon as the emotion finishes leaching all the surplus calcium from your bones."

"Oh, cheery," Clayton said, picking up on Hugh's cue.

"One more round," Hugh said, waving at Arturo. "And this one's on you for all my cigarettes you've been smoking."

"It would be my pleasure. So, Hughie, it's your turn now. Who broke your heart in how many places?"

Hugh snorted, picked up his bottle, swirled it around and grunted dismissively.

"No enormous erect penis eager to penetrate and pound you into a girlish, quivering mess?"

"Girlish? No. I don't think it'll happen to me," he said, voice wan. "They ought to change the phrase fall in love to fail in love."

"Oh my God, oh my God, oh my God, we're going there, aren't we?" Clayton said, for the first time aware that he was drunk. "Let's not go there, okay? I can barely keep track of my own shit." His voice was starting to slur. "I mean, if you don't think you deserve it, you'll never get it."

"Here we go," Hugh griped.

"No, just me. You just have to sit and listen—"

"To you quoting bumper stickers and spouting gibberish and all that pop psychology bullshit." His voice was hard. Clayton connected the dots: Hugh was probably a mean drunk. "I thought you were smarter than that."

"Maybe I'm not," Clayton responded quietly.

Everything ground to a slow-motion crawl. Clayton paused, insides clenched, familiar chemicals flooding his brain and the hurt, paralyzed, receding feelings they bring. *He's kidding. He's kidding. No, he's not kidding. He sits right beside me and insults me. Why am I here? Because it's warm. I am the stranger.*

"I didn't mean that," Hugh recanted, looking stone-faced at Clayton. "Sorry. But you know, you're too sensitive."

"People are mean."

"Meaning me."

Clayton tried to move past his sinking feeling. He found that he was able to do so with what he perceived as a fairly short turnaround. *Just drop it,* he told himself, *and let it lie.* He took a breath in. *We're both drunk. He said sorry. But still...*

Hugh noticed that Clayton was staring dreamily at the bartender.

"You won't get him by gawking at him."

"I know. It's just that... Damn."

"What?"

"He reminds me of someone back home."

"And is that someone the guy you've been so careful to not talk about? Up until tonight, as luck would have it."

"Uh-huh."

"So you want to suck all our information out of us and not offer anything up in return." Hugh said it with a smirk on his face so that Clayton would know he wasn't condemning him.

"Not on purpose. You know, I never know whether I'm right or wrong."

"You lost me."

"I don't know if I fucked up or if he did."

"What if you both did?"

"Then we wouldn't be having this conversation."

"So what's his name, this guy back home who fucks and leaves?" Hugh asked.

"And does both so eloquently."

"Sounds as though he treated you like an asshole."

"José. His nickname on Growl'r is Puff&Stuff."

Hugh roared with laughter. It escalated into a coughing fit. "Puff&Stuff," he repeated when the hacking subsided.

"Yeah."

"Sometimes even a name contains all the information you need to know about a person."

"So it's my fault? Is that what you think?"

"Jesus Murphy," Hugh groaned. "Where did that come from?"

"The depths of my soul."

"At least you didn't say tormented."

"I thought it."

Hugh took a long sip of his beer. "Anyway..."

"I don't want another adolescent forty-year-old," Clayton continued, somewhat uncomfortable but obviously more interested in a way to vent his frustration. "And I don't want an inexplicable reason or a shrug when I ask what the guy sees in me. I want someone who knows what he wants when he sees it in me. Is that too much to ask for?"

"Obviously," Hugh mumbled.

"We've got the sex thing down, well, mostly. So how about the emotional? The spiritual? The glue that binds us together."

"That's not glue, dear."

"What are gay men so fucking afraid of?"

"We don't have all night, Clay. Narrow it down. What are you afraid of?"

"Ha! I think I'm afraid of settling for the wrong person. Again. Or... No! I don't want to waste my time and energy. I want an even match."

"Where'd you meet this guy? Oh, Growl'r, right?"

"Yeah."

"Well there's your answer."

"Really? We keep coming back to this."

"Really. Plus what you said about his nickname, too."

"So all guys—*all* the guys—on the apps are dirtbags?"

"Your word, not mine."

"Fuck off."

"You fuck off. Or go clean the toilets. Arturo's going to need a sample of your work ethic before he hires you."

"Ha. Have you met anyone worthwhile on Growl'r?"

"I'm talking to one right now."

"Really?"

"Uh-huh."

"We were chatting?"

"Uh-huh."

"Oh fuck. Really? I feel like such an ass. Wait a minute, are you... Uh... R-guy?"

"That's me."

"No wonder I didn't recognize you!"

"Why?"

"How old is your profile picture?"

"Flattering."

"But—"

"So it's a few years old. It's flattering."

"You know in most places using a photo that's more than five years old could get your gay card taken away."

Hugh smirked and lit a cigarette. "Where I come from that's *how* we get our gay card. And we get points for hooking up with outdated photos."

"But not from the guys you have sex with."

"Fuck them."

"Exactly."

"But it rarely gets to that point. At least for me."

"See what I mean?"

"Actually... What do you mean?"

"You're just playing games with people as some kind of twisted revenge thing."

"No. I play games with people in the hopes of getting pity sex."

"Pity or piggy?"

"Either. Both."

"Really?"

"Really."

"Really?"

"Really."

"Seriously," Clayton persisted, "You don't think there's one decent guy on those apps?"

"We're both on there, so no. Not one. Two."

Hugh's words hung in the air between them. Clayton was tentative about picking them apart, and decided to change the subject.

A few minutes later, they both got text messages from Ian and Curt saying they were up for last call. Curt banged on Preston's door and woke him up. The gang met in front of Bar Los Amigos. Together they trudged up the stairs, only to find the bar sadly empty apart from some skinny go-go boys who fawned over them in their tiny shiny white go-go pants as they entered. They took turns pissing in the bathroom as Curt threw back a Pacifico. Then, arms crossed in front of their chests, they looked at Clayton as if he were responsible for the empty bar. His heart sank. He shrugged his shoulders. Los Amigos was his favourite bar in Vallarta. He didn't think it should be this empty on a Friday night.

Where are all the vaqueros?

They ended up at Garbo's, sipping brutally strong margaritas and doing their best not to sing along to the piano player's rendition of "Macho Man."

At least it's better than "YMCA," he thought. *No silly dance to go along with this one. Yet.*

"What do you do again?" Ian asked Clayton.

I flit, he thought. He hated the question because he hated wondering what people thought of him when he answered. Jobs were rarely as glamorous as people would like to imagine. "Post production for a TV show."

"Which one?" Preston spun around in his chair.

"At the World's End," Clayton answered, knowing none of them would be familiar with the micro-budgeted Canadian show. "Do

you watch the Weather Network?"

"No. That's why I come here, to avoid having to watch the Weather Network."

"The show I work on aired on the Weather Network in the States. I don't know if they'll pick it up for the second season."

"What's it about?" asked Ian.

"Changes in agricultural practices due to changes in weather patterns."

"Sounds boring," said Quinn.

"Anything without trophy wives pulling each other's weaves is boring to you," Curt snapped at his lover. "You're disqualified from the conversation."

"Another apocalypse-how show about global warming?" Preston's hands rose into the air and he formed air quotes with his fingers while making a face like he'd just done a shot of cheap tequila.

Clayton turned to face Preston. "You don't believe in global warming?"

"It's not Santa Claus, honey," Ian said.

"I believe I'm sick and tired of hearing about it," Preston replied. "I hope you left the show and never return. It's depressing. Change of subject, please."

"You know what I think is depressing?" Clayton jumped in. "Us. Here. In a piano bar in Puerto Vallarta. Look at the clothes. Listen to the—"

"Oh God, he's started in on pop music again!" Curt shouted. "Waiter! A round of tequila and a muzzle!"

Ian moved in close to Clayton, wrapped his arm around him and covered his mouth with his hand. Clayton laughed, the sound muffled by Ian's hand. His penis hardened.

The Wrong Kind Of Wrong

"I don't feel my age," Clayton said.

"What do you mean?" Ian asked from his tiny hotel bathroom as he shrugged out of a snug pair of underwear. From the bed where he lay naked, Clayton watched Ian's reflection in the bathroom mirror through the open door, and saw him reaching into a toiletries bag. He pulled out a condom.

"I mean I know I'm fifty. It's on my birth certificate, passport, driver's license. It's inescapable how old I am, but I don't recognize it."

"Still lost," Ian chimed out.

"I don't feel it. I mean, I don't know how I'm supposed to feel. Or act. Or think. I don't even know how I'm supposed to dress. I mean, do I spend buttloads of money on clothes I don't care about or just fucking give up and shop at Costco? Either way, I don't really care. Much. I don't really care that much."

"Just relax, man. Do you like poppers?"

"You brought poppers to Mexico?"

"Just trying to change the subject," he said. "What's with you and all these loaded, heavy conversations? Can't you just relax and enjoy yourself? Relax! I mean you're on vacation. Vacate."

"I'm trying." Clayton's erection had subsided by this point. He lay still, limbs splayed out across Ian's bed. He had the realization that sex was probably never going to be as moving an experience as the kinds of conversations he had where he learned something about the person. *Maybe I'm doing it wrong. Or... Maybe I'm just doing it with the wrong kind of—Wrong?*

"Ready?"

Ian pushed the bathroom door fully open and stepped into the room. He had a condom pulled over his erection as he walked toward Clayton and sipped the tail end of a can of Tecate. Clayton sat at the edge of the bed, pulling on his socks.

"Something I said?"

"No. Oh, what a nice cock you have. All ready and wrapped up. But I can't. I'm a drunk mess, man. It's just gonna be messy and... Ugh. Sorry. There's no point in doing it if I'm not going to remember it."

"I'll remember it."

"No, I'm sorry. I really am. Do you mind?"

"Come on."

"I wanna tell you something but it won't come up right. Out right. I can... Can you call a cab so I don't..." Clayton scanned the small room and, not finding a telephone, stood up and moved toward Ian, pointing at his penis. "You should be careful with that. You could put someone's eye out."

"The rooms don't have phones," Ian said, following Clayton's gaze.

"That must make ordering room service a fucking pain."

"I'll get dressed and walk you to your hotel."

"No, that's okay. No, no. I'm going to... It's just only around the corner."

"Three corners."

Clayton wrapped his arms around Ian and kissed him on the mouth.

"I'm going now. And I will apologize to you... Apologize to you in the morning if I live to see it."

"I have something that can help with your hangover."

"Do you know how many times I've heard that from naked men in hotel rooms?"

"How many?"

"Well. Just one. That was a historical question."

Ian pulled the condom off and tossed it in the nearby trash can.

Clayton lurched to the door and pulled it open, muttering, "Hysterical, Rhea Pearlman, plutonic," and, finally, "Rhetorical."

"Wait," Ian said, chuckling to himself and grabbing his shirt from a chair.

When he looked up, Clayton had slipped out the door.

Two minutes later the door opened and Clayton swerved back inside the room.

"How come you're the only one here with lights?"

"Did you get lost on your way out?"

"No. I just wanted to say maybe... No, sorry, that I—we—couldn't... Didn't, you know."

"I know."

"No, I don't think you do. Not. I don't... I thick you don't."

"It's okay."

"Fuck."

"What?"

"I'm staying story that we didn't screw."

"It's all right. I'm getting dressed now and taking you home."

"Didn't we just do that already?"

When Harry Met Carrie

When Clayton arrived at the beach the next morning the group was already planted in their chairs. He threw his shirt to the ground and sat across from Ian, and buried his toes in the sand. "Sorry," he said, looking him in the eye.

"What for?" asked Quinn.

"Bad performance? No performance?" Curt asked.

"You just never mind," scolded Ian. "No need," he said softly to Clayton with a wink.

"Did you lure this poor unsuspecting creature into your hotel room last night?" Curt was leaning forward in his chair, eyes flitting back and forth between Ian and Clayton's crotches.

"What are you doing?" Ian asked, catching him.

"What?" Curt replied.

"Your eyes," Ian continued, "Are you... Hello?" he said, waving his hand in front of his face to draw Curt's eyes up. "I'm up here. Come on, man, it was last night. There aren't any cum stains. Different pants. God, watch some porn or something."

Hugh chuckled before yelling out to anyone who would listen, "Could someone please have sex with Curt so we can all move forward with our vacation? Thank you. Applications available on Grindr."

"He attacked me in the bathroom at Garbo's," Clayton said breathlessly with a southern drawl, remembering snippets of visuals sandwiched in between waves of alcohol-induced blur. "And didn't even lock the door."

"Didn't even close it!" Quinn laughed. "Everybody in the bar saw you two in there."

"Don't you remember hearing the music stop at one point?" Preston asked. "Everyone was listening to you guys making out. Even the piano player. He played 'Touch Me In The Morning' and dedicated it to the two guys in the bathroom."

"Great," sighed Clayton, blushing.

"Clayton's a sexy talker," Quinn said.

"And let me tell you, missy, you have quite the vocabulary," Preston said.

Clayton closed his eyes. His head drooped forward.

"I think Hugh got some pics of you two going at it with his phone. You'd better scour Facebook."

"Thanks, Hugh." That was Ian.

"Did your mouth taste like armpit when you got up this morning?" Curt asked, clearly enjoying the awkward moment.

"It usually does," Clayton smirked.

They all laughed. Preston sipped his drink and moved his tongue around the inside of his mouth. Clayton caught him in the act and asked, "Mealy?"

When the skies clouded over, the group disbanded, having already made plans to meet at Frida for cocktails at five. Clayton attempted some work on his balcony before realizing it was time for lunch. He sat down at an empty table at Tizoc, lit a cigarette and continued with his paperwork. Rafael appeared and placed a menu in front of him.

"Uh," Clayton stammered. He gestured to his cigarette and mimed flicking ashes and spoke to the man in Spanish. "Do you have a...?"

"¿Cenicero?" the waiter replied.

He crouched down to Clayton's table and picked up his pen. He leaned in and wrote down a word on the piece of paper in front of Clayton.

Cenicero.

"Thank you. And if I want to ask if it's okay to smoke here?"

The waiter stood upright and handed the pen back to Clayton. "¿Se puede fumar aquí?"

Clayton repeated the words.

"We've got to stop meeting like this," a voice called out.

Curt and Quinn appeared on the sidewalk up the steps from the main dining area. Clayton smiled and shifted in his chair. Rafael scuttled away.

"Have you seen *What's Up, Doc?*" Clayton asked back, but neither Curt nor Quinn got the reference. "That's a line from that movie."

"No. I just said it." Curt looked defiant. Odd looks from Quinn.

"With Barbra Striesand and Ryan O'Neal?" Clayton said.

"Oh, are we playing that twinkie phone game?" Quinn asked as they approached the table.

The couple pulled chairs out, the wooden feet making musical screeches on the smooth tile floor. "You've never seen *What's Up Doc?*" They shook their heads.

"Ever been rimmed? Gone to a tea dance? Are you gay? Come on, it's *What's Up, Doc?*! That's just sad."

Rafael returned with menus and placed them before Curt and Quinn.

"Maybe to you," Quinn said, looking at Curt. Then he turned to the waiter. "Dos margaritas por favor. Lima."

"How old is it?" Curt asked.

"Nineteen seventies. Uh... Seventy-three? Seventy-five? No,

before *Jaws*, that's for sure."

"Shit," Curt said as he jabbed his fingers at the screen of his phone. "You remember every movie ever made. That's tragic." After a moment he looked up. "Seventy-two. I didn't know Madeline Kahn was in it."

Silence, apart from the muted strains of Celine Dion and Peabo Bryson's "Beauty and the Beast" playing over the restaurant's sound system.

"It was her debut," Clayton pointed out.

"Did you order?"

"Oh, yeah. I'm having that one there," he said, pointing at a menu item called El plato Méxicano. "Are you going to join me for lunch?"

"We were going to go have Panini over across the street."

"Really? You come to Mexico to eat Italian food? What's going on with that? Go to Italy for fuck's sake."

"You're the most opinionated faggot I've ever met," Curt quipped.

"I can't tell if that's a compliment or an insult."

"Exactly!"

"So what's wrong with having an opinion?"

"Nothing, if you keep it to yourself."

"And that's what you and all your fellow Americans pride themselves on?"

Curt smirked and picked up Clayton's pack of cigarettes.

Quinn gasped in mock surprise. "And that's a nasty habit," he said.

"I'm on vacation," Clayton smiled, "From health. You know that's something I find hard to understand, why people go somewhere for a trip and they drag their own culture, habits, everything, along with them. Why bother leaving home if you want everything to be like it is at home?"

"*The Accidental Tourist*," Quinn said. "Ever think that some people are here for the weather?"

"It's Puerto Vallarta, Clay," Curt explained in a whine. "There's not much culture here to soak up. Cum, yes. Lots of Cum."

"You're disgusting," Quinn laughed.

"Oh, come on. You're wrong. There's culture. It's just buried underneath all the tourist shit. I mean, come on! Have you ever even wondered about the the lives of people who live here year-round, their history, what goes on here after you leave? And the food? You guys were going to eat Italian for fuck's sake. In Mexico! One of the reasons I come here is to eat Mexican—"

"Ass," Curt interjected. "You come here to eat Mexican ass."

"Don't be crude," Quinn scolded. "He can't help it," he said by way of excusing his partner's behaviour. He motioned at Curt. "He's from Indiana."

The waiter arrived with two margaritas. Curt wrapped his hands around the large, thick glass goblet and took a long sip through the straw.

"Will you eat?" Rafael asked, hovering behind Quinn.

"The chicken quesadilla," Curt said.

"I'll have what he's having," Quinn said, looking at Clayton. "And don't. Don't say *When Harry Met Sally*. Can we find something else to fixate on, please? Like that's all there is to do in the world, talk about old movies. *Bad* ones."

"*When Harry Met Sally* isn't a bad movie," Clayton protested. "Are you insane? And old? You've been listening to too much Shitme Smears."

"Here we go," Curt mumbled.

"Name one romantic comedy of the last five years that's anywhere near as good as *When Harry Met Sally*."

"*Eat, Pray, Love*," said Quinn.

"Oh, my life is so hard. I'm thin and beautiful and wealthy enough that I can go to India to get diarrhea and hopefully shit that man out of my system."

"I think they're pretty much the same movie." That was Quinn.

"You're insane," Clayton laughed. "It's a classic. It's priceless just for Carrie Fisher's dialogue."

"Princess Leia was in *When Harry Met Sally*?" Curt asked.

"What are you guys, just pretending to be gay? How can you not know this?"

"Skinny drôle Carrie or—"

"Don't."

"What?"

"Just don't."

"If a tree falls in the forest..."

"What? So if people can't hear you insult them it's as though you said nothing?"

"Exactly," Curt replied, raising his eyebrows and smiling at Quinn.

"Great. Wow. That's... Really disturbing to hear. Don't you ever—"

"No I don't," Curt interrupted. "I don't. Stop analyzing me, okay?"

"He's cranky today," Quinn said. "Also drunk."

"It's one-thirty."

"Perfect time for a cocktail or ten," Curt smiled, staring at

Clayton and waiting for his response.

"We were at a cocktail party."

"After the beach?"

"Yeah. Guys in the room across from our hotel saw us on the street and invited us up. I'm not sure why we left, especially considering the lecture we've had to endure since we met y—"

"You were hungry and didn't like the decor," Quinn cut in.

"I know this is going to be strange coming from me, but do you ever have anything nice to say about anything?" Clayton asked, smiling at Curt.

"Haven't you been reading my Scruff messages?"

"Actually, no. I stopped reading them because you only send them when you're hammered and they're always about my ass and nipples."

"Fine. I'll block you."

"Don't you love it when people use technology to have a temper tantrum?"

Curt smiled. It quickly turned into a smirk. He stuck his finger in the bowl of pico de gallo. He raised it to his mouth. Immediately his lips curled downward and he grimaced. "Mild," he muttered to himself.

Clayton reached for a cigarette, flicked his lighter.

Quinn stared at his partner and discreetly nudged Clayton with his elbow. "Watch this," he whispered.

"You shut up," Curt snapped. "It's not spicy enough."

"I told you." Quinn beamed. "When he drinks, his taste buds... It's like they stop working and he thinks he can wake them up by devouring the spiciest food he can find."

Clayton smiled, bemused by the couple's antics. "You guys never took your turns on the beach."

"Huh?"

"Your scar story. How did you get that scar on your... Where is it, Quinn? Your shoulder?"

"Oh yeah! That was two years ago. Happened here, actually. We were out in the water and it was rough. But it was our first day and I guess we got carried away or underestimated the strength of the waves. A big one hit and I got sucked under and pummelled around. My acromion snapped and was pushing up. Spent the rest of the trip in bed. No fun."

"You know what's no fun?" Curt chimed in, looking around for the waiter. "This one, immobilized for two weeks. Drinking in bed. That's why we didn't come last year."

"Because he had an accident?"

"Because he was a fucking ass," Curt said, playing with his

straw.

"We were seriously close to breaking up last winter."

"How long have you been together?"

"Eleven years," Quinn said.

"Not counting the courtship," Curt said, and then made a face, looking—unintentionally, perhaps—like Dame Edna.

Quinn laughed.

"He made me wait forever before we did *any*thing," Curt said, leaning forward for emphasis and gesturing at Quinn with his hands. "Ladies and gentlemen, the world's most cautious man. Except when it comes to swimming."

"So you guys had an actual courtship? Wow."

"He was such a princess about the whole thing," Quinn said. "Suck my cock now. Buy me presents. Don't drive drunk. Move in with me. Hurry!"

"And he was having *none* of it," Curt said.

"I don't think I've ever heard any gay man use that expression before. At least to refer to a relationship."

"What?"

"Courtship!"

"Oh, it was a courtship all right," Quinn grinned. "One of the world's longest, I think. I was kidding, by the way. Curt was the one who had the brakes on. Made me wonder where he got his ideas about relationships from."

"John Hughes movies and an episode or two of *The Waltons*," Curt said, grinning.

Clayton laughed. "Ewww."

"It was horrible. No sex until after the fifth date and I had memorized his phone number and the correct spelling of his last name," said Quinn.

"No way," Clayton said, drawing his hand up to his mouth to drag on the cigarette.

"You're telling me," Quinn added. "And you don't know his last name."

Clayton waited. He felt like he was part of a comedy sketch.

"Krzyzewski," Curt smiled.

"Blue balls!" Clayton laughed and exhaled smoke through his nostrils.

"You never told us what records you slipped on."

"Oh, man. This was before there were file sharing programs. I got it into my head to record all the hard-to-find vinyl I could so I got piles of records from my friends. My friend Sam gave me a bunch by television stars from the seventies. You know, Cheryl Ladd, John Travolta, John Schneider, Leif Garret, Patrick Duffy.

Probably a lesser-known Osmond brother, too."

"That narrows it down. Wait a minute. Patrick Duffy recorded an album? I find that hard to believe."

"And harder to listen to, I'm sure."

Quinn put his hand over Curt's mouth. "So you're one of the few people on the planet who can honestly say Cheryl Ladd broke my arm!"

"What about yours, Curt?"

Rafael approached with his hands clenched in front of his chest. "Excuse me, sir, but the food is not... Today they make everything fresh, so first customers. ¿Se entienden?"

"Yes," answered Clayton in Spanish. "No me molesta. It doesn't bother me. Is that right? Or is it, I don't care?"

The waiter looked at the table top and picked up Clayton's pen and, once again, crouched down. He wrote, *No tengo prisa,* on the sheet and then stood up. "Léalo," he said, looking directly at Clayton.

"No tengo prisa. ¿Qué significa?"

The waiter mimed running on the spot.

"No rush," Quinn offered.

"No hurry," barked Curt.

Clayton thought, *Oh, great. Our lunch has turned into an episode of* Party Game.

The waiter pointed at Curt and smiled. "Eso. No tengo prisa. In English is no hurry."

"Technically it would be I have no hurry, right?"

"Sí señor. Bueno. Gracias."

"Excuse me," Curt said as the waiter turned to leave the table. "Is there something spicier than this?"

"He'll be shitting his guts out tonight," Quinn said to Clayton. "Cancel our plans."

"Yes, claro," Rafael said and promptly disappeared, laughing.

Clayton and Quinn looked at Curt dipping a corn chip into the pico de gallo.

"Heat or spice. It's not the same thing here, is it? I mean in terms of food."

"We should ask the waiter, but I think that picante signifies heat, like from chiles, and caliente means heat, like temperature."

"Oh," grumbled Curt, his mouth full of chips and pico de gallo.

"And what about yours then?"

"Mine? Oh, my scar! Nothing spectacular, I'm afraid. Just had my appendix out."

Just Pull On Them

On his last full day in Vallarta, Clayton joined the group on the beach. As he tucked his shirt under his beach chair he felt a weight in his body and a density in the air outside but put it down to a depression that, at its core, was simply about going home.

"Why not extend your trip?"

"I already looked into that yesterday. It would be too expensive just to change the flight, so I just have to bite the bullet. Fuck I hate winter."

There were two new arrivals, Jerry and Mitch, also from Michigan. Jerry was gregarious and outgoing, having no qualms about jumping up from his chair to wander over to a man in the crowd whose bathing suit fit him unusually well. He commented on the design, colour, snugness of the package. It seemed that most men enjoyed being engaged in a deconstruction of their baskets and conversations about the aesthetics of well-tailored bathing suits. Jerry was a painter and photographer. Funny, flippant, and, Clayton thought, sweet, although he wasn't sure how he managed to get all those qualities across. Jerry was fascinated by Clayton's nipples and, unlike the men whose bathing suits Jerry reviewed, Clayton was embarrassed by the attention.

"What do you do to make them like that?"

"Just pull on them," Clayton said.

"Oh, I'd love to."

Clayton laughed and angled his body away from Jerry, whose hands were moving closer to his chest.

"So, no hydraulic pulleys and pumps?"

"No. But I'm sure there are gadgets out there for that," he said with a shrug and then changed the subject to soft drinks and how strange it was that you couldn't buy Jarritos in Puerto Vallarta.

Jerry looked at him with disbelief. "Jesus Christ, Helen, have a Coke!"

That night Clayton went with Preston and Hugh to a drag show at The Palm. Late to arrive, they weren't able to sit together so they exchanged laughing glances and beer-bottle toasts from across the room. Clayton ordered beer after beer from a handsome waiter he assumed was straight. He would spot the man's shirt out of the corner of his eye, and, subtly, his body language would change. He tensed himself as the waiter approached with his Pacifico, the entire process slowing down to half speed as the man leaned forward and placed the beer—wrapped with a white cocktail napkin and topped off with a half wheel of lime—before Clayton. Long, thin, elegant fingers placed the bottle down and then receded out of view. Clayton looked up at the man as he was about to turn away. *His skin. His beautiful face.*

"Gracias," he said. The waiter hesitated, looked back at him and nodded his head. Then he was gone.

After the show and a group photo with its headliner, Misty Mountaintop, they crossed the street and joined Ian, Curt and Quinn at La Piazzeta for a relaxed Italian meal. Clayton had wanted to eat Mexican on his last night there, but acquiesced to the group's wishes: not Mexican. It seems they'd had enough for one week and Clayton wasn't in the mood to try to sway them.

After the meal they squeezed onto a banquette at Garbo's where a man played Elton John covers on the piano, accompanied by pre-recorded backing tracks.

The convivial atmosphere in the bar was palpable; people were smiling, singing along with the pianist, laughing, embracing, passing out business cards for a sensational masseur—but no happy endings, someone was keen to announce. When Clayton returned from the bathroom, he found a row of shot glasses lined up on their table.

"It's your last night," Curt shouted over the crowd. "We had to celebrate."

"What? That I'm going?"

"No, stupid. That you were here! What the hell's wrong with you?"

Clayton sat down, pressed in between Curt and Hugh, who nudged him and then mimed smoking a cigarette. "Nothing," he said. "There's nothing wrong with me that can't be fixed with more of this," he gestured with his glass. "Hey, I have to tell you guys something," he continued, fuelled by alcohol and the failed attempts to shoo away thoughts of his looming departure.

Hugh leaned in and said, "Don't make it a long speech 'cause I'm dying for a smoke."

"Okay. I just wanted to say thanks for making this such a great trip."

"Cheers to Scruff then," Curt said, leaning in and grabbing a shot glass.

"And Growl'r," added Hugh.

The others grabbed shot glasses and raised them in the air. "Rocket Man" was being played and slurred voices lagged behind the pianist's.

"And Marlboro Blancos at three dollars a pack," Hugh added.

"Cheers to all of that," Clayton said.

Clayton moved his shot glass toward Curt's and the sound of

them clinking together was echoed by the others' glasses as they toasted.

"Salud," Clayton said with bravado.

The men retracted their glasses, raised them to their lips and threw back the tequila.

Clayton savoured the warmth of the liquid sliding down his throat. He knew he would remember this feeling, this moment, this trip for the rest of his life. *I'm in.*

Disengaging

The next morning Clayton was the first to arrive at the beach. He watched the waiters begin their daily task of pulling green recliners from the storage hut and out onto the slope of the beach. He put Sam Phillips' *Bikinis and Martinis* album on his MP3 player and dug his toes into the sand. He put his sunglasses down on a nearby table and looked out across the water, at the edges of Banderas Bay, the layers of blue in the horizon that blended seamlessly into each other, the gleaming high-rises of Nuevo Vallarta to the north and the jagged outline of the Sierra Madres further in the distance, the hilly green of the curving landscape to the south and beyond. He took a deep breath in and sighed loudly. A man appeared at the water's edge and, with his back to Clayton, looked out at the ocean, stretched his arms above his head.

When the others arrived, Clayton's awareness of the time pressed down on him, adding weight to the sadness he felt about leaving. He exchanged e-mail addresses, picked up his shirt, towel and lotion, gave hugs to everyone in the circle and slowly walked along the water's edge, carefully moving his MP3 player to his right hand, away from the spray of the waves crashing on the shoreline.

As in previous years, the last thing Clayton did before checking out of the hotel was exactly the same as his first upon arriving: a walk along the beach, alone.

Underneath the resentment of having to go back to the cold of Toronto, Clayton felt an absence. As he walked along the beach, past the Blue Chairs and Tropicana, La Palapa and beyond, it occurred to him that maybe his self-diagnosis had been wrong. Maybe he was likeable. Maybe some people did enjoy his company. He had previously written off the group's attention and affection as the result of too much alcohol, but now, as he mentally prepared himself to drag his suitcase down the hotel's front stairs and into a waiting taxi, he thought that maybe he had been the one all along—after all these years and trips to Vallarta—who had been afraid, aloof, and angry. Perhaps it wasn't everyone else that he saw and disliked or disagreed with. It was just him. A lonely man trying desperately to reach out and yet protect himself from rejection at the same time. *It's funny how you can try to do two opposite things simultaneously and not even know it.* And then he thought about José. *I miss him, but... No. It's not my job to make excuses for him*. And then he let it go.

As he slid into his window seat of the American Airlines plane, more pieces fit into place, seemingly out of the blue. He had carried anger and resentment with him as constant companions for so many years; anger and resentment that he had never found his niche, his group, or even the one man who would be his partner and confidant. Squashed seething frustration that nobody saw in him what he wished they all could. *Whose job is it?* He remembered the feeling after having been dumped by men he should have known better than to fall for; rejection, a closing off inside, the need for some kind of protection. They had gotten the best of him then. Even José had managed to exit with his hands full. *But me? What did I get?* It took a few moments before Clayton acknowledged that José had really broken through a lot of the walls around his sexuality, and he wished he knew of a way to be grateful for that, and to leave it at that, but he wanted more. *I want more.*

His connecting flight in Chicago had been delayed due to a backlog of de-icing. Clayton studied the ceilings and hallways near his gate, took some photos with his camera, and began to form a mental plan of what next year's trip might be like. Would they all reconvene at the same time? Would Ian try to seduce him again? Would there be another public display in a bathroom? Would they get the same spot at the Green Chairs?

He pulled out his phone and opened the messenger app. There was José's name. Status: active. Clayton smiled and took slow breath in as he typed.

—Hello José. How are you?

For five minutes he stared at his phone. Nothing.

Well, that was easy, he thought as he looked at the small screen, waiting for a response—anything—but the screen remained unchanged. Clayton caught himself sliding down a hill and into the pit of rejected lovers. He did not have the luxury of having been deluded into thinking that he was cared for. He was quite convinced, staring into the glow of his phone, that he had just been swept under the carpet—again. *I'm not heartbroken. This isn't news. And Whitney isn't around anymore so I guess there won't be a theme song for this breakup. Breakup?*

An hour later, José had still not responded to his message. Status: offline. Clayton looked up at the LED display listing arrivals and departures. His flight was still N/A. He looked around him, glanced once again at the glowing screen of his phone and then powered it down. He put the phone in the flap of his carry-on bag. *No need to carry that weight around anymore, no? No. No need.*

He remembered earlier that morning turning back on the beach to look at the circle of scarred men. It seemed so long ago already. He had done his farewell trek along the beach and decided to go back and have one last look at the group. He stopped at the edge of the Blue Chairs and scanned the crowd. Quinn, Ian and Curt were in the water. Preston was asleep in his chair. Hugh smoked a cigarette and had an oversized sombrero on his head. Jerry typed something into his phone.

Clayton wanted to take a picture, but only had his MP3 player with him. He stood there a few moments, aware of the fact that the sounds he heard around him were dissipating. The noise of the waves crashing and the din of the people around him were diminishing. All he was left with was the resounding echo of nothing. He had a space inside him. He was open. The space inside him absorbed all his attention as he stood there watching his friends. *That sinking feeling*, he thought. *Here it comes again.* But it levelled. Clayton had it in check. *I can do this again. I'll get better at it and hopefully without the separation anxiety.*

He looked at the irregular circle where they had spent the last five days and thought about the chairs and tables, the bottles of sunblock, meals delivered in see-through plastic containers, the barrage of cocktails and water bottles and the waiters who trudged back and forth along the slope of the beach, weaving in and out of clusters of chairs and bodies, at the rows of men and boys and all their intricate traits and traps, at the vendors, parasailors and surfing locals and the cloudless blue sky, so blue. Clayton took a long look, a deep breath, felt different. Not lighter, but slightly less weighed down.

Acknowledgments

To my family: Sue and John, Betty, Brian and Jonathan and Gretta: Thank you for being there. Tim, whose friendship, inspired suggestions for film, books, music, food and travel destinations are unparalleled: Thank you for your contribution to this project and—pass the kleenex—to my life. To Sean of SERIAL SEAN, thank you for the consistency and quality of your work, suggestions, and your openness and flexibility. To James, for your editorial work: thank you. To Jodi, for your wonderful photographs and effects: thank you so much. A Alfredo Roagui, gracias por tu excelente trabajo para la portada de la edición limitada de *Tiny Grievances*. Querido Armando, mi comadre, por tu ayuda con el español y la traducción. To everyone who was and is a part of the scar circle, from inspiring characters, stories and quips, to offering encouragement, support and suggesting cuts, changes and cocktails: Thank you for your open arms and ongoing friendship... Alex, Angel, Jim, Ryan, Doug, Scott, J.R., Paul, Laura, Felipe, Dale, Michael, Vince, Chris, Rondon.

Descanse en paz, Marco.

Photo by Jodi Thibodeau

Robert Thomson is the author of *Secret Things*, *Need* and *Now... Where Was I?* In the 1990s he worked as a journalist and magazine editor, and his short fiction was widely anthologized. He wrote, directed and edited a number of short films, including "Last Visit," which was nominated as Best Short at the 2011 Barcelona GLBT Film Festival. *Tiny Grievances* is Robert's first book of all-new short fiction in over fifteen years. He lives in Toronto, Canada.

Reviews for *Secret Things*

"Hysterical and bittersweet… Thomson has an extremely engaging, almost inexorable writing style. These stories are unified by his precise and concise speech and images. He has a knack for hooking his reader into the text almost immediately. Mr. Thomson's energetic writing style and succinct format combine to create wonderful glimpses into the personal peccadilloes of anyone's life, gay or otherwise."
—Craig J. Simmons (*XTRA West*)

"Robert Thomson's stories are honest and bold, sometimes hilarious, and always gripping accounts of what it means to be a boy and a man. I read *Secret Things* in one enthralled sitting."
—Lucy Jane Bledsoe (*Sweat: Stories and a Novella*)

"A bold debut. Childhood wounds, wild imagination, a wry and wicked sense of humour, wistfully combined. A wonderful read."
—James Johnstone (*Queer View Mirror 1* and 2, *Quickies*)

Reviews for *Need*

"There is an immediacy to Thomson's writing, a sense that he is capturing the fleeting thoughts which comprise the texture of day-to-day life. The voices of his characters are cacophonic, diverse, made coherent and unified by the common denominator of the author's guiding hand."
—David Crosson (*Outlooks* magazine)

"Thomson's queer credentials are solid—his stories have appeared in the anthologies *Queer View Mirror* and *Brothers of the Night*—but it's easy to praise them for reasons that have absolutely nothing to do with what makes his characters sexually aroused and everything to do with the way he puts them together for his readers... *Need* is full of like characters, striving after the same understanding of themselves and others that mark any piece of serious fiction."
—Ray Robertson (*Toronto Star*)

"...Evoking scattershot, anxious, searching/failing urban gay lives with wonderful clarity."
—Jim Bartley (*XTRA*)

"Honest and candid, these stories explore the frankness of human nature and are highly entertaining. *Need* is a worthwhile investment for the short story enthusiast."
—*Midwest Book Review*

www.ingramcontent.com/pod-product-compliance
Ingram Content Group UK Ltd.
Pitfield, Milton Keynes, MK11 3LW, UK
UKHW021036270726
13967UKWH00013B/2813